CARRIER

*These are the stories of the Carrier Battle Group Fourteen—a force
including a supercarrier, amphibious unit, guided missile cruiser,
and destroyer. And these are the novels that capture the blistering
reality of international combat. Exciting. Authentic. Explosive.*

CARRIER . . . The smash debut thriller about the ultimate military
nightmare: the takeover of a U.S. Intelligence ship.

VIPER STRIKE . . . A renegade Chinese fighter group penetrates
Thai airspace—and launches a full-scale invasion.

ARMAGEDDON MODE . . . With India and Pakistan on the verge
of nuclear destruction, the Carrier Battle Group Fourteen must prevent a final showdown.

FLAME-OUT . . . The Soviet Union is reborn in a military takeover—and their strike force shows no mercy.

MAELSTROM . . . The Soviet occupation of Scandinavia leads
the Carrier Battle Group Fourteen into conventional weapons combat—and possible all-out war.

COUNTDOWN . . . Carrier Battle Group Fourteen must prevent
the deployment of Russian submarines. The problem is: They have
nukes.

AFTERBURN . . . Carrier Battle Group Fourteen receives orders
to enter the Black Sea—in the middle of a Russian Civil war.

ALPHA STRIKE . . . When American and Chinese interests col-
lide in the South China Sea, the superpowers risk waging a Third
World War.

ARCTIC FIRE . . . A Russian splinter group has occupied the Aleutian islands off the coast of Alaska—in the ultimate invasion of U.S. soil.

ARSENAL . . . Magruder and his crew are trapped between Cuban revolutionaries . . . and a U.S. power play that's spun wildly out of control.

NUKE ZONE . . . When a nuclear missile is launched against the U.S. Sixth fleet, Magruder must face a frightening question: In an age of computer warfare, how do you tell friends from enemies?

CHAIN OF COMMAND . . . Magruder enters the jungles of Vietnam looking for answers about his missing father. Little does he know that another bloody war is about to be unleashed—with his fleet caught in the crosshairs!

BRINK OF WAR . . . Friendly wargames with the Russians take a deadly turn, and Carrier Battle Group Fourteen must prevent war from erupting in the skies. Little do they know—that's just what someone wants!

TYPHOON . . . An American yacht is attacked by a Chinese helicopter in international waters, and the Carrier team is called to the front lines of what may be the start of a war between the superpowers . . .

ENEMY OF MY ENEMY . . . A Greek pilot unwittingly downs a news chopper, and Magruder must keep the peace between Greece and the breakaway republic of Macedonia. But what no one knows is that it wasn't an accident at all . . .

JOINT OPERATIONS . . . China launches a surprise attack on Hawaii—and the Carrier team can't handle it alone. As Tombstone and his fleet take charge of the air, Lieutenant Murdock and his SEALs are called in to work ashore . . .

THE ART OF WAR . . . When Iranian militants take the first bloody step towards toppling the decadent west, the Carrier group are the only ones who can stop the madmen . . .

continued on next page . . .

book eighteen

CARRIER
Island
Warriors

KEITH DOUGLASS

J
JOVE BOOKS, NEW YORK

CARRIER: ISLAND WARRIORS

A Jove Book / published by arrangement with
the author

PRINTING HISTORY
Jove edition / August 2001

All rights reserved.
Copyright © 2001 by Penguin Putnam Inc.
This book, or parts thereof, may not be reproduced in
any form without permission.
For information address: The Berkley Publishing Group,
a division of Penguin Putnam Inc.,
375 Hudson Street, New York, New York 10014.

The Penguin Putnam Inc. World Wide Web site address is
http://www.penguinputnam.com

ISBN: 0-515-13115-6

A JOVE BOOK®
Jove Books are published by The Berkley Publishing Group,
a division of Penguin Putnam Inc.,
375 Hudson Street, New York, New York 10014.
JOVE and the "J" design
are trademarks belonging to Penguin Putnam Inc.

PRINTED IN THE UNITED STATES OF AMERICA

10 9 8 7 6 5 4 3 2 1

ONE

Ku K'ai-Chih stared straight ahead as the water crept up his torso. It was cold, around fifty-five degrees farenheit, but his insulated dry suit made it more a pressure than a temperature change. Water continued to pour into the small lockout chamber of the submarine at a rate that would have panicked many men, but Ku had done this too many times to be concerned. Another few minutes, and he would no longer have the option of breathing the air that was rapidly hissing out through the exhaust tubes. Then, the lockout procedure itself: undogging the hatch by forcing the heavy wheel to turn, and swimming out in the black, featureless water.

The first few seconds were always the worst, the shock of going from the dim red lights of the lockout chamber into the utter blackness of the ocean. The sub would be shallow, and reaching the surface would not take long.

The weather predictions called for a mostly cloudy

night, with even a slight chance of rain. The moon was a mere sliver, its pale light blocked out by the cloud cover. It would hide him from prying eyes, from anyone who might wonder what a swimmer was doing out in the middle of the ocean.

Not that they would wonder for long. Not if the submarine realized they were there. A sailboat might sneak by, but anything with an engine would be picked up by the submarine's sonar.

It was a shame, really, but some innocent fishermen might have to die simply because they were in the wrong place at the wrong time. But such are the fortunes of war. The innocent always suffer along with the actual military forces, and indeed, with every Chinese man serving a two-year tour in the armed forces and then a lengthy reserve commitment, the line between military forces and civilians was virtually undetectable.

He wondered how it would be, to be on such a fishing boat. Perhaps they had had a good day, drawn their nets in, and were quietly transiting to a new fishing area. Most of the crew would be asleep, only a small duty section on watch. Someone to guide the ship, perhaps an engineer— no more than two or three.

They would not even have time to wake the rest of the crew. A very alert lookout might catch a glimpse of the torpedo in the water, but probably not. It would travel through the water submerged, leaving the wake that could be detected only under clear conditions, and probably not at all at night.

Ku smiled slightly at the thought. All those innocents, asleep, believing themselves as safe as anyone ever was at sea. Perhaps they would be dreaming of their families, of the end of the voyage when they would return home marginally richer, or at least with sufficient funds to put food on the table for another few weeks. They would live mainly on fish and rice, supplementing it occasionally with a few vegetables bought in those ridiculous markets.

Or maybe they would have bad dreams. Perhaps someone would be tossing in his bunk, contemplating getting up and taking a turn around the deck to settle his head. Perhaps he would even be walking along the weatherdecks, staring up at the cloud cover and wondering why he couldn't sleep.

Perhaps, indeed. In a way it might be better to remain below decks, where death at least would be swift and certain, if decidedly unpleasant. No, someone wandering the weatherdecks would have a chance of surviving at least the initial explosion.

The torpedo would intercept the keel of the fishing boat, which would be deep in the water. Fishing boats were like icebergs, with most of their mass out of sight. It would easily penetrate the old wooden hull, passing through several layers of bulkheads quite easily. Once it had reached several meters inside the hull, it would detonate, immediately shattering strakes, bulkheads, and every other structural member of the ship. How long the ship would stay afloat after that would depend on which part of the hull the torpedo hit, but the conclusion would be inevitable. The frigid sea would crash in, breaking down any barriers between storage holds, immediately flooding the lower regions and going to work on the upper. The boat would be dragged down, perhaps by its stern.

Inside, the crew would have only moments to do anything useful, and the odds of anyone managing to deploy a life raft or small boat in time were virtually nil, if indeed they even carried such equipment.

Even supposing that they did, the chances of surviving for more than ten minutes was nonexistent. *Jungwei* was under strict orders—no survivors.

It was the government's fault, wasn't it? Ku considered this question again as the water filled the remainder of the lockout.

Sun Yat Yat-Sen was across from him, another veteran of lockouts. It had become their habit not to talk during lockout. He wasn't certain exactly why, but they'd fallen into that routine many years ago, and neither one wanted to be the first to break the silence.

Yes, if fishermen died, it would be Taiwan's fault. They were Chinese, rightfully a part of a great nation. Just as the islands to the north, the Kuriles were, which had lived for so long under the oafish Russians' domination. And to the south, the Spratley Islands, with their oil-rich seabed floors. Yes, by marriage or conquest, over the centuries, all of this part of the world was properly a part of the Chinese hegemony.

And soon Taiwan would return to the fold. It had been carefully explained to him. Indeed, Taiwan would have rejoined the mainland many decades ago as one united nation had it not been for the continual interference of the United States.

But now, ah, now . . . it was time to strike. With most of America's forces deployed to the Middle East, quelling the constant conflict there, and her mightiest carrier, the USS *Jefferson*, seriously damaged, it was time to strike. The United States could do no more than howl ineffectively over the latest series of Chinese long-range missile tests.

The diplomatic protests would be a mere formality. Both Taiwan and the United States had been lulled into some degree of complacency by the missile tests in the past. Prior tests had skirted Taiwan by a large margin, and at least half the time the missiles failed to launch at all. Yes, it had been a long and careful plan of deception.

This time, it would be different. The missiles would fly on schedule and begin their trajectories just as every other test had in the past. But at some point, the missiles would turn south and burrow into the city of Taipei, destroying the treasonous rebels by the thousands, if not millions. And the most delicious part of the entire scheme would be that the United States would believe Taiwan was at fault. If Ku carried out his mission successfully, he would be single-handedly responsible for severing the relationship between the U.S. and China's wayward province.

Ku glanced at the waterproof pack at his side, and looked over to double-check Sun. The homing beacons were advanced, the best that China could produce. During the next missile tests, the missiles would veer off course "accidentally"—on purpose, of course—and strike several military targets. There would be plenty of evidence in the electromagnetic spectrum to show that Taiwan herself had caused the disaster.

The water covered his face now, as the last of the air hissed out. He waited another few seconds, and nodded at Sun. His massive partner reached up and easily turned the locking wheel, opening the connection between the sea and the lockout chamber. For just a moment, Ku felt a surge of nervousness, which he quickly repressed. Six hours, that was all. Then they would be back at the submarine, safely extracted, and on their way back to China. No one would even know that they'd been there—although they might suspect after the next test went so terribly wrong.

Ku stretched one last time, feeling his muscles and bones crack. Then he pulled himself up the ladder, fluttering his leg slightly, and swam out into the cold dark sea.

Once they were ashore, the mission went without incident. As had Ku and Sun's stealthy approach on the hospital, and the actual planting of the laser beacon. Now, with everything done, he was tempted to relax. But no, that would not be wise, not until he was back on the submarine.

Still, despite his best intentions, he found his concentration slipping. Part of it was from the sheer physical exhaustion of the swim, and the dread of having to do it again. Oh, of course he could—that wasn't even a question. But he dreaded the prospect of the hours undersea again, fighting down the moments of worry, and waiting to be picked up. He did not anticipate any problems—he had done this too many times before, although not under these exact circumstances.

Ku made his way back to the edge of the water where he'd stowed his gear. Right here, high above the water

line, well out of the reach of anything except a tidal wave.
He walked confidently to the location, moved to the rock
he'd picked as a landmark, and then stared.

No gear.

Had he somehow been mistaken? Perhaps it was the
next one over—or the next. He searched location after location, wandering further and further away from his original spot, his concern growing with every moment. It was
not possible that he had forgotten exactly where it was—
no, not possible at all.

Then he stopped dead at the sound of someone clearing
his throat, and turned, coldly certain at that moment what
had happened. Behind him were five man garbed in camouflage uniforms. Even the camouflage paint could not
change the shape of their eyes or the lanky structure of
their bodies. Americans—not Taiwanese.

One of them spoke, and although Ku understood the
dialect, he elected not to reply. He had been discovered—
his mission goal had changed. With the missile beacons
planted, his only remaining objective was to maintain his
silence until he died.

One of the men stepped forward and secured Ku's hands
behind him with a plastic strap. Two others conducted a
fast but thorough pat-down search, missing nothing. A
fourth took his knapsack and searched it. Within minutes,
they surrounded him and prodded him to move forward.

Americans. This would be easy. They were not trained,
hardened warriors, at least not in the traditions of honor
and mercilessness that Ku's own culture demanded. Prison,
even a military one, would be child's play to endure.

But the Americans did not take him to their own facilities. Instead, he was tossed into a Humvee and taken to
Taiwanese military headquarters in Taipei. There, surrounded by men of his own blood, Ku began to know fear.

Ku had dreaded the swim ashore. It was nothing compared to what he would experience in the next five hours.
And, in the end, he died without speaking.

•   •   •

Outside the Taiwanese compound, the senior member of the American SEAL team powered up his portable, secure satellite communications set. His radioman scanned the horizon with the parabolic mike, then grunted when the link was at maximum strength and clarity. With a nod, he passed the headset to the lieutenant.

"Yeah, the Taiwanese have got him," the lieutenant said, once he'd been quickly patched through to Don Stroh at CIA headquarters. "But we kept the gear we found. No maps, no charts, nothing like that. But what I got is enough." He held up his hand and surveyed the small piece of equipment he'd found there. "Transmitter—he had one spare, maybe in case something broke. And from the looks of it, it's got long-range capabilities."

The lieutenant listened for a moment, nodding in agreement with the man on the other end. Stroh had been in this business of deploying covert forces to problem spots all over the world far longer than the SEAL officer had, and he understood immediately what was going on.

"No way we could search every building within range, and there's no telling how long he's been ashore," the lieutenant said finally. He glanced overhead, as though already seeing the flights of missiles inbound. "But yeah, I gotta agree—there's something up with this, and the missile test they announced last week looks like a good candidate."

The other men in the squad moved uneasily. Armed men on the ground or in the water were one thing—dangerous business, but business they'd been trained to take care of. Missiles overhead were an entirely different matter. The only successful tactic was to be somewhere else, and each one of the SEALs had a deep aversion to cut-and-run.

The lieutenant handed the headset back to the radioman. "Okay, that's it. Like we thought, they're going to pass the buck to the Taiwanese forces. They may already know more than we do, if they got that bastard to talk." The lieutenant remembered the cold, flat expression in the Chinese frogman's face. "Or maybe not. He didn't look like the talkative sort. Anyway, Stroh's going to sanitize the source and dump the warning into all the normal channels. It'll put the good guys on alert, anyway."

"Alert for what, El-Tee?" the radioman asked.

"Good question, Barker. A very good question." Without saying anymore, the lieutenant lead them back to their operations center.

TWO

Retired Master Sergeant Colin Waterson whistled softly as he studied the data on his screen. It was faint, but it was there—a heat bloom.

"Judy, Judy, Judy," he said as he tweaked the gain on the screen. "You funning me, girl, or are we going all the way?"

Processing error? An innocent explanation, like a hot water geyser? Or the start of something that could get way, way out of hand?

Waterson glanced over at Jim Vail, the junior sensor analyst on this shift. As usual, Vail seemed lost in his own world, his eyes focused blankly on his screen but his thoughts clearly elsewhere. In contrast to Waterson's stocky, bullet-shaped body, Vail was a slender man, one who looked more like a poet than an analyst. In the three months they'd worked together, Waterson had come to the conclusion that Vail needed to find the guts to quit and find something that suited him better. It wasn't that Vail was a bad guy—to the contrary. He just didn't have the fire in his belly that Waterson liked to see in an analyst.

After three decades in uniform as an Air Force intelligence specialist, Waterson had found that stalking elusive trout in his Montana hideaway hadn't proved as fulfilling as he would have hoped. While his military retirement check covered all of his necessities, it couldn't provide the one thing in life he was missing—the sheer raw excitement of his military career.

In his last tour, Waterson had been the senior enlisted man at Cheyenne Mountain, the facility dug deep into rock that controlled all strategic sensors and weapons. Waterson was a veteran of countless periods of increasing tension and had seen what happened when someone thought that the next world war was about to start. It was heady stuff, and despite the long hours, days and weeks during which absolutely nothing happened, he missed those moments when everything was on the line, when the slightest screw-up or hesitation could spell the difference between war and peace.

So he'd gone back to it, at least part-time. Not in Cheyenne Mountain, but as a senior analyst onboard the USNS *Observation Island*, a ship operated by the Military Sea Lift command that was primarily composed of antennas and sensors. The Judy in his life was Cobra Judy, the sensor system fitted on the ship.

Cobra Judy was one leg of a detection triad that kept a close eye on every area of the world that possessed ballistic missile launch capability. Waterson's Judy consisted of a solid-state based array fitted into the stern of the USNS *Observation Island*. The four-story high structure monitored the exo-atmospheric portions of Russia and Chinese ballistic missile test flights. Cobra Judy operated in conjunction with Cobra Dane as well as a dedicated satellite network.

Waterson had been to Cobra Dane, the massive shore-based radar located at Shamir Air Force Base on Shemya Island. He'd stared up at the single, circular-phased array radar thirty meters in diameter. The face of the radar was

covered with more than 35,000 elements and faced south-
west, covering an arc of one hundred and twenty degrees.
Initially operational in 1977, Cobra Dane was upgraded in
the nineties to improve its capabilities. It could follow one
hundred targets at once, as originally configured, and as
part of an early warning network, could track two hundred
targets.

The final leg of the triad, and the only one Waterson
hadn't visited in situ, although he had seen one of them
before launch, was a defense support program consisting
of satellites positioned about twenty-two thousand miles
above the equator. The satellites monitored other areas
known to have ballistic missile launch capabilities and,
along with large ocean areas' satellites sensors, detected
the heat generated from a missile launch and transmitted
data to ground stations.

All three legs of the triad were operated by and reported
to the United States Air Force Space Command, which
provided strategic warning of detected missiles to the National Command Authority.

"Got it on Dane and overhead," Vail said. The correlating data blipped into being on Waterson's screen,
confirming the detection his Judy had brought him. "Cheyenne's got a copy on the data."

Waterson felt his stomach tighten. Suddenly, he had the
urgent need to take a leak, as his body responded to the
flood of adrenaline.

Observation Island operated alone. No fighter cover, no
missile cruisers, nothing. For self-defense, she possessed
two close-in weapons system setups, as much as a reas-
surance to the crew as for any real protection value.

They all knew what the score was. If the balloon went
up and the world went to shit, their ship's life expectancy
dropped dramatically. The last thing Russia or China
wanted was an extremely sensitive radar detection ship
keeping an eye on the goings on, and Waterson figured
they'd be in the initial targeting package any staff put together.

It was something that they'd all been briefed on when they'd come on board. Just a fact of life, that your survivability might go to shit in the blink of an eye. It wasn't something they talked about—part of life in a blue suit, Waterson figured—and the crew onboard *Observation Island* sure wasn't the only one in that boat.

But before, it hadn't seemed quite so damned personal.

"Tracking," Waterson announced. "I got a target line—medium confidence—looks like it will hit open water twenty miles north of Taiwan."

Twenty miles. Within the margin of error for earlier ballistic missiles, but everything Waterson had seen on the latest technology being tested by China indicated that they'd gotten their targeting accuracy down to a matter of meters. Although the U.S. was still far ahead of them, measuring their missiles' accuracy in inches, Waterson figured that it didn't matter that much in the short range. You were just as dead if a Chinese missile hit ten meters away or two inches away. It was on the longer flights that it came into play, when a missile traversing thousands of miles to reach the continental U.S. might develop much larger variances and end up hitting, say, Burke, Virginia, instead of the Capitol building in D.C.

Twenty miles. That ought to be enough. Not saying I'd like it much if I were fishing the waters north of Taiwan, but enough so that it ought to miss land.

Unless there's a screwup, right? And isn't that why you do live fire tests, to find out if the wonderful targeting accuracy that every one of your computer models swears exists is actually ground in truth?

The data and symbology on his screen blinked once, then disappeared into a flurry of harmless pixels. "Self-destruct?" Vail asked hopefully. "Or we lose data link?"

"Yeah," Waterson answered. "Data link is okay, but I got snow—they must have self-destructed."

Silence fell in the compartment as they all kept close watch on their respective screens, praying that it was over but afraid just yet to hope that it was.

"Nothing else," Waterson announced finally as the static cleared from his screen. "Clear scope."

And thank God for that. It means this probably is a test, probably there won't be a missile launched at us, and I may just live long enough to see those grandkids start first grade.

It was at moments like this that life back in Montana looked very, very appealing.

The Taiwanese frigate **The Marshall P'eng**
Off the western coast of Taiwan
Tuesday, September 3
0300 local (GMT +8)

The blood of ancient warriors ran in Taiwanese Navy Captain Chang Tso-Lin's veins. Both family oral traditions and written records traced his lineage back to ancient days. He himself was named for a warlord from the last century. He carried on that tradition with a quiet pride.

He was well regarded by both his superiors and his subordinates. His crew worshipped him, regarding him as a patriarch of their shipboard family. Many of them had ancestors who had served with Chang Tso-Lin's ancestors, and they were proud of that connection. He was regarded within the Navy as a rising young tiger, selected early for command, and known as an astute tactician. He was a humble man in bearing but he insisted on perfection in his crew and demanded even more of himself. He was a naval officer any nation would be proud to claim.

That he was assigned to command *Marshall P'eng* was no accident of timing. The Taiwanese had seen this day coming for decades, and were well aware that their fragile freedom rested on the shaky goodwill of their American friends. They were exceptionally conscientious in selecting captains for ships that would work with the Americans directly, but there had been no question about Chang Tso-Lin. He was, simply, the finest the nation had to offer.

Chang had completed his early education in Taiwan, but once his potential became apparent, he'd been sent to the United States for graduate school. His command of English was fluent and colloquial, on par with a professional linguist. He understood not only the language but the American culture as well, and, in his heart of hearts, had even briefly considered the possibility of emigrating. But his sense of family honor and duty to his country was far too strong to permit it to be any more than a brief fantasy. He put it aside almost immediately, turned his attention back to his work and did as his nation had asked him.

The Marshall P'eng steamed in calm waters today, her boilers providing power to turn the shafts. The ship was an old U.S. Knox-class frigate, considered too weary and battered for further service in the American Navy.

A wasteful attitude, as far as Captain Chang was concerned. The ship was structurally sound, and with careful maintenance and dedication, had been restored to a virtually pristine condition. Her engine room was spotless, her radars tightly tuned and deadly. She was in a higher state of readiness and efficiency then she ever had been in the American Navy.

He had to admit, though, that his nation's policy of not transferring people as often as the Americans did had something to do with it, as well. Men were stationed on *Marshall P'eng* for years, and knew her quirks and peculiarities. They had more ownership in her than their American counterparts had had, and it was a matter of personal pride to every man that she both looked and performed her best.

Currently, the only American presence in the area was an Aegis-class cruiser, the USS *Lake Champlain*. She'd been on station for two months, popping in and out of port on liberty visits as often as her schedule permitted, and Chang had come to know her captain well. Captain James Norfolk was a typical American, brash and blunt, overflowing with vital energy and good cheer. His ship itself was a marvel to Chang, containing advanced electronics and weaponry that his country would not see for decades. It seemed to entrust such technological capabilities to what—by Taiwanese standards—amounted to a pickup crew. The cruiser captain himself would be in command for only eighteen months. Chang's tour, by contrast, was a minimum of five years.

Nevertheless, Chang and Norfolk quickly came to understand each other as only professional sailors could do. Chang privately considered some of the captain's tactical plans to be foolhardy, but he recognized that the superior weaponry and fire control systems could quickly compensate for any overconfidence on the part of the cruiser's crew.

The cruiser was ten miles to the north, conducting a slow, methodical search of her assigned operating area. The ship's last liberty had been cut short when the Taiwanese government began to notice escalating tensions. Norfolk was not so sure he agreed, but he was an accommodating fellow. He rousted his crew and put to sea with almost everyone onboard. The helicopters were still ferrying back and forth almost daily to reprovision them and bring along stragglers.

Chang walked to the bridge wing and stared off to the east. Somewhere over the horizon lay China. Not that being over the horizon mattered anymore. In terms of weapons and fire-control solutions, they were virtually next door.

This latest missile test would bring them even closer. It would be fired from a Chinese destroyer. The intelligence reports Chang had seen were worrisome. She supposedly carried sea-skimmer missiles that might be virtually impossible to detect before it was too late. Additionally, the cruiser in company with her carried long-range land attack missiles.

The Chinese claimed it was a test. Chang considered the exercise as preparations for war.

Without the Americans here, he had little hope of intercepting the missile with his own missiles. Even with her best efforts, the systems she was designed to fight against were decades old, and no amount of care and maintenance could make up for the technological gap between the two ships. And no one could doubt that the American sailors, for all their frequent transfers, were superbly trained.

No, the critical differences lay far deeper than that. First, Chang and his crew knew these waters, knew the tricks and traps of both the electromagnetic spectrum and the seething currents under their hull. Second, the *Marshall P'eng* was defending her homeland. The chain of command was shorter, Chang's orders more direct, and his motivation strong. Countering this missile attack, if indeed one took place, was what he had been born, bred, and trained for. He would prevail. That was not in doubt.

USS Lake Champlain
Twenty miles north of **The Marshall P'eng**
0300 local (GMT +8)

James Norfolk, the *Lake Champlain*'s commanding officer, had just finished soaping up for a shower after his late night workout when the general quarters gong filled the ship. He swore, jammed his thumb down on the water flow button on the showerhead, and blasted the hot water on his face just long enough to get the soap away from his eyes. That done, he grabbed his towel and took one quick swipe over his body before pulling on his pants and slipping on his shoes. With his shirt and his socks in his hand, he ran for his station in combat.

Speakers lining the passageway continued the gonging for five seconds, then a voice broke in. "General quarters, general quarters. All hands man your battle stations. Reason for general quarters: ballistic missile launch from Gungzho base."

Shit! Those little bastards! Norfolk vaulted up the ladders leading to the bridge, in close formation with the other sailors hauling ass all over the ship. Those heading forward or up used the starboard passageways, those heading aft or down used the port, but there was still enough movement, particularly with a large portion of the crew rousted from their racks, for asses and elbows to go flying. Many of them were far less dressed than Norfolk was, but all carried their clothes in their hands. When there was time, they'd get dressed, and not a person on the mixed gender crew gave a shit who had what on, not with general quarter going down.

Norfolk burst into combat and ran over to the TAO, Lieutenant Calvin Ackwurst. "What you got?"

"Ballistic missile launch from the shore site. Coming in over national assets, confirmed by Cheyenne. It's for real, sir." Ackwurst pointed up at the symbols on the monitor mounted just above eye level. "Trajectory still unknown."

At least to us. Somebody somewhere knows where it's going and they ain't saying. Norfolk had spent enough time in joint command centers around this part of the world to know just how fast the detection and analysis process could work. And even now, when he was still shoving his soapy arms into his shirt, there was some poor bastard somewhere waking the President up to tell him what was going on.

"We're still inside our box, speed twelve, course one one zero," Ackwurst said, and then continued with an abbreviated brief on the equipment status of the ship. Even as he spoke he was moving toward the hatch leading off the bridge, because Ackwurst's own GQ station was in engineering.

The boatswain's mate of the watch shoved Norfolk's GQ gear into his hands, and Norfolk automatically donned the steel helmet, the flash gear, and slung the bio-chem gear along his side. Seconds later, he said, "I relieve you," and after a brief announcement to the watch crew,

Ackwurst scurried off the bridge. The whole process had taken less than a minute.

Norfolk took a deep breath and surveyed the crew in combat. Everyone was in place, alert but not panicked. That was the reason for the frequent drills, to turn it into a reflex, to reduce the confusion factor.

"Captain?" a voice came over his headset.

"XO, it's going to pass to the north of us, but not by much. Let's come right, put us bow on to it. I don't think we're a player in this, but let's not take any chances."

"Aye-aye." Norfolk felt the ship turn as the XO gave the orders, knowing that it wasn't really necessary. Turning toward the trajectory would present a smaller profile to the missile, should it turn out to be something other than what they thought. But with modern targeting systems, it wouldn't make a whole lot of difference. The ship's self-defense systems were equally effective at any target angle.

But even though it wasn't tactically necessary, it gave the crew something to do, a maneuver to focus their attention on and a chance to make sure everything was working as advertised. Action calmed nerves, and the sense that they were turning to face it was beneficial as well.

"CPA, thirty miles," Ackwurst said almost immediately. "Confirmation over intell circuits, Captain. I don't want to stand down, though, until we figure out what's going on."

"Open ocean impact, sir?" Norfolk said, mentally working out the picture in his head.

"Affirmative. Unless something goes wrong."

And something always goes wrong, Norfolk thought. *It's just a matter of how and when.* "Does *P'eng* know?" he asked.

"I'm just letting them know now," the TAO replied, his voice grim. "And Captain Chang ain't liking it one little bit."

Can't say that I blame him. It's like living in San Diego and having a missile heading for Oceanside. That close.

The Marshall P'eng
0305 local (GMT +8)

Captain Chang beat the *Lake Champlain* by almost a full minute in setting general quarter, but by the time he'd settled into his station, the verdict was already in. The missile would miss Taiwan, and, except for the remote possibility of impacting a fishing or commercial vessel, posed no threat to his country.

No threat, that was, other than the promise of more to come. How long would they be required to tolerate these increasingly menacing test flights before a mistake was made? The Chinese were either deliberately provoking them and the Americans or they were attempting to lull them both into complacency until the moment that they eventually struck. And strike they would, of that Chang was certain.

A radioman dashed up and handed him a hastily printed-out message. Chang took it and scanned the contents. He sucked in a sharp breath, then passed the message to his watch officer.

Taiwan had had enough. His government was officially requesting that the American ship cruising with them employ her weapons to destroy the test missile. It was invading Taiwanese air space and hazarding vessels off Taiwan's coast.

Enough is enough. Let's see if our ally really means what they tell us—that they are committed to a free and democratic Taiwan.

USS **Lake Champlain**
0311 local (GMT +8)

Norfolk stared at the message on the screen in front of him. Equal measures of deep concern and glee coursed through him. This was the moment every cruiser captain waited for, the time to use all the power of the ship as it was intended to be used. But another part of him dreaded what was to come. Not necessarily for him and his crew— no, they could take care of themselves. The unconscious arrogance that nothing, absolutely nothing in the world could penetrate his ship's defenses was as much a part of a cruiser's officers and crew as it was of any naval aviator. Inside this ship, the one they'd trained on so hard, kept up so well, they were all invulnerable.

But not everyone was so well-situated, foremost among them the Taiwanese frigate to their south. And not only the frigate—Taiwan itself was not heavily defended, not ringed with the Patriot batteries so common in the Middle East and Europe, not surrounded by flights of fighters. And while *Lake Champlain* could protect herself and her crew, and most probably the frigate as well, there was no way they could cover every approach. Sooner or later, a missile would reach its intended target, and the bloodshed that would follow already haunted him.

But for now, he had one task—destroy the missile in flight now, and hopefully, by doing so, dissuade China from launching more. He turned to his TAO, who had already assigned anti-air missiles to the target and was waiting for weapons release authority. A quiet, expectant air filled combat.

"Weapons free," Norfolk said quietly. "Make every shot count, TAO."

Because there's no telling what this is the start of. Maybe it's just a missile test shot, and this will all blow over. But maybe it isn't, and if it isn't, there's a chance that I'm going to want every single missile I've got on-board later on.

A low rumble swept through the ship. Norfolk watched the monitor mounted in one corner. The picture showed the foredeck, the vertical launch cell hatch popping open, and then the nose of the missile emerging. He had just a split second to marvel at its size before a boiling cloud of steam and smoke swept across the deck and obscured the picture. As visibility crashed down to zero, the ship gave one hard shake, as though it were a dog coming out of the sea, then settled back into the water.

Norfolk shifted his gaze to the computer monitor. There was nothing more to see on deck—within seconds, the missile would be out of view and the radar return would provide the only information.

"Two shots fired, no apparent casualties," the TAO reported. "Standing by for third shot."

"Wait on it," Norfolk said as he studied the geometry. Something clicked inside of him, and he knew without a doubt that the first missile would find its target. He knew, even before the computer-generated solution could flash onto the screen, that the second missile would find no more than carbonized metal and hot gases in the air.

Forty seconds later, Norfolk's intuition was confirmed. Raw video on the radar scopes flared into tight balls of static, then faded to reveal empty air. The data link screen to his right flashed up the computer's assessment: CON-FIRMED KILL.

"Good work," Norfolk said. "We could have made do with just one, you think?"

A flurry of cheerful comments, the aftermath of the tension, flooded the compartment. They were proud, more confident than ever, now that they had their first kill under their belts. It had gone flawlessly.

Perhaps too flawlessly. Because they don't yet know just how screwed up your tactical picture can get in combat. Let 'em enjoy it now, but don't let them get overconfident. If this is just the beginning, then they'll learn soon enough what it's like. And if it's not, well, then, this could be the last time that they ever get to do it for real.

But something tells me this isn't the last time. Not the last time at all.

With those sobering thoughts on his mind, Captain Norfolk settled in to wait.

THREE

Commander Hillman "Lab Rat" Busby was slowly savoring his way through a bowl of the best clam chowder he had had in at least five years. He had watched Tony prepare it, saw the sauce steaming, until the cook had gently stirred in the clams. It'd simmered just long enough to barely cook them, just to the point of tenderness, and then been dished out immediately into his eagerly held bowl.

A sprinkle of pepper, just the right amount, Lab Rat meticulously counting each grain. Then he positioned his bowl just so, and opened a packet of crackers to rest on the side of his plate. Then, reverently picking up his spoon, he dipped into the steaming bowl. He scooped out a small serving, making sure it included some clam bits—indeed, they were almost impossible to avoid, as thickly as they were cluttered in the rich white broth. He let it cool just a few moments, and then slid it into his mouth.

The sensation was completely indescribable. Lab Rat

groaned a low moan of pleasure. The other diners glanced around nervously, but he ignored them. There was nothing, absolutely nothing, like clam chowder on the Chesapeake Bay.

"Everything all right, sir?" his waitress asked, evidently reacting to the concern of the other diners.

Lab Rat swallowed, regretfully leaving his mouth empty. "Yes, perfectly fine. Absolutely perfectly deliciously—fine."

He glanced over at the grill, and saw Tony smiling back at him. The burly Virginia-born and -bred fisherman understood. It was the rest of these people, the tourists who didn't have a connoisseur's appreciation of clam chowder and the jaded locals, too accustomed to the luxury of perfect chowder, who didn't understand.

"Gloria!" Tony shouted, loud enough to be heard over the noise in the seafood shack. "Leave the man alone— he's from the West Coast."

Sudden enlightenment graced every face, and they all murmured sympathetically. A few couples looked at him with pity.

Lab Rat didn't care. He scooped up another spoonful of chowder, his mouth eager to continue the gustatory orgasm.

Suddenly, the screen door burst open. Lieutenant Commander Bill Frank strode into the room, a look of concern on his face.

Frank was Lab Rat's second in command of the intelligence detachment from the USS *Jefferson*. With the carrier in dry dock for repairs, she had little use for the highly specialized talents of her intelligence spooks. Admiral Everette "Batman" Wayne, never one to waste precious Navy manpower, had promptly formed the CVIC department into an independent detachment and sent them packing. The Navy had opined that with the Middle East situation still in flux—and when exactly wasn't it? Lab Rat had wondered—that Lab Rat and his sailors would be most effective working in direct support of USACOM, the type commander with cognizance over the Atlantic theater of operations. Lab Rat and sixty-two others were currently making a nuisance of themselves at the Joint Intelligence Center, or JIC, at Naval Station Norfolk.

Frank plopped himself down in the chair opposite Lab Rat without speaking. The native of Alabama was never one to interrupt a man when he was eating, but Lab Rat could already see that bad news was coming. If he waited long enough, Frank would tell him, feeding him short phrases in a brief summary delivered in that slow drawl of his.

Lab Rat sighed and put down his spoon. "What now? Can't I even enjoy my chowder in peace?"

"Back to the office, sir," Frank said, no trace of apology in his voice. Whatever he'd been doing when his duty officer beeper had gone off, Frank evidently thought it was a good deal more interesting than immersing himself in a bowl of chowder. Given Frank's disheveled appearance and the slight smudge of black on his collar—eye makeup, perhaps?—Lab Rat thought that he could make an educated guess as to what Frank thought was more important than a bowl of chowder.

"But what for?" Lab Rat asked, knowing even as he spoke the words that anything that warranted a recall was far too classified to be discussed here. Frank just shook his head.

Lab Rat stared down at the bowl of creamy chowder, almost ready to cry. He waved Gloria over, and said, "I'm afraid I'll have to ask for this to go." It would be cold, or least chilly by the time he got to eat it. Although he could eat in his car—no, not safe, not unless he left his here and rode back to base with Frank.

The sheer unfairness of it all came crashing in on him. "And," he said, with sudden ferocity, determined to wring some sort of concession out of life, "I want another quart. To go. In an insulated container. With extra crackers. LOTS of extra crackers."

Gloria stepped back slightly, then smiled and nodded. "You sure are from California, aren't you, sir?"

Pier Thirteen
Collins Shipyard, San Diego, California
1500 local (GMT −8)

Admiral Everette "Batman" Wayne and retired Admiral Matthew "Tombstone" Magruder stood on the pier and surveyed the battered hull of the USS *Jefferson*. She was in dry dock, her keel resting on individually crafted cradles, the water drained out of the dock so her entire hull was exposed. In dry dock, the carrier looked more like an office building than ever before. She was massive, overshadowing every other structure around, an imposing figure. It seemed impossible that she was upright, supported only by the cradles, ripped from the sea to stand naked and exposed to the world.

"The old girl has seen better days," Tombstone said quietly.

"Yes. But it's not as bad as it looks, they say. Another week, and she'll be back together."

To an aviator, an aircraft carrier was a shape-shifting creature of magic. At night, to an approaching pilot hoping desperately for the first glimpse of her lights through foul weather, *Jefferson* seemed impossibly small, a mere postage stamp in a vast ocean. In every approach Tombstone had ever made, there had been one fragile moment when it seemed inconceivable that the massive aircraft strapped on his ass could somehow land on that deck that looked so short.

But that moment passed in an instant, and within seconds, *Jefferson* looked like a granite cliff, massive and inhospitable. Her stern would rise up from the ocean almost one hundred feet, depending on how the waves caught her and how heavily laden she was. She stretched

several football fields in length. Below the water line, there
were another eight decks, in addition to the twelve above
the water line, and that wasn't even taking into account
the height of her antennas and radar masts. Her deck was
massive, stretching out for miles and miles, and finding the
elusive three-wire seemed the proverbial needle in a hay-
stack.

Once you were onboard again, *Jefferson* shrank by a
factor of ten. Aircraft from eight squadrons crowded her
deck and hangar space, and with thousands of sailors and
officers running over her exposed surface, repairing, preparing for launch flight, and directing the aircraft around
on the hot nonskid of her flight deck it seemed impossible
to taxi to your appointed spot without sucking at least a
dozen of them down your jet intakes.

And it didn't end there. Even when you weren't flying,
Jefferson seemed impossibly larger on the inside than on
the outside. Few people on the ship had been to every
compartment—in fact, most sailors had never even visited
each of her decks. The decks below the waterline that held
her machinery, nuclear reactor, and everything that kept
her steaming through the ocean in excess of thirty-five
knots, was well out of the way for most except engineers.
Above that, the decks were crowded with enlisted berthing
and the enlisted dining facility, as well as some officers'
quarters. Then the 03 level, the one immediately below the
flight deck. That housed the guts of the combat capabilities. Forward, the ship's combat direction center, staffed
by ship's personnel, coordinated the actions of the battle
group. Six decks above, the ASW commander, or Des
Ron, took control of the undersea warfare battle, coordinating flights of S-3B and other antisubmarine warfare aircraft and assets, including helos and surface-ship towed
arrays and sonars.

Back on the 03 level, aft of the ship's CDC, were the
flag spaces. They were curtained off from the rest of the
passageway by blue plastic curtains pulled back to each
side. They were sometimes tied back to provide passage-

way, but other times met in the middle. The tile on the deck there, too, was blue. Blue meant flag spaces—ship's personnel were to steer clear and use the long passageway on the other side of the ship rather than trespass on that ground.

The blue tile area was short compared to the rest of ship, housing all the administrative and combat functions of the admiral's staff. Both Tombstone and Batman had filled that billet, Tombstone first being pressed suddenly into power from his billet at CAG. Batman had just spent two years as the admiral in command of the battle group, and was still technically embarked on the battered ship.

The blue tile passageway was where elephants danced, and the rest of the ship ventured in there at their own peril. The short stretch of office space housed not only the admiral, but the Carrier Air Wing Commander as well. Technically, his billet should have been abbreviated as CAW, but the historic acronym for the earlier title of Carrier Air Group commander stuck even after changes in command structure rendered it obsolete. The senior, post-command Navy captains that filled the new billet were convinced to a man that CAW sounded exceptionally—well—stupid, although they'd generally phrased that thought in more traditionally colorful language.

The CAG owned all the aircraft onboard the carrier, and he was the immediate superior of each one of the individual squadron commanding officers. He, in turn, reported to the admiral onboard, the Carrier Battle Group Commander, and it was CAG's responsibility to task missions and sorties to support the CVBG's plans.

The final elephant dancing onboard the carrier was the carrier's commanding officer, also a senior, post-command aviator captain as fully qualified as the CAG to run flight operations. In contrast to the CAG, the carrier CO owned the airfield just overhead the flag spaces as well as all the non-squadron maintenance facilities onboard. The ship's CO also provided the infrastructure for the squadrons and the battle group staff in the form of messing and berthing for all the officers and sailors, medical, dental and religious staffs, communications and the carrier intelligence center, or CVIC. Both the CAG and the ship's CO were normally rising stars, ones that could reasonably expect to rise to admiral rank and someday own the coveted blue tile passageway themselves.

But *Jefferson*'s last deployment might have permanently benched the CAG and ship's CO. Batman had been in command as Battle Group Commander when *Jefferson* had taken the fatal shot, trapped in the Gulf during what looked to be a final flare-up in the Middle East. As *Jefferson* escaped the confined waters, she had hit a mine that the mine sweeper had missed. The resulting damage put her out of action, and brought her back here to the shipyards and had probably put a fatal black mark on the CAG and CO's records.

"The keel is okay, it's mostly the steel plates. Some damage to one shaft." Batman's voice was soft. "I hate to turn her over to anyone else in that shape, Stony."

"Where do you go from here?" Tombstone asked.

Batman shook his head. "No word yet. The more senior you get, the harder it is to figure out the billets. And getting *Jefferson* all banged up while I was in command doesn't help any."

"You thought about retiring?" Tombstone asked.

"Yeah. I know I'll have to some time—hey, if you can do it, I can too." Batman tried on a smile that didn't fit too well. "Nothing's decided yet . . . for now, I'm overseeing her repairs, awaiting further assignment."

They were silent for a moment, surveying the damage. Technicians scurried around her massive flanks like ants, clinging to scaffolding and ladders. The last of several massive steel plates was being lifted into place, where it would be riveted and welded to complete the repairs. Further down the pier, the damaged plates were piled up like giant potato chips, impossibly warped, burnt and twisted.

"Good thing the *United States* is ahead of schedule,"

Tombstone said. "She can fill the gap, at least for a while. Until *Jefferson* is repaired."

The newest addition to America's nuclear ship arsenal was moored four piers away, and she was a stark contrast to the battered *Jefferson*. The USS *United States* had yet to see action, and her hull showed it. She was pristine, gleaming in the spring morning, still waiting for a final coat of haze gray paint that would help her blend into the horizon. Her radar antennas were glistening black, her pennants and fittings impossibly clean.

It wasn't that *Jefferson* had been a dirty ship—far from it. But after a decade of being on the front lines of every conflict in the world, her age was starting to show. She had seen more action than any aircraft carrier since the world wars, and although she had held up well, there was no magical potion to restore the fresh gleam of youth to her cheeks. The new steel plates stood out smooth and unblemished like scars against the rest of her worn, oxidized hull.

"*United States* starts her sea trials today," Batman said reflectively, turning the conversation away from himself. There was too much uncertainty in the future—he didn't want to be reminded of it. "Remember those days?"

Tombstone groaned. "Do I ever. Long days, longer nights—God save me from ever having to do sea trials again."

"I don't think we're in much danger of having to." Batman's voice was grave. He turned to his old lead and said, "So when are you going to tell me something about this?"

Tombstone shook his head. "When I can, I will."

As Tombstone made his way home, his mind was racing over the possibilities. For the last two weeks, his uncle and he had been going over every conceivable scenario that might require the services of a covert air group. Between the two of them, they figured they covered most of the bases. Now they were in the final stages of contacting candidates for staff positions and asking them if they were interested in something very, very secret and very, very important. Tombstone had taken it on himself to personally contact the members of his previous pickup game in Hawaii, and was waiting for their answers. His uncle also had a number of men and women in mind, people he had served with over his decades in the Navy. Between the two of them, they were about to embark on a looting mission within the ranks of the United States Navy.

His uncle Thomas Magruder was brother to Tombstone's father. Tombstone's father had been a naval aviator during the Vietnam War. During a daring inland mission to destroy a critical resupply bridge, Tombstone's father had been shot down. For decades, he'd been listed as missing rather than killed. It was only during the last five years, as Tombstone had acquired enough power within the Navy to give him some degree of flexibility in his assignments, that he'd begun to suspect the truth. During an encounter with a Ukrainian naval officer, Tombstone had learned that there was a possibility that his father had survived the ejection and been taken prisoner. Following the old path through Vietnamese prison camps, Tombstone had found evidence that his father had been taken to Russia. In one of his most grueling missions ever, Tombstone had finally found his father's grave in Russia.

Uncle Thomas, a naval surface ship officer, had stepped into the gap in Tombstone's life as a surrogate father. He'd been the one to teach Tombstone to throw a killer curve ball, to encourage him in his studies and coach him in his early years in the Navy, to stand by his side as best man when Tombstone finally married Tomboy. And now, as both of their careers were coming to an end, his uncle had been the one to lead him back to his real passion—flying.

As a former Chief of Naval Operations, his uncle's possible second career opportunities had been virtually unlimited. But instead of signing on as a highly paid consultant to a defense industry contractor, his uncle had heeded a call to head up a specialized black operations unit composed of men and women who were willing to do what had to be done to prevent war before it started. They were so far off the books that their missions were completely deniable.

Foremost among the scenarios Tombstone and his uncle had planned for were ones involving China. The potential for difficulties in that region was enormous. And, with so much of America's might committed long-term to the Middle East, there was every chance it would flair into chaos in the near future. Tombstone knew those waters well, having dealt with the Chinese on far too many occasions.

Most of the aircraft would be requisitioned rather than permanently assigned, along with the necessary complement of maintenance technicians. That was one way to keep the budget numbers low enough to cause no alarm elsewhere. The cover story made recruiting the most difficult part of it all. Tombstone's face was too well known to too many of the operating forces all over the world, and there was little chance that he could avoid being recognized. He even briefly considered plastic surgery, but decided against it.

Ever since his return to the civilian world, Tombstone had felt a lightening up of spirit. The tragedies of the last year were no less real, but for the first time, he thought he might be able to survive losing Tomboy during the last attempted invasion of Hawaii. He had watched helplessly as her plane had gone down, unable to save her. In one sense, his life had ended when his RIO wife had died. Had he simply retired from the Navy at the same time, he thought the pain would have been unbearable. But the prospect of flying again full time had been the only sliver of hope and light in his otherwise dark world.

No, life would never be the same. For as long as he lived, he would feel this aching emptiness, this sense of a part of himself being irrevocably gone. But at least he would have a purpose in life, something on which to focus his energies. And eventually, he might even have a chance to strike back at the bastards that had taken Tomboy from him.

"Look," Batman said, elbowing him in the side and bringing Tombstone back to the present. "She's getting underway."

FOUR

USS **United States**
Pier Alpha, Naval Air Station North Island
San Diego, California
Wednesday, September 4
1505 local (GMT−8)

Admiral Willis E. "Coyote" Grant leaned over the railing, staring at the pier below. Even though the ship was moving away from the pier, the V-shaped configuration of the carrier resulted in the flight deck overhanging the pier for a considerable distance. The carrier would be well off the pier before he would see water between the ship and the concrete.

Not much was likely to go wrong, not now. Every senior ship-handler onboard was watching, bringing centuries of experience to bear on the evolution of moving away from the pier. Even his Chief of Staff, Navy Captain Jim Ganner, was watching, staring aft as though he could read the radio signals connecting the Officer of the Deck, the forward and aft observers and the tugs.

"Looking good, Admiral," Ganner said finally, as though Coyote had been waiting for his opinion. Ganner had a way of sounding like he thought that any aviator around really needed the adult supervision of a surface officer. And that included his own admiral. No matter that Coyote had had command of *Jefferson* himself, as well as a previous command of a deep draft surface ship, both vessels far larger and more like the carrier than the destroyers and cruisers Ganner had commanded. In truth, Coyote judged himself a better ship-handler of a carrier than any surface sailor who'd commanded only smaller ships.

But it was only Ganner's second week onboard, far too soon to be characterizing minor character flaws as mortal sins. Coyote would give him some rope, let him run with the bit for a while before he had to start jerking the man up short. He'd get him settled in before the first cruise— and if he didn't, well, there were plenty of Navy captains around who'd jump at the billet. Plenty of 'em who'd know when to speak up and when to just stay out of the way. Like Ganner ought to be doing right now.

For the last thirty minutes, Coyote had paced the flag bridge, unable to settle down in any one spot. On the deck below him, the captain of the ship and his crew were making the final preparations for getting underway. Four tugs were already around the massive carrier, the lines firmly affixed. He heard the whistle blast from one that signified they were ready to commence operations.

Coyote knew all too well what was going on one deck below him. It was a nerve-racking game, to maneuver an aircraft carrier away from a pier, even with the assistance of tugs. Even more so when she was brand-spanking-new, not a scratch on her, with a price tag higher than that ever paid for any aircraft carrier before.

The flight deck looked strange empty, as did the hangar bay. There was not a single aircraft onboard yet. Oh, they would soon come flocking, just as soon as they cleared the harbor area and controlled sea lanes and could make their way to the flight operations area. Then the deck would be

insane, as systems were tested real-time for the first time
and the inevitable glitches sprang up.

In addition to flexing the flight deck and flight deck
crew, the ship would also be testing every system in her
engineering department. That meant full-speed runs, crash
backs or emergency stops and emergency reverses, and a
variety of tight turns and weaving maneuvers designed to
give everything every possible chance to go wrong. There
would be man-overboard drills, engineering casualty drills,
firefighting drills, drills, drills, and more drills, until the
entire crew and wardroom were ready to scream. And then
there would be more drills.

But as grueling as the next two weeks would be, the
honor of being a plank owner, or member of the first crew,
made up for it. There would never be another acceptance
sea trial, never another set of plank owners.

The handheld radio next to Coyote crackled to life as a
stream of orders began issuing from the bridge to the tugs.
Coyote listened critically, ready to step in if he thought
the captain was hazarding the ship, but he could detect no
flaw in the captain's performance. Ganner kept up a running commentary, as though Coyote needed an explanation, before Coyote finally told him to keep quiet.

"Admiral?" A chief petty officer approached, a clipboard held in front of him. "Flash traffic, sir. I thought
you'd want to see this."

"Thanks, Chief." Coyote reached past Ganner to take
the clipboard, resisting the temptation to slap Ganner's
hand as he reached for it. Coyote had served a brief stint
as Chief of Staff and he knew what the job entailed.

Yeah, so a chief of staff was supposed to run interference for his admiral and ensure that he only had to deal
with stuff that really required his attention—so what? The
chief radioman had been around the Navy just as long as
Ganner and had been making the calls on radio messages
for admirals for at least ten years. Sure, having Ganner
screen routine stuff was a necessary part of the chain of
command, but there were limits to that, too. What worked

well in peacetime wasn't always a good idea when flash traffic started flying around.

The carrier was moving so slowly than it was impossible to tell that she was leaving the pier and getting underway except for the one long blast sounded by the ship's whistle and the order over the 1MC, "Shift colors." Other than that, the only clue was the gradual opening of the distance between ship and the pier and the low vibration running through the deck.

Coyote scanned the message, then whistled softly. Without comment, he passed it over to Ganner, who scowled as he read it. "There goes the deployment schedule," Ganner said when he'd finished.

"Maybe, maybe not," Coyote said, perversely driven to disagree with Ganner although he had a feeling the man was right. "One antimissile shot's not the end of the world. Nobody harm, no foul." Even as he let the trite saying slip out of his mouth, Coyote knew he didn't believe it.

Why didn't they just let the missile go? According to the trajectory, it was headed for open ocean. Why shoot this one down when they've let others go before?

"Could be nothing at all," Ganner agreed easily, although Coyote could see that he didn't agree at all. Regardless of his faults, Ganner was no fool. "But it wouldn't hurt to be ready for a change in the schedule. If we *do* get shipped out early, the time schedule's going to be short. Not only supplies, but personnel as well. With your permission, I'll tickle the system a bit, see if we can't get some orders expedited."

"Make it happen," Coyote said. Maybe he'd been too judgmental—from the sounds of it, Ganner knew exactly what a chief of staff ought to be doing.

As the *United States* used her massive rudders and her propellers to twist her stern away from the pier, the tides pulled mightily on the bow, resulting in a sideways motion that brought her clear of the pier. The tugs remained tied off to the carrier until the ship had negotiated her turn toward the channel, and then, at the earliest possible moment, cast them off. The USS *United States* was underway, making way and ready to answer all bells.

Coyote finally saw a strip of water between the ship and the pier, a dark swath of oily, dirty ocean that he was glad to be away from. Yes, the USS *United States* was ready— but ready for what? They might have a chance to find out sooner than any of them had planned.

Naval Station Norfolk
1230 local (GMT −5)

By the time they'd transited the toll road running from Virginia Beach to the naval base, there was evidence of additional activity at the gate. The guards were checking ID cards and the already long line of cars was growing. The threat condition assigned on a board located next to the guard shack had gone from condition white to condition yellow. As Lab Rat watched, two men came out from the OOD's office and removed the sign completely.

"Dear God," Lab Rat said. "They've gone to condition Red. What the *hell* is going on around here?"

"I don't know what it is, sir, or I'd tell you," Frank said. Lab Rat had elected to leave his rental car at Tony's Chowder Shack so that Frank could drive and he could eat. "The duty officer made it sound like it was for real, though. Full recall for selected commands, the JIC among them."

"Not good," Lab Rat commented around a mouthful of chowder. It was starting to cool and he was eager to get it all consumed before it clotted up. "Not good at all, from the looks of this mess. Selected commands around here must mean most of the base." The crackers were still in a paper bag in front of him. All he wanted was chowder, and more chowder.

When they finally made it inside the front gate, the traffic was relatively light, although most of the parking lots were filling up. They waited until they were inside the foyer of the Joint Intelligence Center and then through the security hatches to talk further.

With *Jefferson* in the shipyard for the foreseeable future, one of the first priorities had been to find temporary positions for her ship's company complement. Those that would be in no way involved in repairs, such as the staff of the intelligence center, were quickly sent to temporary duty elsewhere. Everyone was insisting it was temporary—there was no discussion that might indicate *Jefferson*'s eventual fate.

They were finally admitted through the locked doors to the inner sanctum of the intelligence center. Senior Chief Armstrong Brady, one of the most perceptive intelligence experts Lab Rat had ever known, was the first person they saw.

"Okay, quick version," Lab Rat said. He pointed at Brady.

"Chinese missile test near Taiwan, except this time we think it will be an actual attack." Brady stopped, to give Lab Rat a chance to absorb it.

Of course, it was not completely unexpected. The Chinese had been posturing in this way for decades. Not that they'd actually had the balls to do anything about it. That part of the world was extremely conscious of the potency of a force like the U.S. military, given the evidence of Nagasaki and Hiroshima so close at hand. In the back of their minds, there always lurked the memory of how completely devastating an attack on U.S. forces could be.

The only nation in the world to use nuclear weapons, and we're surprised that nobody else forgets it, Lab Rat thought. He shrugged off the dilemma, and nodded his appreciation for Brady's one-liner. "So what else? What's the story?"

"That's a problem, sir," Brady continued. "Most of it's human intelligence, HUMINT. This stuff from the SEALs—I gotta say, I agree with their intelligence estimates. But as for hard evidence . . ." Brady shrugged. They all knew that hard evidence was something you couldn't expect in intelligence work.

"What's the staff doing?" Lab Rat asked, referring to the intelligence personnel permanently assigned to JIC.

"They've already got a standard intelligence brief prepared for the area, of course," the senior chief said. "Given that we've been there, they want us to look it over—see if there's anything we can add from our personal experience."

Lab Rat nodded. "Any indication from force commanders on what forces will be deploying?" he asked, knowing that was indeed the five million dollar question.

"Even with everyone working at top speed, *Jefferson* is at least a week away from getting underway." Frank spoke with authority, since that was his area of expertise and he spoke daily with the maintenance forces back in San Diego. "Of course, if all they need is seaworthiness and no flight deck capabilities, it could be a lot sooner."

"They could carry Harriers, at least," Lab Rat said. "And helos, and logistic support. Maybe some aircraft maintenance depot stuff."

"Yes, sir. And as for *United States*, a lot will depend on how her sea trials go."

Lab contemplated the ceiling, the pieces falling into place in his mind. "Don't count *Jefferson* out completely," he said softly. "No, it's far too early to do that. Okay, everybody, listen up. Suppose—just suppose, mind you— that there was a call to immediately staff the *United States'* CVIC. I'm not saying it is going to happen, but I'd like a list of people who want to go, and a list of people who don't. Senior chief, you handle that." He turned to Frank. "Go sneak around. Find out what the thinking is at all the Fleet headquarters."

"Yes, sir, I certainly will. If that new carrier is going to deploy anywhere suddenly, she deserves to have the best intelligence crew around onboard her."

"And where you going, sir?" Brady asked.

Lab Rat was heading for his office to change into his

khaki uniform. He paused for a moment and grinned. "San Diego. I'm going to go see my old friend, Admiral Coyote Grant."

"Hope you're a strong swimmer, sir," Brady said, dead-pan.

"Why?"

Brady handed him another message. "I figure if you can do fifteen knots in an overhand crawl, you ought to be able to catch up with her. She left for sea trials this morning."

JIC, North Island
1000 local (GMT −8)

Batman swore quietly as he thumbed through the message traffic. With his own communications and intelligence staff temporarily reassigned, he was reduced to thumbing through the station's message file like any other officer. After a couple of years of having his very own message boards, meticulously maintained and organized for his convenience, trying to read grubby-edged, blurry copies left him singularly cold.

Halfway through the most sensitive message board, Batman stopped breathing. He read over the details again, up to and including the *Lake Champlain*'s after action report, his heart thudding. When he finally realized that he was getting dizzy, he leaned back in his chair and took a deep breath. The fresh oxygen invading his temporarily starved brain cells brought a host of ideas flooding in as well.

It was bad—real bad. Even though nobody was saying it, Batman knew that it wouldn't stop with this one missile shot destroyed or the one incursion into Taiwan. No, it was all going to start going to shit soon enough, and going to shit in a big way. China, Taiwan, and then most probably Russia. The former Soviet Union would be tempted to stand by and let China and Taiwan and perhaps the United States battle it out, hoping that they'd exhaust themselves and be easy pickings. But Batman thought that they'd probably be unable to resist the opportunity to nudge things along a bit, maybe picking off some easy targets or taking advantage of the hostilities to make a covert grab for the Kurile Islands again. Whatever they'd have in mind, the fur was going to be flying over there.

And Batman was going to miss it all. Nobody wanted an admiral without a ship around.

But I do have a ship. So maybe she's in a couple of pieces right now, but she's still a ship.

Batman slammed the message board shut, startling a junior lieutenant at the other end of the battered table. The lieutenant stood, not entirely sure whether or not he'd done something to annoy the admiral, but not taking any chances of compounding the error by being rude.

"As you were, Lieutenant," Batman snapped.

"Yes, Admiral." The lieutenant swallowed hard, but didn't sit back down. Instead, he stayed braced at attention while Batman immediately forgot about him and stormed out of the secure area. When the last door swung shut, the lieutenant sat down and breathed a sigh of relief that he didn't work for the fellow.

Outside, Batman's car and driver were waiting. The admiral snapped, "Back to the ship, ASAP." He settled himself into the back seat, his mind racing, and then reconsidered his destination. Right now, what he needed wasn't on the ship at all. He already knew what CAG and the ship's CO would say—there was no need to even consult with them.

"Sup Ships," he said, using the short hand term for Supervisor of Ship Repair, the maintenance facility responsible for the major repairs now in progress. "I got a few favors to call in."

While Sup Ships was not entirely enthralled by the idea, he immediately saw Batman's rationale. If things were going down, better to be ahead of the power curve than behind it. Barring a return of the USS *United States* and any priority repairs she required, Sup Ships agreed to divert every available resource—as well as a substantial part of his end-of-the-fiscal-year slush fund to pay for overtime— into getting *Jefferson* back into operation. Batman left the man's office completely satisfied with the promised effort, if wondering whether he'd sold his soul to the devil.

By the time he made it back to *Jefferson*, the tempo of operations was already increasing. The pier was swarming with more technicians, and they crawled along the massive exposed flank of the ship in huge clusters.

Batman's maintenance officer met him on the pier, concern in his eyes. Batman waved off his concerns. "Sure, we have a pick-up team right now, but that will change if you can get her back in commission. This is going to be a come-as-you-are deal, and we ain't no wallflowers." Batman fixed the maintenance officer with a fierce glare. "Now, you make up your mind. Your nation needs you— my ship needs you. Are you part of the solution, or part of the problem?"

The maintenance officer gulped, then reached his decision. "Part of the solution, Admiral. Please inform your staff that the USS *Jefferson* will be ready to answer all bells in two days. Now, unless you have something further for me, I've got work to do." Without waiting for Batman's answer, the maintenance officer turned and strode back down the pier.

Batman stared after him, at first mildly pissed and then truly pleased. His ship might be crammed with maintenance weenies and repair folks instead of operations specialists and pilots, but maybe, just maybe, he could turn them into what he needed.

FIVE

United Nations
1400 local (GMT −5)

Ambassador Sarah Wexler, the American ambassador to the United Nations, had just finished wading through a thick stack of briefing papers on her desk when Brad knocked on the door. He rapped lightly, opened it at once and stepped in. "You've got a visitor—Department of Defense. JCS."

Wexler leaned back and stretched her tight back muscles. Any diversion would be welcome at this point. There was no way she could avoid reading all of the briefing papers and position summaries her staff drafted for her every day. Indeed, she depended on those to remain aware of the more subtle nuances in the world. But sometimes the paperwork threatened to overwhelm her, and she wondered if it was all that necessary. Over the centuries of the history of diplomacy, much rested on the personal relationships between men and women in power. Harsh reality had little to do sometimes with the alliances that were formed, the decisions that were made, and a general conduct of the business of nations.

"Any idea of what he wants?" she asked.

Brad shook his head. "Says it's for your eyes only."

Now that was alarming. It wasn't the first time that it had happened, but every time it did, it presaged a major challenge for the United States. At least she would have advance warning of it, whatever it was.

And that, she suspected, was due to Brad. As soon as she had given him his head in allowing a closer relationship between the CIA and her office, it seemed that the information flow had . . . well, not exactly increased, but taken on a new accuracy and timeliness that she found exceptionally helpful. Along the way, she'd acquired a new working relationship with the Department of Defense as well. Also a good thing, in her opinion. It meant that the first notice she had of major problems came from somewhere besides ACN, the premier news network in the world. Her only concern was that her new acquaintances might decide that they were entitled to a degree of reciprocity she was not yet willing to grant. However useful it was to share information, have advance notice of potential problems, and otherwise coordinate the entire American national security plan, she was still convinced that it was critical to maintain a clear distinction between diplomacy and the military means of enforcing it.

How could the other ambassadors trust her to keep their confidences if they saw CIA agents in her office every day? And what would they think of international military objectives she supported if Department of Defense officials looked like they were holding morning quarters outside her office? That the president had approved her decision to develop a closer working relationship with the CIA, and had not even attempted to deny it when she asked him if he'd known all along that her aide, Brad, was a former CIA employee, had troubled her. But in the end, they all worked for him, so she did her best to adhere to his wishes.

Brad showed the JCS representative in. She was a female Navy captain, and young for the slot by the looks of her. She came to attention in front of Ambassador Wexler's desk and said, "Ma'am, I'm Captain Jane Hemingway, from JCS, Department of Contingency Evaluation. We came across some disturbing information and thought it might be wise to share it with you. If I may?"

"Please, sit down." Wexler had not met Hemingway before, but immediately liked the looks of her.

"Thank you." Hemingway took a chair at the corner of the desk and opened the attaché case she carried. She extracted a file, and slid it across the desk to the ambassador. "If you like, I can give you a brief overview."

"Yes, do that," Wexler said, not touching the file yet. She'd listen to the overview, see if she wanted to know the details.

"China," Hemingway said immediately. "China and Taiwan. Yesterday, without warning, China launched a ballistic missile test. Acting on orders from the National Command Authority via JCS, The USS *Lake Champlain* shot it down."

"And the reason for that?" Wexler asked. "There've been missile tests before."

"We've got information that it wasn't exactly a test. We think it's at least possible that this is the beginning of a major initiative to reunite Taiwan with the mainland."

"Well, that wouldn't be any surprise. What do you have to support that view?" Wexler opened the folder and leafed through it.

There wasn't much, not in the way of original source material. A report from an intelligence specialist debriefing a defector, two satellite shots with attached photo intelligence interpretations. The longest item was a three-page analysis by—she glanced at the end page—yes, Captain Hemingway herself. She skipped through it, going straight to the last page: recommendations. She read through quickly, and then laid the folder on a corner of her desk. "Not much to go on, is there?"

Hemingway shook her head. "No, ma'am. There's not. But I've been following this region for a significant period of time, and you develop instincts. Everything I know about this area of the world screams at me that this time it's real. The timing, for one thing—you don't know how stretched thin we are, particularly in that region. And this defector—I interviewed him myself." She spread her hand in a supplicating gesture. "Obviously, I can't go into some details. But I found myself personally persuaded by his story. And when I add his data up with the rest of the things I see, it only spells trouble."

Wexler frowned. "When?"

"Next month, I think. They have a couple of major surface combatants still in outfitting, as well as a major upgrade on some fighter avionics. They'll finish that before they make a move."

"Not much time, then."

Hemingway smiled. "More advance notice than we've had a lot of times, though. The question is what we're going to do about it."

"I suspect this is primarily a State Department and DOD issue," Wexler said.

"Yes, of course. But if things go down the way I think they will, it's going to be happening fast. If I give you a background briefing now, I believe you'll be better prepared to deal with what comes up over here."

Wexler waited for a moment, then asked, "That's it? That's all you want to do, give me a heads-up?"

Hemingway looked faintly amused. "Astounding, isn't it? But yes, that's all. No favors to ask, no politicking, no trying to enlist you to confirm or deny our intelligence. It's just a briefing, ma'am. One that I hope will be the first of many." Hemingway picked up her file from the ambassador's desk, stowed it in her attaché case and locked the case. "With your permission?" she asked.

"Wait," Wexler said. "Do you like tea? Not the grocery store stuff—I mean really, really good tea."

A speculative look crossed Hemingway's face. "Why yes, as a matter of fact, I do."

Wexler smiled. "I thought so. Unless you've got some pressing business, Captain, why not sit down and have a cup with me. I need a break from my paperwork and you can tell your boss I'm a slow learner."

Thirty minutes later, the two had established that they had a good deal in common. After they'd talked, Hemingway finally asked, "Who handles your electronic security around here?"

"Brad, my aide. You met him when you came in."

"But who actually handles it?"

Wexler frowned. "I don't know. That's always been his department. Why? Do you have some reason that I ought to be concerned?"

"Yes, I do." Seeing Wexler's look of consternation, she added, "And I can't tell you why. But if you want, I'll bring a team over here tomorrow and double-check your aide's work. I'm not trying to imply anything about him, of course . . . but . . . well . . . what could it hurt?"

"His feelings."

"And that matters?" Hemingway asked.

"No. Not if it's a question of security." Wexler drained the last of her tea, suddenly weary. "All right. Bring your people over tomorrow. Around one p.m.?"

Hemingway stood. "At one, then. And I hope I'm wrong about what I suspect."

SIX

Within twenty-four hours of starting sea trials, every man and woman onboard the ship was convinced in their heart of hearts that there would never, ever be a problem with this ship. They were invincible, invulnerable—the ship met and exceeded every performance characteristic tested. Her acceleration was significantly above what was predicted, her emergency crash backs virtually bone-jolting in their ability to reverse propellers and generate full reverse power. Her turning radius was tighter, her electronics more reliable—hell, even the radars look like they worked better. There was something special about being on a brand-new ship, one that had never known combat.

Each plank owner had been through numerous schools and rigorous training during the pre-commissioning days. Now, when they were finally allowed to strut their stuff on their new ship, they shone.

This morning would be the first test of the flight deck

systems. For the first few days, the ship had tested engineering and damage control without the burden of having the air wing onboard. No aircraft would come onboard until Coyote and the carrier's skipper were convinced that they could effectively fight a flight deck fire and provide power to the ship under casualty conditions.

Most of the aircraft technicians had walked on from pier side, but the actual aircraft and flight crews themselves were waiting patiently onshore.

Coyote left the flag bridge and headed for Vulture's Row, three decks above, to watch the first trap. While everything might look great on paper, and even in trials, there was no real test of flight deck operations other than actually doing it.

CAG had elected to be the first one to land onboard the pristine flight deck. He was flying a Tomcat, his weapon of choice, with a tail number of zero zero, otherwise known as the double nuts bird. Coyote wondered briefly who the backseater was, then dismissed the thought. It didn't matter—this was completely a pilot's show.

In addition to the dangers of there being an undetected mechanical problem, taking the lead for the first landing brought with it other worries. Everything had gone so well so far—indeed, had gone perfectly. If the first landing was screwed up in some way, even in a minor one, that might shake the confidence of the crew. A wave off, or God forbid, a bolter, would be a bad omen.

No, to do it right, CAG had to make it onboard on his first pass, and had to catch the three wire.

Coyote listened in to the approach chatter on a headset. CAG had to know how critical this first landing was, but he could detect no hint of nervousness in the man's voice as he made his final approach on the ship. The landing signals officer, or LSO, sounded just as casual—slightly bored, professional, with no trace of nervousness.

He could see the Tomcat in the distance now, sunlight glinting off her wings.

"Tomcat double nuts, say needles," the LSO said.

"Needles show on course, at altitude," the CAG said.

"Roger, concur with needles. Fly needles. Tomcat double nickels, call the ball," the LSO concluded, indicating that the CAG should let him know when he had the Fresnel lens clearly in view.

"Roger, fly needles." There was a short pause, then the CAG said, "Roger, ball."

The litany continued, the careful phrases and measured interaction that characterized most routine landings. "Looking good, sir, looking good, watch your attitude, attitude," the LSO said quietly, coaching the senior officer onto the deck.

Final was only two miles long, and the Tomcat was looming over the flight deck almost immediately. The deck was rock steady, the weather perfect, clear visibility unlimited.

CAG executed a perfect carrier deck landing, catching the three wire neatly. The noise on the flight deck immediately increased as he shoved the throttles forward to full military power. That was standard operating procedure, in case the cable snapped or the tailhook somehow skipped out of it, the latter being known as a kiddy trap. Full military power ensured that the pilot could get the aircraft off the deck again and airborne in order to come around and make another pass.

After a few moments, a loud cheer broke out across the deck, audible even to Coyote high up the superstructure. He joined in. The sheer excitement and relief was almost overwhelming.

Finally a yellow shirt flight deck technician stepped out front of CAG's aircraft and gave the hand signals to decrease power to the engines. The reasoning for standing in front of the aircraft was that the enlisted people were too smart to step in front of an aircraft if they weren't absolutely convinced that the aircraft was securely trapped on deck. The yellow shirt was putting his life on the line if something went wrong as was the pilot who was cutting power.

The CAG let the Tomcat roll back slightly, neatly re-
tracted the tailhook, and increased power slightly to taxi
forward and follow the directions of the yellow shirt to a
spot near the island. All around the perimeter of the
marked off landing strip, technicians were clustered, cheering, shouting out greetings and congratulations. The CAG
returned the waves as he taxied, and he pulled off his oxygen mask so that they could all see the broad grin on his
face.

The Tomcat reached its appointed spot. Even before the
CAG could pull back the canopy to egress, the aircraft was
surrounded by hordes of cheering sailors wearing every
possible color of jersey. No matter that there were other
aircraft stacked up in a holding pattern, waiting their looks
at the deck. For just this moment, the only thing that mattered was that they'd made it through the first trap, and an
excellent trap it had been indeed.

Coyote had been leaning over the railing, his elbows
resting on it, and now he straightened up to turn to his
chief of staff. "One less thing to worry about."

Ganner nodded. "For all our modern technology, sailors
are still a damned suspicious bunch—superstitious, even."

Just then, the young enlisted radioman walked out onto
Vulture's Row. He held a clipboard in his hand. "Good
morning, Admiral. P4 message for you."

The "personal for", or P4, was a designator for communications between the Navy's highest ranking officers.
The messages required special handling, on the theory that
that that would prevent the contents from being broadcast
over the ship. It was not necessarily that the message itself
contained classified material—it was just that the information was often sensitive, and best not shared with the
entire fleet.

"Must be congratulations on our first trap," Coyote re-
marked, as he took the clipboard. "But how did they get
off so fast? AIRPAC must have had the message all written and waiting in the queue so—" He stopped abruptly
as he began scanning the message.

It was short and to the point. The *United States* was directed to break off sea trials and immediately make best speed to Taiwan. She would be resupplied enroute, and the remainder of her air wing, qualified or not, was ordered to immediately embark.

Coyote passed the message to Ganner. "We ready for this?"

His chief of staff nodded. "Yes, Admiral. Not as ready as I'd like to be, but I moved up some of the provisioning schedules, and we should be able to make it."

"We can do carrier quals on the way over there," Coyote said.

Of course they could. It was done all the time. And there was no real reason not to sign off on this warship right now. No, they hadn't completed every test. And in actual fact, it would take months before they really knew how she would hold up. It was one thing for everything to be working when they went to sea. It was another entirely to stand up to the endless day in and day out use that went with a deployment. Still, if he had to bet, Coyote would come down on the side of the *United States*.

"Get everybody in the conference room," Coyote said. "Maybe we're worried about Taiwan for no reason. There might be another explanation for this, a good one."

"Maybe." The chief of staff's voice was doubtful.

As his chief of staff left, Coyote turned back to the flight deck. Pristine, unscarred—well, that would change. And sooner rather than later, it looked like.

"Admiral! Someone here to see you." Ganner stepped aside to reveal Lab Rat standing at the hatch to Vulture's Row.

"Hey! What the hell you doing out here? You're supposed to be in Norfolk. You didn't . . . ?" Coyote glanced down at the Tomcat now being positioned just forward of the island.

"Yes, sir, I did indeed." Lab Rat's voice was calm. "I called in a few favors—nobody ever cares who's in the back seat, do they?"

"I wouldn't put it that way, buddy." Coyote slung a companionable arm over Lab Rat's shoulder. "But there's times when it's the most important thing in the world, and there's times when it's not."

"This was a not, then," Lab Rat said.

"So to what do we owe the honor?"

"I'll get right to the point, Admiral. Right about now, you should be getting a—"

"A P4?" Coyote interrupted. "Yeah—just saw it. That your doing?"

"Some of it," Lab Rat admitted. "But the thing is, you're not completely manned up yet. And I've got my entire CVIC sitting ashore twiddling their thumbs. I was wondering—"

"Why, hell yes!" Coyote said. Lab Rat had forgotten that it was sometimes difficult to finish a sentence around the exuberant Texan. "You want to bring that whole little pack of yours on out here, you go right ahead. Save me having to break in a bunch of newcomers, right? And give your people something to do."

A frown crossed the chief of staff's face. "Admiral, with all due respect—Commander Busby's people just came off cruise. I suspect they may need some down time, a chance to recharge. Isn't that so, Commander?" He turned to the intelligence officer.

"I asked if they wanted to go—every single one of them volunteered, sir," Lab Rat said. He appreciated Ganner's concern, although he was slightly miffed at the implication that he himself hadn't thought of that. "They want to be plankowners, sir. It's not something they'll get the chance too often to do in their careers."

"Well, pack 'em up and bring 'em on out," Coyote said. "COS here will take care of the details. Right, COS?" There was a slight challenge in Coyote's eyes, and Lab Rat had his first hint that there might be some issues to work out between the new battle group commander and his chief of staff. "I mean, we got this sweetheart through precomm and sea trials, we ought to be able to handle wrangling Lab Rat's boys and girls on out here, right?"

"Of course, Admiral," the COS said smoothly. "I'll make that happen." He nodded to Lab Rat and then said, "With your permission, Admiral, I'll get right on it."

"Carry on, carry on," the admiral said, waving him off. He watched the man go back into the interior of the ship before turning to Lab Rat. "Surface guy," he said, his voice confiding. "You know them." In Coyote's view that said it all. The man was not an aviator—therefore, by definition, he sweated the small stuff, didn't know the sheer joy of flying, and would tend to get his panties in a wad over things that might make a tremendous amount of difference to some paper pusher in DC but that Coyote didn't give a rat's ass about.

"Seems like a good fellow, though," Lab Rat added tactfully. He could see the problem looming, and he had no intention of being part of a tiff between Admiral Grant and his chief of staff. "Got a sterling reputation."

"Sure. You can't believe everything you hear, though," Coyote said, and for a moment his eyes looked bleak.

And just what is that all about? Lab Rat wondered. Ganner was a cruiser man who'd commanded an Aegis cruise and then a deep draft follow on command. Those two command tours had pegged him as a man to be watched, one who was being put through the crucible in order to evaluate him for later selection to flag rank. That he'd been assigned as Coyote's chief of staff was not a step up—it was a sideways move, indicating that there was some doubt that he was still on the fast track to promotion to admiral.

If it bothered Ganner, you couldn't tell it by looking at him. He was a darkly tanned man, one with brown sun-streaked hair swept back from his face, short but not Marine short, dark brown, almost black eyes and a powerful physique. He had the look of an admiral, the sense of presence and command, and from what Lab Rat had heard, he had the brain power to back it up.

So what had happened? What had knocked him off his

preordained track to higher rank? Lab Rat considered asking Coyote, but decided against it. While Lab Rat himself
was considered part of the aviation community, he was not
per se an aviator. Therefore, Coyote might have been reluctant to confide in him the way he would in another pilot.
Besides, it was always better to know things that no one
else knew you knew. Sooner or later—and Lab Rat was
betting on sooner—he'd know exactly what had happened
in Ganner's career and be able to evaluate how it affected
his position on the ship. Maybe Ganner was resentful over
whatever had happened and envied Coyote. A bitter or
disillusioned COS could make life difficult for one of the
admiral's perceived favorites, and joining the battle group
like this could make Lab Rat and his people look like just
that. There were a thousand ways a COS could sabotage
a more junior officer.

In the meantime, it was important to avoid getting
caught between Coyote and his COS. Stay on the good
side of both, keep your head down, and do your job. Because clearly the COS hadn't pissed Coyote off enough to
get his butt relieved, so Coyote would be reluctant to completely torpedo the man's career. But the situation would
bear watching.

"So git," Coyote said. "You got a ton of stuff to do,
starting with finding a ride home, right? You need to get
your people packed up and orders cut and berthing arranged and all that paperwork shit, I bet."

"Sir, they're packing out right now." Lab Rat could not
repress a slight smirk. "I got reservations on comm air for
all of them and a couple of COD's standing by at North
Island to get them out here."

Coyote gave him a long, level look. "Pretty confident,
aren't you?"

"Not in *me*, sir." Lab Rat grinned openly now. "In *you*."

SEVEN

Shortly after the last secretary had straggled back from lunch, Captain Hemingway appeared at Wexler's office, accompanied by four enlisted technicians carrying black plastic cases. Hemingway did not give their names, and Wexler did not ask.

Most of the staff was still at lunch, although a few were eating at their desks. They looked up, puzzled, as the technicians immediately began spreading around the room, rapping on the walls, examining cracks and ceilings, checking telephones and computer lines, and generally taking possession of the entire office.

Hemingway turned to Wexler. "This takes about an hour. I also have people down at the central switch boxes tracing out the circuitry. You'd be amazed how often that is overlooked. And yes, I know you're on fiber optic communications, but there are ways . . ." She didn't finish her sentence, but merely looked at Wexler significantly.

Just then, Brad returned from lunch, his face flushed. Another quick round at the racquetball court, Wexler surmised. But his color rose even higher as he saw the people swarming over their office complex. He turned to Wexler, a question on his face.

"Just a redundancy check," Wexler said calmly. "Captain Hemingway was kind enough to offer the services of her office. She provides the same service for JCS, and I felt we would welcome a second set of eyes."

Brad's face looked anything but welcoming. He went into his own office without speaking to Hemingway, dropped his gym bag, then came back out, all traces of emotion gone from his face. "Madam Ambassador, could I see you in private for a moment?"

"Of course." Wexler led the way back into her office, and Brad shut the door firmly behind them.

"You didn't discuss this with me," he stated.

Wexler nodded. "That's right. I didn't."

"I'll resign immediately, if you like," he said steadily. "That's really the only course left open if you don't trust my judgment in these matters."

Wexler waved him off. "Oh, do sit down and stop being such a dick, Brad. It's just what I said—a double check. I thought you'd welcome a second opinion telling me how wonderfully capable you are at your job."

Brad leaned forward and planted his hands on her desk. "Have they been in your office yet?"

"No."

Brad pointed at the telephone. Then he motioned her to follow him into her small personal room behind her office. He shut the door again behind them. "I can't believe you don't see the danger in this," he said. "Did it occur to you that they might be planting a bug rather than looking for one?"

Wexler regarded him levelly. "Yes, of course it did. I need to sort out who the players are, Brad. One way of doing that is to give people a chance to make their intentions clear. As soon as they leave, I want you to run a complete check on our spaces. See if anything has changed."

"That's what this is?" Brad asked incredulously. "You're giving the Joint Chiefs of Staff the opportunity to bug your office to see if they take advantage of it?"

Wexler nodded. "And if you can think of a way to run the same scam on the State Department and the CIA, I'd like to do that as well."

Brad laughed. "You're betting a lot on my competence, Ambassador. What if they've got some new system that we don't know how to detect?"

"Then we're in a lot more trouble than I thought." She stared at him, challenge in her eyes. "You keep telling me that there's nothing to worry about—well, then prove it."

Just then, she heard a cry from the other room.

"This conversation is over," Wexler said. "I am counting on your cooperation."

Brad nodded, although he was clearly still not in favor of the idea. They walked out together into the outer office to find Captain Hemingway in deep conversation with one of her technicians. She turned to face them, a mixture of triumph and concern on her face. "Look at this."

The technician held out a pair of tweezers and what looked like a grain of rice between the prongs. Hemingway held out a magnifying glass to let them get a closer look.

"That's it?" Wexler asked, surprised at the size of it.

Brad looked grim. "Where?"

"In the ambassador's door jamb," Hemingway answered.

"Any idea how long it's been there?" he asked.

She shook her head. "As you can see, it's colored to match your wall paint here. I don't know if that means it was designed that way, or whether it was painted over the last time the office was redone." She shot a speculative look at the walls. "Do you know when it was last painted?"

"Eighteen months ago," Brad said immediately. His face was pale now, his jaw pulsing with anger.

"You mean," Wexler said carefully, "there is a chance that that . . . that . . . device has been listening in on con-

versations in my office for the last eighteen months?" Her
horror was evident in her voice. She cast her mind back
over that time, reviewing the conflicts the United States
had been involved in, the delicate negotiations and outright
confrontations that had taken place in her office. Was it
all compromised? Did someone else know everything that
she did as soon as she did it?

*Oh, dear God. This is a disaster. Please, tell me this
can't be happening.*

"Tell me everything you know about it," she said firmly,
focusing on the current issue at hand. What was important
was that they figure out who had planted it, whether there
might be any more, and then deal with the damage already
done. "They will know we detected it, I suppose?"

Hemingway looked faintly amused. "I have certain . . .
ways . . . of dealing with that very issue. At the moment,
there is a dummy load in series with it, transmitting nothing but static. Whoever is listening may think they're getting some short-term interference. Sun spots, that sort of
thing. They'll wait for it to clear up on its own before they
decide the device is compromised."

"So they don't know?"

Hemingway nodded. "If you want, we can replace it. In
the long run, sooner or later, you'll slip up. But in the
short run, you may be able to plant some disinformation
that may help undo any damage. What precisely that might
be, I don't know. That's for you to decide." She glanced
around the room. The support staff was staring at them,
shock on their faces. "And it will be quite a lot to orches-
trate. Remember, you'll all have to behave precisely as you
were before, with the exception of being very careful about
what you say. At the same time, you'll have to act natu-
rally enough that they won't know there's a problem." She
shook her head discouragingly. "It's very difficult to pull
off. We've had instances where people have tried, and
failed miserably."

"Could you move it?" Wexler asked. "Reposition it so
it only hears inside my office alone?"

Hemingway looked startled, then quickly understood what Wexler was suggesting. "Yes, of course. And it's much easier for one person to manage to carry on the charade than an entire office. That might work."

"Next question, then. Who's responsible?" She resisted the temptation to growl when she saw Hemingway and Brad exchange a significant glance. "Well? Who? The CIA, perhaps?"

She could see by their body language that Hemingway was tossing the ball into Brad's court. He sighed, then looked away from her. "This is, I believe, a device known as 'Little Insect.' It is normally not intended as a long-term surveillance device. Somewhere behind a wallboard, we'll find a small battery to power the transmitter. But because of its size, it's normally for short-term use only. Unless you can make arrangements to have someone come in and change the battery."

More horror. "But at least there's a chance it's short-term, yes? How long is short-term?"

"Depending on a number of factors, it is effective for up to three weeks."

Finally, some good news, if it could be called that. "Let's assume the battery hasn't been replaced, for the moment. I imagine you'll be able to tell more when you locate it, yes?" She saw two heads nodding in unison. "Very well, then. For now, we'll operate on the assumption that it has been in place only three weeks. Now, answer my original question—who?"

There was a long silence, and Brad said, "The 'Little Insect' is manufactured in China. As far as we know, it is not available on the export market." He held up one hand to forestall comment. "As far as we know. Every time we have seen it so far, the circumstances have indicated China."

China. T'ing. Oh dear Lord, not this, too.

In the last year, Ambassador Wexler's relationship with the ambassador from China had gone from mutual respect to warm friendship. He had been responsible for saving her life in the last Middle East crisis, and she'd come to depend more and more on his advice and friendship.

"China." She looked away, her face carefully composed. "That would answer a lot of questions, wouldn't it?" She glanced at Brad. He simply nodded.

"Replace it," Wexler said firmly. "Fix it so it will only hear what's inside my office. And you two," she pointed at Brad and Hemingway, "and I need to have a long conversation. Somewhere else. I have a plan, and I'm going to need your help."

EIGHT

USS **United States**
Thursday, September 5
1800 local (GMT –10)

Coyote stared down at his cup of coffee, fascinated. The surface of the liquid jittered with standing waves, the concentric circles radiating out from the center, a response to the vibrations thrumming through the ship.

It was odd to feel the carrier trembling under his feet. Odd to actually feel the power of her four turbines driving her four shafts, the slant on the deck as she made turns, the dip and yaw as she smashed through the seas.

Normally, the carrier had no more sense of motion about her than an office building. The deck was stable underfoot. Coffee cups and plates did not slide around on tables. Things stayed where you put them. Except for the howl of aircraft and the reverberating slam as aircraft hit the deck—and the occasional typhoon, of course—you could have been ashore.

But not now. Flight operations actually provided the most stable times, since the carrier reduced speed from flank, sought favorable winds and kept the deck level to within a few degrees of roll. But once a flight cycle was completed, the carrier immediately ramped back up to flank speed, channeling every atom of superheated steam from her reactors into pounding the ocean into submission with her propellers.

Coyote glanced up at the tactical plot and saw that they were making excellent time. Would it be fast enough? Hard to say—but short of fitting the carrier with jet engines and turning her into a hovercraft, they were making the best time that was humanly possible.

Could have been a bit faster, I suppose. But a carrier without an airwing and qualified pilots isn't much use at all.

CAG had gotten the airwing onboard in record time. The deck was still clobbered with the newly arrived squadrons sorting out people and planes, looking for assigned spots, and generally going through all the gyrations that they would have had a couple of weeks to work out normally.

But the air wing wasn't the only problem. In addition to Lab Rat's people, there were hundreds of additional personnel to embark, and in between fighter traps and carrier quals, the decks were crowded with C-2 Greyhound CODS disgorging massive loads of people and gear. While they were still within range, the heavy transport helos picked up part of the load, but soon they would be out of the helos unrefueled range, and the CODs would have to handle the rest of it alone.

And the carrier quals—my God, had there been such an increase in new pilots into squadrons in the last year? It seemed like every third pilot was completely out of qual and had to get ten day traps and five night traps to even be considered minimally safe. And that didn't even count the ones who needed a few extra looks at the deck to get back into the saddle.

Yes, getting the airwing back onboard and up to speed had cut into their speed of advance, or SOA. But there was no help for it. Cutting corners would just get people killed down the road.

"How long, do you think?" Coyote asked. He glanced over at Captain Ganner.

"I think we'll make it in three weeks, easy," Ganner said. "We might shave off a couple of days along the way if everything works well."

"Let's just hope China doesn't bomb Taiwan back into the Stone Age while we're hauling ass across the ocean. Dammit, what were they thinking, leaving the area without a carrier around?"

Ganner cleared his throat. "Sir, we could cut some time off if we proceeded ahead alone. I don't like the option, and I know you don't either. But the support ships and small boys are slowing us down. Between refueling and a slower speed of advance—well, I wonder if you'd reconsidered."

Coyote grunted. What Ganner was proposing was something that they'd all known, but hadn't had the balls to say out loud. The *United States* was powered by a nuclear reactor. She didn't need to take on fuel, except when the hungry aircraft finally depleted her massive stores, and that wouldn't be for quite a while. And she had storage space and reefers to hold more than enough food for the transit. Oh, sure, they might run short on FFV, or fresh fruits and vegetables, but it was something that they could deal with in the short run.

The escort combatants and supply ships, however, were in an entirely different situation. Not only were they conventionally powered and needed fuel en route, but they also had slower max speeds. Sure, some of the gas turbine ships could keep up, but not without taking a terrible toll on equipment and personnel. Speeds that translated to a little roll onboard a carrier were gut-wrenching and exhausting rolls and yaws on a small boy. The motion would make solid sleep virtually impossible when every movement of the ship threatened to throw you out of your rack, and eating was a constant challenge. And that wasn't even counting the sailors—about a third, Coyote reckoned—who would be seriously sea sick most of the time. All it took was one sailor puking in Combat to set off the rest of them.

And the replenishment ship—well, there was no way that they could match the *United States*'s speed. And that included the USS *Jefferson*.

"*Jeff* holding up all right?" Coyote asked.

Ganner nodded. "For now. The fact that she's underway at all . . ."

Ganner didn't need to finish the thought. *Jefferson*—and Batman—had pulled off something like a miracle. Coyote shuddered to think what corners might have been cut in getting her seaworthy, but in a frank conversation with Batman, the more senior admiral had assured Coyote that *Jeff* was more than capable of giving the newer carrier a run for her money. Although the flight deck and associate gear was not fully operational, *Jefferson* was fully loaded with everything that both carriers would need for the deployment. Everything from bullets to beans, as the saying went. During the two days she'd spent in dry dock, supply troops had packed every empty inch of her hull with the stores intended for the *United States*, and those supplies would be ferried to her via helo. Logistics make or break a battle group, and having *Jefferson* along had solved at least one major problem for Coyote and his staff.

"But she's stressed just like the rest of them, not as much from the seas as from being shorthanded," Ganner continued, bringing a surface sailor's perspective to evaluating the issue, one that Coyote acknowledged without fully comprehending. There were things his COS knew deep in his bones, intuitions that he had about surface ships that Coyote would never be able to match. But then again, the COS would never really understand at a gut level how a barrel roll or a wingover affected a pilot and crew.

"Letting them drop behind is a ballsy move," Coyote mused. He stared at the plot, imagining the howls of protest he'd get from the small boys. And how would Batman onboard *Jefferson* react?

None of them would want to be left out. To let the

carrier go ahead of them, unprotected, would go against
every fiber of their being. The cruisers and destroyers, he
suspected, would be poised on the edge of virtual mutiny
at the idea. Sure, they'd understand the necessity and they
could damned sure do the numbers themselves. But protecting the carrier was their primary role on this mission,
and to be left behind would be a direct insult to their capabilities.

Still, with over-the-horizon targeting and non-organic
sensors, the cruisers *could* still provide some potent protection to the carrier. And if it looked like things were
starting to go down, he could always slow and let them
catch up.

"Get the staff together," Coyote ordered. "We're going
to take a hard look at this. I'm leaning toward doing it,
COS, but I have to admit it worries the hell out of me."
He stared glumly at the tactical plot, already imagining the
storm of protest he'd face. "Draft the message. Let's have
it ready to go."

USS Jefferson
1910 local (GMT +10)

Batman stared down in disbelief at the message in his
hand. "What the hell—he can't do that!" he roared. He
slammed the message down on the desk. "This is insanity."

All around the battle group, similar reactions were taking place in the other wardrooms. Pens were picked up as
skippers drafted hasty howls of protest, and the communications circuits flamed with P4 and highly classified messages. Washington and Seventh Fleet got into the act as
well, albeit without the sense of personal outrage that the
escort ships had.

Twelve hours after Coyote recovered his last aircraft and
send the message off, the decision was made. The situation
in Taiwan was critical, so critical that it justified the risk.

The USS *United States* would proceed at flank speed toward the island and her escorts would catch up as they could, having due regard for the safety of their ships and crews.

"Well, I'm not going to stand for it." Batman turned to his chief engineer and fixed him with a steely glare. "You make sure I've got the juice to keep up with her. We have to stay within easy aerial resupply range, you got it? No excuses—not now."

The most immediate result of Coyote's message was an impromptu naval Olympics, as Batman's orders were echoed on every surface ship attached to the battle group. The competition between the surface ships to maintain position on the carrier was fierce. As they chivvied for position, each one eking out a few extra turns on the propeller and sacrificing a few hours of sleep for speed, it quickly became apparent that despite her injuries and hasty repairs, the USS *Jefferson* would be the winner.

NINE

Pacini's Restaurant
New York
Thursday, September 5
1930 local (GMT −5)

Pacini's was not the most popular restaurant in New York City, but Wexler thought it probably served the most authentic northern Italian cuisine in America. It was quietly and tastefully decorated, and its patrons paid a premium price for privacy. Pacini's didn't advertise. It wasn't reviewed in food magazines or in newspapers. Its clientele patronized it weekly, had standing reservations, and kept it a secret. The arrangement suited both the owner and his customers.

"Has Ambassador T'ing arrived yet?" Wexler had made plans for dinner with the Chinese ambassador even before she'd learned of the bug in her office. An audacious move, one suggested by Brad, but one that made sense as soon as he mentioned it. China was outraged over the destruction of her missile, and thus T'ing was obligated—at least temporarily—to be furious with Wexler. But both of them were too experienced in the ways of diplomacy to let the respective emotions of their parent countries close down the flow of communications between their diplomatic envoys. T'ing, even more than Wexler, was certain to understand this. Now that the initial flurries of confrontations and demands were over, it was time to get down to work. And even apart from the issue of test missiles and shooting them down and such, Wexler had other reasons for wanting to maintain contact with T'ing. Very small reasons.

Late yesterday, Captain Hemingway's team had repositioned the Little Insect bug, shielding it from anything other than conversations that took place in her office. It was Wexler's job to try to find out just what T'ing knew about it.

But they don't know for sure yet, do they? I mean, even though Brad said he'd never seen another nation use it—and just how much did he know about that sort of thing?—it didn't mean it couldn't happen.

And even if it were a Chinese entity of some sort, that didn't mean that T'ing knew anything about it. In fact, she was quite certain he wouldn't know about it. They would shield him just the way she was shielded from the more distasteful practices of their respective governments.

But if that was true, why did she feel so apprehensive about seeing him? She knew she was capable of dissembling with the best of them. Years of experience in diplomacy had taught her to hide her thoughts, maintain a bland expression no matter what she felt or thought. Could she pull that off with T'ing? She wasn't sure. And nervousness had made her, the one who was usually late for their appointments, early tonight. So she sat alone at their favorite table.

Finally, she saw T'ing appear at the entrance to the restaurant. The maitre d' greeted him warmly, and led him to their regular table. There was a small expression of surprise on his face at seeing her already seated there.

"You're quite early, Sarah."

She forced a small laugh. "I shall have to do this again just so you won't be so surprised. I finished up early and if I'd stayed another moment, Brad would have brought in another pile of papers for me to sign. You know how he is."

"Oh, yes. I do." T'ing slid into his chair, then pulled the wine list from the center of the table. He glanced over at her. "The white or the red?"

"White," she said. "If I can ever make up my mind which one, I'm going to have fish."

He studied it for a moment, although there was no real need for him to do so. They both had the small but exquisitely chosen list memorized. T'ing closed the wine list and handed it back to the steward.

For a moment, Wexler panicked. How did their conversations usually start? She couldn't exactly remember. They'd been so free and natural after the first couple of months that she'd quit thinking about how and what to say.

T'ing saved her from having to decide. "I have had quite a rewarding day myself," he said. "Our good friend from the United Kingdom, one of your favorites, is he not?" He glanced over at her and smiled. Ambassador Wells had been a pain in the ass for both of them in his early days. He had come under orders to disrupt Ambassador Wexler's relationship with T'ing. The plan might have worked had she not found him so consistently annoying. It had been the inconsistency between the face he presented to the world, that of a genial, bumbling fool, and what she knew must be true of any representative from the Court of Saint James. He consistently rang a false note, and it was only when they were forced to level with each other in the last Mid East crisis that he'd finally revealed his true colors. No, he was not the polished, elegant statesmen that his predecessor had been. Certainly he had all the right breeding, all the right connections, but his manner was less understated, more likely to attempt a sly, manipulative approach to a problem rather than the quietly elegant solutions of his predecessor. Nevertheless, once she had grown accustomed to his manner, he'd proven to be a fine representative of America's oldest ally.

"And what is our dear friend up to these days?" she asked, grateful for the opening. "Still fuming over the fact that the British Empire no longer rules both of our continents?"

"That, always. He speaks quite good Mandarin, you know. I was most impressed."

"You're kidding. And just how long was he going to keep that a secret?" she asked.

T'ing shrugged, an oddly sinuous movement on him. Although he was dressed in a conservative western suit, elegant tailoring and fine fabric made it hang on him like robes. "I got him to admit it after I asked him about his studies at Sandhurst. He attended their specialized language institute, you know."

"No, I didn't. They normally keep that information rather classified."

T'ing smiled and said nothing. It wasn't the first time he admitted knowing more than anyone thought he should, but under the circumstances, it gave her a decidedly uneasy feeling. It would be foolish not to expect him to have considerable espionage resources at his disposal—indeed, he had been the first to clue her in on the fact that her aide, Brad, wasn't all that he appeared to be. And although she considered T'ing a good friend, she did not believe that he would have any difficulty reconciling their friendship with having her office wired for sound.

"Have they declared war on China?" she asked lightly. Now wouldn't that have been an interesting thing for someone to overhear? She wondered how long it would take to make it into a gossip column.

"Nothing so straightforward. Indeed, I'm not sure quite what to make of it myself. He is, I believe, quite concerned about China's intentions regarding Taiwan. He conveyed a gently worded warning—but a warning nonetheless—that we take no precipitous action to disrupt the balance of power in our area of the world. Of course, we both know what that means." He glanced over at her, mild curiosity in his eyes. "And he mentioned that your country is quite concerned as well."

She knew what he was hinting at. If the United States was so concerned, why hadn't he heard about it from her directly? She searched his face for a trace of hurt but saw only curiosity and perhaps a trace of disappointment.

"I wonder where in the world he got that idea?" she asked. "Did he say?"

"No." He leaned over and placed his hand over hers, his palm cool and smooth. "Please do not misunderstand me. I know that the United Kingdom and America have a unique parent-child relationship. She fought on your soil, and yet even after your independence, your two nations have so much in common. But I must tell you, even the best of friends have interests that do not always completely coincide. And it would be worth considering that at times that may be the case with England and the United States."

She leaned forward, matching his intensity with her own. "What are you getting at?" She made a motion to withdraw her hand, and his tightened on it.

"Just this. I suspect that our British friend has sources of information in your office of which you are not aware. He knows too much and there is no explanation for what he knows. And he was letting me know that. Why, I do not know. Any more than I would know why you would convey a message to me through him."

"I didn't. If I had something to say to you, I would say it directly."

He regarded for her for a moment, then nodded. His pressure on her hand lessened. "Then you must consider the possibility that he has a spy in your office. That, or some way of intercepting your most confidential communications."

A shiver ran through her. Why tonight, of all nights? There were too many possibilities.

First, T'ing, despite all the precautions, might know that they had detected the listening device. This was an offensive strike, intended to divert her suspicions to the British.

Second, that Wells had some plan of his own, still trying to disrupt her relationship with T'ing. She would not put that beyond him.

Or perhaps Wells was trying to give T'ing the impression that he did have confidential sources in her office. And why would he do that?

And the final possibility—that T'ing was right, that Lord Wells did have sources of information in her office that she was unaware of. Perhaps a back door, with the CIA and British intelligence cooperating through Brad. Perhaps the Little Insect listening device they had discovered. Or perhaps both.

And she was supposed to tolerate this? Not being secure in her very own office? The last time her life had been in danger, and she and T'ing had been on the run, they'd bolted to the security of the United Nations building as soon as they were able to. Brad had mobilized a strike force of people she had no idea he even knew.

And now this.

For a moment, she considered confronting him. Telling him about the listening device, and asking him bluntly whether or not China was responsible. But no, that would do no good. He was even better than she was at concealing his expressions, and she would know only what he wanted her to know. In the shifting game of alliances and deception, how was one to know who one's allies really were? And despite her long-held belief that personal relationships were an important part of diplomacy, would their friendship have any effect on the conduct of affairs between nations?

"The mustard catfish, I suggest," he said finally.

"What?"

"For your dinner. It is one of your favorites, and I noticed several others enjoying it tonight. Perhaps that would be a good selection." He withdrew his hand, then picked up his own menu to study it.

The world is about to go to crap, and the representatives

of the two principals are trying to decide what to have for dinner. Hell of a contribution to world peace. But it could be the last time for a long, long time, if China goes ahead with those missile tests. And the last one ever if they actually have the balls to target Taiwan.

She looked over at T'ing. He raised his head from his menu and smiled, a pleasant, genial expression that betrayed no hint of his real thoughts. And that he had some real thoughts, oh yes, she had no doubt of that. He always knew more of what was at stake than she did, and had a connoisseur's appreciation for subtle layering of national interests and the complexities of international affairs.

She withdrew her hand from the table. "Yes. The catfish, I believe."

TEN

USS **Jefferson**
Admiral's conference room
2100 local (GMT +10)

With his makeshift staff assembled around his conference room, Batman opened the folder in front of him. He glanced around at the faces, evaluating what he had to work with.

Better than it could have been, but not as good as a regular battle staff. Most of the officers seated at the table were either maintenance experts, exceptionally skilled in managing the supply system and flow of work that kept an airwing flying, or supply officers carrying long lists of everything onboard. The hangar bay had been hastily out-fitted as a high-level maintenance depot, and the ship was manned with the appropriate personnel. He had jet me-chanics, avionics specialists, and electricians instead of pi-lots and operations specialists, supply clerks instead of radiomen. Still, they were sailors, and there were certain skills they would have their disposal. Chief among them was the ability to take orders and think creatively.

"Okay," Batman said, "so far, so good. I know this is a short-notice deployment for everyone, and I expect to be advised immediately of any problems that arise because of this. Our primary mission may be as an aircraft repair facility and the supply resource, but let's not forget one thing, ladies and gentlemen—this is an aircraft carrier. And as such, I expect all of her systems to be fully operational. That includes the catapult, the arresting gear, and every combat system we have on board." He held up one hand to forestall protest, and continued. "No, I'm not expecting you to get the hangar queens working, learn to fly them, and go on combat missions."

That garnered a slight chuckle from two of the maintenance officers. One of them spoke up. "Admiral, I'm willing to give it a shot, if you are." Batman remembered from his service record that the man had flunked out of the Tomcat training pipeline.

Might be interesting to see just how much he remembers.

"That won't be necessary, but I'll keep it in mind. No, we need to be able to recover aircraft and launch them again. God forbid, if something should happen to the *United States*, having an extra big deck ship around might come in awful handy for Admiral Grant. In all probability, it's not going to happen. But if we have the capability, I want to be able to exercise it."

"I've got a couple of techs who were air traffic controllers before their nerves gave out," one officer said.

"Yes, and I've got an operation specialist. Dumb as a rock—so they sent him to fix aircraft instead of talk to them." The officer shook his head, disgusted. "But a good man, a hard worker—we get him some help and keep an eye on him, he can manage."

One by one, the other officers around the table volunteered the latent capabilities within their units, and Batman was surprised at the breadth of experience. Finally, he turned to the senior engineer present and said, "Effective immediately, in addition to your other duties, you will be my chief of staff. I want a full, fleshed-out roster of how we're going to set flight quarters for both launch and recovery, as well as an analysis of the impact on damage control capabilities. I want names, specifics, not just 'to be determined.' "

Then Batman pointed at next most senior officer. Odds were that every maintenance officer onboard had started life as an aviator and flunked out of flight school. "Fallen angel, right?" Getting a nod of affirmation in response, he said, "Okay, you're the air boss. Pick your mini boss and your tower crew. What you don't have, train. Let me know your proposed training schedule and give me an estimate of how long it will be before you're ready to conduct underway flight operations.

"And the rest of you—I want this entire evolution supported. Your full support, you understand—I don't want to see anyone just going through the motions. If you know something that somebody else doesn't, you tell them. It's going to take all of us working together to pull this off, but we can do it."

I hope we can do it, he added silently.

"Admiral, with all due respect," his new chief of staff said, "do you really expect anything to happen to the other carrier, sir? I mean, do you know something we don't know?"

Batman nodded. "Yes. I know that you fight the way you train. If we don't train to do this, we won't be able to pull it off. I don't know how or when we'll need these capabilities, but if we do, I want to be ready."

Greenwich Village
2200 local (GMT −5)

Wexler leaned back against the leather seats and went over the evening in her mind. Apart from his cryptic warning about the British ambassador, there had been nothing out of the ordinary in T'ing's conversation or conduct. Not that she really expected to catch him in an unintended reaction. She just hoped she'd upheld her ambassadorial inscrutability as well as he did.

The driver pulled up in front of the townhouse she occupied for most of the year. The man sitting next to the driver got out, took a quick look around, and said, "Okay, Madam Ambassador. It's clear."

Sarah Wexler got out of the car. She still was not comfortable with the new security measures Brad had implemented, but under the circumstances, she had little room to complain. And she had to admit, she appreciated not having to fight the traffic herself. Riding in the quiet elegance of the back of the Lincoln town car, she read briefing papers, signed correspondence and dictated answers to letters. It was, she found, the most productive part of her day.

A car pulled up behind the ambassador's, and a gun immediately appeared in her escort's hand. "Get in—take off," he snapped at Wexler and the driver. "Head for—"

"Wait," Wexler ordered. "I recognize the car."

"Who is it?" The guard demanded, his gun still in his hand pointed at the front windshield.

Wexler shook her head. "I'm not going to tell you. If they're approaching me like this, then they don't want anyone to know they're here. Go on, leave. I'll be fine. Either wait inside or get back in and drive off. Either way, I need you to clear the area now."

"But Madame Ambassador, I really don't think—"

She cut him off. "I don't care what you think. Now move." She put a bark into the last words.

When she saw that they were inside her townhouse, she walked back to the car behind her. She approached the back seat, not even bothering with the front. As she came close, the window rolled down. She leaned forward and poked her head into the car. "Good evening, Mister Ambassador," she said.

"Good evening to you, madam. I apologize for approaching you in this manner."

She nodded. "These are difficult times for us all. I understand your caution. I would invite you in for a nightcap or a cup of tea, but under the circumstances, I suspect you might wish to decline."

The ambassador from Japan inclined his head ever so slightly. "As pleasant as that would be, I'm afraid you are right. However, there are things that we must discuss."

"And my office is . . . ?" she prompted.

He didn't answer for moment, and said, "You have many new friends. What I have to say is for your ears alone."

A cold shiver ran through her. Did he know about the bug? Or was he just referring to the visits by Captain Hemingway?

"Perhaps we could take a drive?" she suggested.

The door lock clicked, the Japanese ambassador opened it. "Yes. That would be acceptable."

USS **United States**
Friday, September 6
1100 local (GMT +10)

By the time the USS *United States* was in blue water operations and out of unrefueled flying range, Lab Rat had all of his staff and material onboard. In fact, as he gazed at the mass of boxes and steel security containers stacked ceiling-high in most of his spaces, he suspected he had a good deal more than his own gear. It was entirely possible that the U.S.'s shore detachment at North Island had taken the opportunity of a few more COD flights to pack in some extra ship's company gear. Not that that bothered him, no. But untangling the ship's practical and decidedly unclassified gear from his own top secret and higher material was going to take up more of his time. And time was the one thing that Lab Rat and his people didn't have.

"More classified material to be signed for, sir," Chief

Brady said as he passed a clipboard to Lab Rat. "I think
that's the last of it, though."

"You did an inventory?" Lab Rat asked.

"Of course, sir. That's my signature on the bottom line."

Over the last eighteen hours, COD flights had been
pouring in with more material for the newly-staffed CVIC.
Senior Chief Brady had been running ragged trying to keep
up with it all.

"Sir? There's a Captain Ganner asking for admission,
sir. Is he cleared?" a petty officer asked.

"Of course. He's the chief of staff—have we got the
people and clearances sorted out yet?" Lab Rat asked, turning to the senior chief.

The senior chief maintained a determinedly neutral expression. "Without the pictures, yes, sir, but it's going to
take few days for all the watchstanders to learn all the
faces."

"Yes, of course. Let him in. Unlimited access," Lab Rat
said.

A few moments later, Captain Ganner sauntered in to
the most sensitive area of the intelligence center. He took
a look around, noted the open boxes, gear on every flat
surface, and bustle of technicians. The area was in complete chaos.

"How long before you people are going to be open for
business?" Ganner asked. "Because I got to tell you, it
looks like the war will be over before you can get all those
boxes put away."

"We're ready now, sir. It's not as disorganized as it
looks," Lab Rat lied. "Is there something I can do for
you?"

"Yes, as a matter of fact, there is. I need five sailors to
help on the flight deck. And since most of the boxes clob-
bering the deck are your gear, I figured you'd be eager to
help out. Oh, and by the way—you'll be standing watches
in TFCC. Under instruction, of course. You have the midwatch tonight." Ganner's face was bland, but Lab Rat had
the sense that he was watching carefully for a reaction.

"Sir, could we speak privately?" Lab Rat asked.

"No, that won't be necessary," Ganner said. "I believe you have your orders."

A hush fell across the intelligence center. Ganner jutted his jaw out and waited for a reaction.

Lab Rat tried again. "Sir, if I could just have a few moments—"

"See you on the midwatch, Mr. Busby." Ganner turned and stalked out of CVIC.

Senior Chief Brady waited until he'd left the intelligence center and said quietly, "Man, who did you piss off, sir?"

"I don't know exactly, Senior Chief. But I stepped on it somewhere. Listen, is there any way we can cut loose five people to help on the flight deck?"

The Senior Chief sighed. "I can, but it's going to slow us down in here, sir. And every minute that we're not fully operational, well . . ."

He didn't have to finish the sentence. Every day that the intelligence center was not fully operational could spell disaster for the battle group. Sure, they were performing the basic functions now, but there was no time for the sort of in depth analysis and projections that Lab Rat preferred to be able to develop.

"Five men," Lab Rat said quietly. "We'll go along with this for now. A midwatch more or less won't hurt me, either. Won't be the first time I've run short of sleep, and it certainly won't be the last time, will it?"

"I guess not, sir," Brady said. "But, this is one of those things, sir—you give them an inch, the surface sailors take a mile."

"I'm not ready to draw lines in the sand yet," Lab Rat said. "We'll do what we can to be team players for now, but if it starts affecting operations, I'll go to the admiral."

The petty officer guarding the entrance stuck his head back in the compartment. "Sir? That captain, just before he left—he told me to tell you that he's going to do a zone inspection on our spaces tomorrow. And he told me to get a swab and get started on the deck. He said our spaces look like a disaster, and that they'd better look better by tomorrow."

Lab Rat heard Senior Chief Brady swear quietly beside him.

Greenwich Village
Thursday, September 5
2210 local (GMT −5)

"Such an interesting part of town," the ambassador from Japan murmured as they drove through Greenwich Village. "We have nothing like it in Japan, of course."

She bit back a reply. She suspected there was indeed a Greenwich Village somewhere in Japan, if not quite as visible or as flagrant as Greenwich Village was here. Instead, she said, "I know the area quite well. Perhaps I can give you a tour someday."

"That would be very kind of you," he said. She noticed a frown of disapproval on his aide's face.

"Then sir, I must ask you . . . the hour is somewhat late, and you have gone to a great deal of trouble to talk to me privately. May I ask what this is about?"

"China." The Japanese ambassador spat out the word as though it tasted bad. "And Taiwan. Our position—perhaps I will not give you exact answers. It is difficult . . . the interest in that region . . . our own position . . ." He spread his hands as though helpless.

She knew what he was getting at, and couldn't decide whether or not to force the issue. Japan was a relatively small nation in terms of land mass and military forces, and it would be very risky for her to offend China. Not only for military reasons, but because of the potential effects on economics and trade as well.

Yet it was equally risky to offend the United States. Thus, he had not wanted to be seen talking to her, not quite so publicly. And yet he needed to convey his country's difficulties to her so that the United States would not be offended by Japan's apparent silence on the issue.

"I appreciate your position," she said quietly. "But you understand mine as well."

"Of course. And that is what I want to tell you—that, as you suspect, we do not wish to be drawn in to this conflict. Consequently, I believe that within the next several days my country will impose stringent overflight and transit landing restrictions on your military aircraft." He held up one hand to forestall comment. "This is not an official notification—it is simply my best guess based on experience. Furthermore, should things become . . . more intense . . . I suspect my country will withdraw landing privileges altogether."

Now that was going too far, wasn't it? She expected some resistance, perhaps some limitations on how many military aircraft could be on the ground at any one of the bases at a given time, but certainly not this. "The spaces are subject to long-term lease agreements," she said. "Are you suggesting you will break those agreements?"

"I am suggesting nothing. This is purely preliminary. But what I have to say is this—if that happens, if there are serious restrictions imposed on overflight and landing, my government wishes to assure you that we will do nothing that would place American forces at risk. Furthermore, in the case of imminent danger to your people, such as a rescue at sea, we will cooperate most fully."

"So we're out on the front lines and we shouldn't expect any help at all. You'll abide by international law, and that's all?" she asked, rather more sharply than she intended. But dammit, what was the point? Allies were supposed to stick up for one another.

"I'm also authorized to tell you," he said, as though she had not spoken, "that Japan very much wishes to enter into the conflict on the side of the United States. But not, however, until there are sufficient forces in the theater that you can protect us if this should be necessary. We risk much if we support you against China—I think you must not expect any support for months to come after your aircraft carriers are in the area."

"What about the rest of the Pacific Rim?" she asked. "Where do they stand?"

"To a great extent, their positions mirror ours. They wish to support the United States, wish that most fervently. But the danger is not insignificant, you understand. Especially for the smaller nations."

Economic powerhouses the Pacific Rim nations might be, but there was no way they could stand up against the military might of China. No, it only made sense for them to try to sit on the sidelines for now. But she had thought that America could at least count on Japan's support once an American aircraft carrier was near their coast.

"And what is it that you expect in exchange?" she asked.

"Continued friendship, and support for our historic territorial integrity." His significant glance said everything his words did not.

Ah, so that was it. Japan wanted to ride the fence as long as she could and end up with the U.S. supporting her claims to the Kuriles and Spratley Island chains. The Kuriles, the jagged line of islands extending up to Japan's north, were currently under the control of Russia. The Spratleys, with their oil-rich seabeds, were to the south, and were a point of controversy between China, Japan, the Philippines, Malaysia, and anyone else who could muster up a boat big enough to get out to them.

"That won't do," she said sharply. "You know it won't—and you know I can't agree to it."

"Ah. But we had hoped we could count on America's friendship in the future?"

"It has been adequately demonstrated to you time and time again, my friend. And now, if you don't mind, I really must get back home. The hour grows late."

The ambassador spoke to his driver, and the car turned and headed back toward her townhouse.

"Later than any of us think," he murmured. They rode in silence for the rest of the way.

ELEVEN

Brad intercepted Wexler in the passageway outside her office. She took one look at his face, then followed him down the hallway, waiting until he judged they were in a secure position. Then he turned back to her. "Hemingway's back."

"More bugs?" she asked.

He shook his head. "Naval operations. JIC is in an uproar. It's like a feeding frenzy. There's still no hard evidence, but all the area experts are saying it's about to come down to a confrontation."

"When will the carrier be in the area?" she asked.

"Another two weeks. According to Hemingway, they're setting a new speed record for transiting the Pacific."

"Not soon enough, I suppose?"

"No. Hemingway needs to talk to you . . . but under the circumstances . . ." He stopped, knowing she understood what he meant.

"I suppose it's time," she said heavily. She felt obligations and bindings descending on her at the thought of

what she was about to do. But really, there was no other
choice, was there? Her own spaces were demonstrably not
completely secure. Hemingway had insisted that there
were no further listening devices, but Wexler could not
shake the uneasy feeling that she was never completely
alone in her office.

She pulled her shoulders back and raised her chin.
"Okay. I'll do it. When?"

Brad seem slightly surprised and uneasy over the situation. "Hemingway can take you right over, if you want.
I'd like to go along."

"What for?"

"I might as well hear about it at the same time, right?"

She stared at him, trying to understand what he was
thinking. Did he think she wouldn't tell him everything
she heard at JCS? Or did he have other reasons of his own?

Suddenly, an insight. "Is there a turf war between the
CIA and naval intelligence on this?" she asked, suddenly
certain she was right. "The CIA doesn't have a source
there, do they? They want you to take a look at things,
figure out what's being withheld and get everyone singing
off the same page."

She could see him consider denying it, and then he
sighed. "I don't know exactly. Ever since the big summit
that you and the president and the CIA had, I feel like I'm
out of the loop. And this agreement—well, they don't trust
me as much as they used to. Divided loyalties, you know."

Now that was ironic, coming from him. It was T'ing
who had warned her about Brad and told her of her aide's
CIA connection himself.

She pointed a stern finger at him. "I will be leaving the
office, accompanying Captain Hemingway, in precisely
twenty minutes. Within that time, I expect to have a telephone call from the CIA requesting that you be allowed
to accompany me and explaining their reasons for the request. Without that, not only do you not go, I will not tell
you what happened when I get back."

TWELVE

For two weeks, *Marshall P'eng* and *Lake Champlain* patrolled the western coast of Taiwan, intent on just holding out until the USS *United States* arrived on station. But the entire area was oddly silent, and none of their intelligence sources were exactly sure why. Yes, China was finishing up a major upgrade to most of her fighters. Yes, she had several major combatants just completing periodic maintenance.

But if that were the reason, why the missile test in the first place? Why stir things up, looking like you were going to take advantage of the lack of air power, and then stand down? Had they simply been impressed with *Lake Champlain*'s capabilities? Captain Chang tried to believe that was the case, but he simply couldn't convince himself that it was so. He'd even tried to ferret out some explanations during a brief return to port for refueling, but no one knew anything more about it than he did. At least he'd had the opportunity to see for himself the tactical data link that showed the American carrier—two of them, actually—

almost off the coast. Soon, very soon, it would be absolute suicide for China to attempt an invasion.

Since the carrier was now within unrefueled flying range, an exchange of liaison officers was proposed. Taiwan Central Command provided an army officer, Major Ho, to serve as a representative onboard the USS *United States*, a move that bothered Captain Chang somewhat. Major Ho was an extremely competent army officer with extensive training and joint forces experience under his belt, but when all was said and done, he was still an army officer who knew a bit about naval operations, not a navy officer. Captain Chang wanted to send someone from his own crew, but simply didn't have the bodies.

In return, the American carrier detached a lieutenant commander by the name of Charlie Goforth as their liaison. Goforth was a *nisei*, a second-generation American with a Taiwanese mother, and spoke their language fluently. Major Ho was equally fluent in English. In discussing the matter with his own XO, Captain Chang had decided that for the time being, he would keep his own excellent command of English secret.

The exchange of pleasantries ashore had been abruptly cut short by a call from *Lake Champlain*, who politely requested *Marshall P'eng*'s assistance at her captain's very earliest convenience. Chang, who knew of no reason that an Aegis cruiser might require the assistance of a former Knox-class frigate, nonetheless immediately put to sea with Lieutenant Commander Goforth onboard.

As soon as Captain Chang saw the radar contacts appear on the surface plot, he knew there was trouble. Whether *Lake Champlain* had given him the heads-up based on her own radar coverage or outside intelligence assets, Chang had no idea. The latter, he suspected, since Captain Norfolk's information on course, speed and intentions on their common adversary was quite detailed.

The task force itself was worrisome enough. Every major combatant from the Gungzho military base was underway, formed up in a tight pattern, and headed their way.

Four cruisers, two destroyers, and three amphibious landing ships crammed with troops—no, this was not an exercise or standard workups.

Two hours after he was underway, Chang flew over to the cruiser for additional briefings. As his old Sea Sprite helicopter hovered over the deck, then settled gently, guided by the American flight deck crew, he mentally assessed the condition of the ship. It was well cared for, that was true, but no more so than his own small frigate. Remarkably, the Americans seem oblivious to the marvels around them. The *Marshall P'eng* required constant chipping and painting, and it was an endless task to maintain her in pristine condition. This ship, with its newer, tougher exterior, seem to require virtually no maintenance. And under the haze gray paint was a layer of solid Kevlar, the tough, fire-resistant fabric that absorbed the impact of projectiles and protected her superstructure from fire.

He was quietly pleased with the competence that his Sea Sprite pilot showed settling onto the deck, and nodded politely to the pilot, who understood immediately what was being conveyed. They had put on a good show in front of the Americans, and Captain was pleased.

The executive officer, a bluff, hearty man Chang had met before, was standing at the edge of the flight deck, waiting to welcome him. Chang would not have expected the captain himself, no, not under the circumstances. That he'd chosen to send his XO was intended to convey his respect for his Taiwanese allies.

Captain Chang let his translator lead the way across the flight deck and out from under the helo's rotors. For now, they would maintain the pretense that Chang spoke little English. The XO immediately popped into a sharp salute, then led him away from the rotor blast of the helo.

"Welcome aboard, sir. We're pleased to have you." The XO gestured to a younger officer standing next him. "Lieutenant Jones would be pleased to have your pilot and copilot accompany him to the wardroom for a cup of coffee and perhaps a meal while we talk to the captain. If that meets with your approval?"

Chang listened as the translator conveyed the XO's words, matching the translation to the tone of voice and expression of the man standing in front him. "Tell him my flight crew would be pleased to accept the honor," Chang replied. "I believe they have developed quite a fondness for ice cream during their visits here."

The XO chuckled. "Ice cream it is."

The XO led the way off the flight deck and through the central passageway of the ship. The bulkheads were spotless, the fittings polished and shining. Fire hoses, communications gear, and emergency equipment were all apparently brand-new.

The XO took him directly to the captain's cabin, knocked on the door, and opened it without waiting for a reply. "Captain? I've brought Captain Chang." The XO stepped aside to allow Captain Chang to go first, and then followed and closed the door behind him.

The captain stood as they entered, crossed the room and extended his hand. Chang stood at attention as they shook hands warmly, because that was what was expected in this culture. After the handshake, he bowed slightly, as he would to an equal.

"Well, then, we don't have much time, I know," Captain Norfolk said. He motioned to the table in the middle of his room. "You'll forgive my abruptness, I hope, but perhaps we should get to work."

Their directness was one of the things Chang liked about the Americans, although he had to admit he still found it jarring. "That would be agreeable," he said to his translator, and waited for Norfolk to seat himself at the table before taking the chair across from him.

Norfolk shoved a chart across the table at him, and then a short message. "I'm hoping you can shed some light on this," he said. "We've seen a number of deployments by the Chinese forces in the past, but never quite this composition. The long-range missile shooters, the destroyers, the amphibs—but I have to say, it's the mine-laying capabilities that worry me as much as anything else. We've had some recent experience with those, as you know."

Chang nodded politely, but did not comment. The American's experience in the Gulf and the serious damage to USS *Jefferson* were well-known to the world's navies.

"And here's the worst of it. We've got information that they're planning another spate of missile tests. And not normal missile tests," Norfolk said. He locked eyes with Chang, his expression deeply concerned. "Even with the carrier in the area, this could be the start of a major offensive. While I don't want to alarm you unnecessarily, that's what I'm hearing from my sources."

Sources. Intelligence. Spies. How much of the same information does my own government have, and why is it not provided to me?

Chang studied the chart for a moment, then the composition of the ships headed his way. They would be here in about ten hours. Not much time—not much at all. And that was just for weapons-release range—to come closer within visual range would take another six hours, even moving at top speed. Still not much time to prepare.

"But of course, we are already prepared," Chang said finally. "I agree with you, and I am afraid I can shed no additional light on the matter. Your sources are perhaps more . . . forthcoming . . . that mine are." He saw his translator struggle to get exactly the right nuances in his choice of words to accurately convey Chang's tone of voice.

Norfolk sighed. "I was afraid of that. If the weather holds, we may see the carrier tomorrow. Her escorts will be another week behind her, so it's up to you and me to provide cover for her." He saw Chang grimace, and nodded in agreement. "Right, it's not the way we like to work. But under the circumstances . . ."

Under the circumstances, you want your air power here. You'll pick up the antiair coverage for the cruiser she's leaving behind, and you want me to handle any submarine problems in the area, because between here and there, she will be going too fast for submarines to be a problem.

Norfolk then confirmed Chang's reasoning by saying, "If it meets with your approval, I'll concentrate on the air problem while you handle the subsurface and surface issues. I'll chop my two helos over to your operational control to use as you see fit. Once the carrier gets within range, it will be a different ballgame, but for now, that looks like the best use of our capabilities. Any comments or suggestions?"

Chang shook his head. "No. And I think it is an excellent plan."

"Well, then. Perhaps you could join us for lunch before returning to your ship?"

Chang shook his head, suddenly anxious to be back on board *Marshall P'eng*. "I hope I will not offend if I decline. But given the matters that we have discussed . . . well, there are some measures I must take immediately."

An odd expression crossed Norfolk's face for a moment, and he looked at the translator. But then he said, "I understand. Perhaps another time?" He gestured to his mess cook. "I was afraid this might indeed be the case, but I have been eager to show off my mess cook's talent. Perhaps you would accept this package for you and your senior officers on our behalf. And, I am afraid I must admit, that I have taken the liberty of providing several gallons of ice cream to your helicopter crew. I hope that your officers and men will enjoy them as a token of our friendship."

"Thank you. And I hope we'll see you onboard *Marshall P'eng* for dinner sometime when circumstances permit." With mutual assurances of their undying respect and confidence in each other's capabilities—and in this instance, each man actually meant it—the two men parted. Chang followed the XO back to the flight deck, preceded by his air crew scrambling to get to the helo before he did, and the captain returned to Combat.

THIRTEEN

United Nations
Friday, September 20
1000 local (GMT −5)

Despite the occasional cry of wolf from the intelligence
community, life remained relatively normal during the carrier's transit to Taiwan. Wexler and T'ing repaired a few
frays in their friendship and soon resumed their easy conversations over dinner. Although Wexler found the presence of Little Insect in her office troublesome, she spent
the time putting the final touches on her plan for uncov-
ering the source.

China's opening diplomatic salvo came as a surprise to
both Wexler and her allies. None of the Asian nations even
saw it coming, and it came from a most unexpected quarter.

Brad came into her office after the morning session, his
face serious. He handed her a petition addressed to the
United Nations, signed by the ambassador from China. It
protested in the strongest possible terms the presence or
intended presence, or potential presence, of radioactive
materials in her territorial waters. China lodged her objection in general, and then specifically noted the aircraft car-

rier USS *United States* as a potential source of the objectionable materials.

Wexler scanned the petition hastily, picking out the pertinent points. China was making much of the fact that the aircraft carrier had not even completed sea trials before being deployed. The petition claimed that under the circumstances, her safety precautions could hardly be considered adequate. China requested—no, demanded—that the United Nations take measures to ensure that the aircraft carrier not enter Chinese territorial waters—which, according to the Chinese, extended one thousand miles out past the coastline.

"Complete and utter nonsense," Wexler said, tossing the petition on her desk. "There's no way they'll get any support for that."

"I don't know, ma'am," Brad said quietly. "From what I hear, they might not be alone in this."

"Who?" she demanded.

"Russia."

At that, she let out a hearty laugh. "They're the biggest offenders in the world in the area of nuclear safety," she said. "They'd get laughed out of session."

"Maybe." Brad's voice was dubious. "Maybe not."

"Do you have information I don't?" she demanded.

He shook his head. "I just have a bad feeling about this one."

An idea occurred to Wexler. She turned to Brad and carefully touched her right ear. It was their prearranged signal. A look of surprise flashed across his face, and then he nodded his understanding.

"It's a good thing," Wexler said in a normal tone of voice, "that the President agreed to send those Patriot batteries to Taiwan. I think they'll come in handy."

"Sure will," Brad said.

"Although," she continued, "I have to tell you, I'm not sure that we'll really be able to keep the Chinese from finding out about it. And labeling the boxes as farm equipment—well, who is that going to fool? No, I think we've got to plan for the possibility that China will find out, although I dread the possibility."

"Let's hope everyone just does his job right," Brad answered.

"Let's hope," she said.

And let's see who does *find out!*

Later that afternoon, Wexler would learn that Brad's premonition had been true. Russia, as well as a host of smaller nations, and of course Australia and New Zealand, joined in the protest. The United Nations Secretary-General sent the matter to committee for further study, which would stall the matter further, but there was every chance that with China and Russia acting in concert, the matter would be back on the floor for a vote in record time.

The Beltway
Washington, D.C.
1114 local (GMT−5)

From the outside, Tombstone's uncle's new quarters looked like any one of the Beltway Bandits that thronged around the center of the country's government. They sprang up overnight like mushrooms, bid against each other, merged a week later, and competition for economic survival was fierce.

The entrance sign gave no hint of what was inside. AD-VANCE SOLUTIONS, it said, the letters picked out in gold paint over plastic, swirling in a cursive script, impressive and prosperous unless you looked too close. Beltway firms were experts at looking well-capitalized while expending as little money as possible.

Even the double doors leading to the suite were in keeping with Advance Solutions' public image. The darkly stained wood doors opened onto the portion that was unclassified, complete with a receptionist and a couple of computer technicians. Indeed, Advance Solutions had already bid on three government contracts, although never successfully.

But what was important was what lay behind the metal doors at the far end of the suite. The door frame itself housed a number of security measures, including metal detectors and a fluoroscope. It opened onto a secure vestibule. Entrance beyond that was controlled by a retinal scanner as well as a security number pad. Both were required to gain access. And beyond that armed guards sat behind one-way mirrors, Marines for the most part.

Tombstone passed quickly through the outer area, garnering a cheery greeting from the receptionist. Had anyone asked her, she would have informed them that Tombstone was a technical adviser working on the company's bid to design the analysis factors that would go into the final bid requirements for advanced fighter ECM system. And she would have been able to discuss quite convincingly—and often did in response to phone queries from job seekers—the firm's requirements, staffing, and past and future plans. Indeed, she was probably the most well-prepared part of the entire cover story.

Once past the steel doors, all pretense of corporate luxury ceased. The walls, overhead, and deck were reinforced, and sensitive electronic monitors in every corner kept watch to prevent eavesdropping. The windows were insulated, covered with metal, covered with another layer of sound-deadening material, and sealed off. All in all, it was the most secure classified area that existed outside the Pentagon.

"Good morning, Uncle," Tombstone said. His uncle had a desk in one corner, a small, functional metal one. Tombstone had his desk in the opposite corner. "What's up?"

"Our first mission," his uncle said, his voice a model of controlled excitement. "Dammit, Tombstone, they're actually going to let us do it this time."

Tombstone slouched down in the comfortable executive chair he'd insisted on. "About time," he said. "Four months of desk work are starting to get to me."

His uncle shot him an amused look. "It hasn't been all desk work, as I recall. There is a little matter of two hundred hours in a Tomcat."

"There is that. But I took it as simply a signing bonus."

His uncle laughed out loud. Tombstone stared at him with some degree of amazement, delighted in the changes in his uncle's demeanor over the last months.

How had it been that he had missed his uncle's slide into the grim formality that had characterized his tour of the CNO? How could he have missed the absence of the warm friendliness that always characterized their relationship, the occasional bad joke his uncle used to make? No, it was only now that his uncle was freed of those burdens that he saw the man he remembered from his childhood days emerge again. His uncle was like a child with a new toy, only this toy had a budget that was truly mind-boggling and bigger, better, faster toys than anything either of them had experienced as a child.

"So what's the deal?" Tombstone asked, as he propped his feet up on his desk. "Is it time to save the world?"

"A small part of it, maybe," his uncle said. He came over to Tombstone's desk, and tossed a couple of photographic surveillance photos in front of him. "Take a gander at these."

Tombstone studied them, pretending to puzzle out whatever it was he was supposed to notice. But in truth, he as well as his uncle depended on the enlisted intelligence staff who were experts at this sort of work. Interpreting satellite images was still more of an art than a science, and it took years of looking at seemingly random collections of light and dark before the brain started making sense of what the eyes reported.

Once he made the obligatory show of studying them, Tombstone held out his hand. "Okay, care. Where's the report?"

His uncle handed him two sheets of paper.

Tombstone scanned them quickly, sparing a fleeting moment to appreciate the terse style in which they had been written. The terrain was just north of the Kurile Islands, and those specks of white on the infrared shots were troops. Lots of troops. Just off the coast were Russian landing vessels. The analyst concluded that there were at least two regiments and ships to carry them waiting to deploy to the Kuriles.

"The Russians making a grab for them, are they?" he asked.

His uncle nodded. "Yep. No indications from other sources yet, but we've got some feelers out."

"Well, you got to have troops to hold land, that's for sure. And it looks like they've got enough of them."

"Take a look at the last paragraph again."

Tombstone looked again. According to the analyst, there was no indication that there were antiair defenses in place, and no indication that they would be installed. He looked up at his uncle in amazement. "Pretty stupid. The Japanese are more than capable of taking them out."

"The Japanese aren't. We are."

"What!?" Tombstones bolted upright in his chair.

His uncle stuck out his hand. "You heard me. Congratulations, you're a plankowner."

Tombstone clasped his uncle's hand in both of his own. "We're actually going to take them out?"

His uncle nodded. "The Pentagon figures that one good bombing run could disable all three ships and decimate about half of the ground troops. They'll know who's responsible, don't doubt that. But they won't be able to say a thing. Because just as we're not going to be there, they're not there right now. Everybody's cover stories will fit together neatly."

One bombing run—yes, that could do it. Tombstone studied the satellite photographs again, now that he knew what they represented, and saw it was entirely possible. Two antiship rounds, maybe three—the rest Rockeyes or some other antipersonnel weapon. He called up a picture of the region in his mind, and verified that there was one serious problem with the plan. "How am I supposed to get there?"

"The Aleutians. Your last stop will be Adak. You'll refuel there, and then make one hell of a long-assed haul down to the Russian position. You'll be met enroute by KC-135 tanking support."

"Tanking from the Air Force? That's going to compromise our mission, isn't it?"

His uncle shook his head. "Son, there's a hell of a lot you don't know about the way the world works. The Air Force has been providing this sort of service for ages. They don't ask, we don't tell. After all, they get paid the same whether they're refueling satellites or aircraft."

Tombstone looked stunned. "Satellites? You're kidding; they *do* that?"

His uncle's face was dead serious. "Yes. Of course I'm kidding." Then his face cracked into a broad smile and he laughed aloud again. "Don't be silly, Tombstone. Refueling a satellite . . . come on, it was a *joke*."

"I knew that."

"Right. So. You up for this? Remember, I told you that you could refuse any mission you didn't want to carry out."

"Are you kidding?" Tombstone said. "Of course I'm up for it."

"Remember, there are going to be risks," his uncle said somberly. "For most of the transit, you'll be a long way from land. You're going to get the best aircraft that money can buy, but there's always the unexpected. And it's possible the Russians will move air defenses in place between now and then."

"When is then?" Tombstone asked.

"Tomorrow. Unless you need more time."

"Tomorrow! You're not kidding when you say things move fast." Tombstone shook his head admiringly, thinking of the things he could've done while on active duty if the Navy establishment had been so flexible. So much trouble could've been prevented, nipped in the bud, by a force capable of doing just what his uncle was proposing.

But then, did he really know for sure that there hadn't been a predecessor to Advance Solutions?

He started to ask, and saw his uncle shake his head. "I know what you're thinking. Don't even ask. I can't tell you, even if I knew."

"Well. I just wish . . ." Tombstone's voice broke off.

His uncle laid a reassuring hand on his nephew's shoulder. "I miss her, too. She was good for you."

His last, shattering memories of Tomboy came flooding back. Her face, the feel of her skin next to his, the way she had of continually challenging him, making him better than he'd ever thought he could be. God, but he missed her. And to be denied even the cold comfort of burying her—well, it didn't bear thinking about. Nothing could change what had happened.

"So tomorrow," Tombstone said at last. "I better get some sleep, then." Another question occurred him. "Who's my backseater?"

"Some good news, there," his uncle said. "The aircraft you're taking was originally configured as a trainer, so you'll have dual flight controls. You can have a pilot instead of an RIO, if that's what you want."

"I'll take Jason," Tombstone said promptly.

Jason Greene was the newest addition to their team, a hotshot young F-14 pilot who had leaped at the opportunity to join up. He had already foreseen the way his career would go, that eventually responsibilities and duties would take him further and further away from the cockpit. All Jason wanted to do was fly—he didn't care about additional responsibility, about command, or any of the other things that a good naval officer should care about. That made him perfect for Advance Solutions.

"Jason's a good choice," his uncle said approvingly. "I don't think you'll have any difficulty convincing him."

"Difficulty? Hell, I'd have to shoot him to take off without him."

FOURTEEN

Marshall P'eng
Saturday, September 20
0800 local (GMT+8)

Captain Chang gazed out over the relatively placid Yellow
Sea. He knew this body of water like he knew his own
house, its moods, the peculiarities of its sound velocity
profile, and had developed an almost instinctive feel for
how sonar propagation curves would look. He glanced up
at the sky and took a careful look at the horizon. Everything he saw agreed with his gut feeling. There would be
no storms today, none of the sudden squalls that could lash
the sea into unbelievable chaos. And a good thing, too.
While a storm might not bother the massive aircraft carrier
off its port now, the crew of the small frigate would definitely feel the effects. Even worse, increased sea state
would definitely degrade their USW capabilities.

But even a body of water he knew well could hold surprises. Somewhere over the horizon, the Chinese surface
task force was supposedly conducting a training exercise.
Their intentions worried Chang, but not as much now as
they had earlier. Within a few hours, the aircraft carrier
would be within range to deliver antisurface missiles,

should the need arise, and Chang found the prospect of a snowstorm of Harpoon missiles immensely reassuring.

What bothered him more than the surface ships was what might be below the surface. The latest intelligence reports showed that one Chinese diesel submarine was missing from its berth in port. Yes, Chang had held them, tracked them, even simulated killing them. But who was to know just how much of that was realistic? It would not be beyond a Chinese to feign incompetence in order to induce a false sense of confidence in the Taiwanese.

Oh, he knew them too well. They had ancestors in common stretching back over time on a scale that these Americans could not even contemplate. These Americans—the new toys, their advanced electronics, the brash, abrasive way they had of dealing with each other. Such a young nation, with officers like children—it could be, at its very best, simply annoying. At worst, the differences in their culture led to serious misunderstandings that took much patience and tolerance to work through.

Chang walked back onto his bridge, noted that all was going well, and then proceeded aft to Combat. The quiet murmurs inside there fell silent as he walked in, a mark of respect. His watch officer, a young man from a good family, stood and bowed politely.

"All is well?" Chang asked.

"Yes, Captain. We maintain our station, and have been transmitting reports regularly on our contacts." The lieutenant hesitated, as though deciding whether to speak further.

For just a moment, Chang felt nostalgic for the days when it had been just the *Lake Champlain* and the *Marshall P'eng* in this part of the world. The arrival of the aircraft carrier USS *United States* had complicated life by a factor of ten, not the least by the micromanagement of his own USW patrol area.

Oh, Chang understood the reason behind the sudden rudder orders and the polite requests that *Marshall P'eng* be somewhere other than where she was headed. The car-

rier usually pleaded pending flight operations or replenishment evolutions with the USS *Jefferson*. After all, it wasn't
like they could order him out of certain areas of his own
sea, but he could tell that that was just what they'd like to
do.

There was an American sub somewhere around, there
had to be. There was a sub in his water, and no one wanted
to tell him about it. Nor did they want him accidentally
stumbling across their sub and prosecuting her.

Chang conducted a few careful maneuvering evolutions
to determine exactly when and where the Americans got
nervous. By careful observation, he had a pretty good idea
what the boundaries of their sub's operating area was, and
he confirmed his suspicion by noting that no American
ships ventured into that particular square of water.

But the American submarine was not his only problem.
Even with the aircraft carrier's escorts a few days out, the
tension had already started to affect his crew in more subtle ways. No longer were they the premier warship in the
water, a pretense they'd been able to maintain with only
the *Lake Champlain* around. The massive bulk of the aircraft carrier, the sheer volume of radio traffic and aircraft
and everything else that she threw into the air brought
home to each *Marshall P'eng* sailor just how powerful the
other ship was.

That was the down side, as the American's said. The up
side was that the Chinese task force seemed to have
stopped dead in the water. They remained approximately
two hundred miles off their own coast, ostensibly conducting training operations, perhaps to draw attention and
resources toward the surface ships and mask covert maneuvers by their submarine. Chang felt a flash of pity for
the ground troops sweltering in the close confines of the
troop transport ships.

"And?" Chang prompted gently, waiting for the watch
officer to continue.

"I am not sure they listen to our reports, sir. Oh, they
are quite polite on the circuit—sometimes I must repeat

numbers and names, but eventually they understand. But look at the display," he turned to point at the newly installed tactical data system.

Unfortunately, it was a one-way system on their ship. They received an integrated tactical picture from the battle group, but could not manually input their own contacts. "Why have they a need of our reports when they have all this?" the watch officer asked.

Chang had wondered the same thing himself, but the decision had been made at higher levels. "It is to develop coordination," he explained, hoping to sound like he meant it. "We will get used to working together, now, when there is time. There may not be time later."

"Yes, Captain." His watch officer said nothing further, but his eyes mirrored a shadow of doubt.

USS United States
TFCC
0810 local (GMT +8)

Lieutenant Commander "Bird Dog" Robinson clicked down on his mouse again, this time punching it harder. Nothing happened. His JTIDS, or joint tactical information display system screen remained infuriatingly locked on what the sailors called "the eagle prompt," meaning that the giant American Eagle logo was displayed. A nice logo it was, indeed, with the eagle well drawn and suitably fierce, but no substitute for the array of tactical data that should have been there.

Bird Dog glanced over at the watch supervisor's console, the small one mounted directly under the racks of computer gear. It showed a complete tactical data picture.

"Why the hell has he got it and I don't?" Bird Dog demanded. He glanced over at the lieutenant sitting at his side, his watch officer. "It's just not fair."

"I don't know, sir." The watch officer paused for a moment, as though wondering whether to proceed. "Were you adjusting the background color displays again? Or the geographical features?"

"Maybe. What's that got to do with it?"

"It's just that if you overload the computer with high-density graphics, sometimes it drops offline."

Behind Bird Dog, Taiwanese Major Ho Kung-Sun walked into the compartment silently, and stood at the back to study the screen. Even in his few days on board, he knew what the eagle prompt was.

That American officer, abusing his computer again. Ho Kung-Sun had listened to the technicians and other officers explain to him time and time again what would drop it offline, yet the lieutenant commander never seemed to understand. If he did, he certainly didn't modify his behavior. Instead, he insisted on experimenting with different color mixes, changing the range displayed continuously, tracking contacts and putting up graphics, all of which quickly overloaded the system.

"Well, call the geeks and tell them to get up here," he heard the brash lieutenant commander say.

Ho Kung-sun stiffened. That word—how dare he! Long exposure to American culture, as well as a careful reading of the documents provided to the American officers, had made it clear to him that the term "geek" was an old, offensive word, a racial slur applied to many Asian races. And to use it here, in front him—well, no matter how they protested about their desire to work together in harmony with the Taiwanese Navy, this made their feelings clear. Had there been any real desire to work together as equal partners, no American would have even thought—much less spoken out loud—the racial slur.

Ho Kung-Sun turned and stalked out of the room, infuriated beyond measure. This would be reported, it would indeed, and the American officer would rue the day he dared to use such language.

The watch officer turned as he heard heels staccato on tile, and caught a glimpse of Ho Kung-Sun leaving the room. Bird Dog swiveled around as well to follow the man's gaze. "Wonder what he wanted?" the watch officer asked.

Bird Dog shrugged. "Who knows? He seems like a nice enough guy and pretty sharp. That little boy of theirs, he's a hell of a good station keeper, isn't he?" He concluded in an admiring way. "They've got that Helen Keller sonar on board, but once they've got something, it's not getting away. And aggressive?" He pointed at the watch officer's log. "They've called in more detailed contact information in the last hour than our lookouts report in two weeks."

"Yes, I know what you mean. It's a shame that there's a language barrier—I bet he's a hell of a nice guy when you can get him to loosen up."

"Oh, his English is pretty good. He just has problems with a couple of the vowels, that's all."

The watch officer turned to stare at the door, an odd thought crossing his mind. No, it couldn't be—of course not. He dismissed the thought. And it wasn't until much later, when the situation had deteriorated considerably, that the watch officer first voiced his hesitant thought. "He has a problem with vowels."

USS **United States**
CVIC
0815 local (GMT +8)

The senior submarine officer on board copied down the coordinates then plotted them quickly against his detailed area chart. Certain areas of the ocean were exclusively for the submarine's use, at given depths and at given times. The *United States* would not launch sonobuoys or deploy other assets against the submarine operating in its own area.

The submarine officer laid down his two-point dividers and said, "Admiral, the *Marshall P'eng* is on the very edge of the sub's keep-out zone. And he hasn't said anything, but I think that frigate captain knows what's going on. He's no dummy, sir." He shook his head, a frown deepening on his face. "I don't like it a bit, sir. No telling what can go wrong. You know it's an absolute, that we never share water space with anyone else."

Coyote sighed. Yet another problem, another one arising out of incomplete information exchange between the two forces. It was bad enough that the LINK was not a full duplex operation, although it certainly made safeguarding classified information easier. But in times such as this, when Captain Chang inadvertently stumbled into areas of waters they didn't want him in, it could be hard to explain. Nevertheless, the *Marshall P'eng* was under Coyote's operational command, and he'd already seen that the Taiwanese frigate was eager to be a part of his battle force.

Coyote turned to his TAO. "We can't tell Captain Chang why, but he'll figure it out. He's a smart man—the second we start moving him out of some operating areas, he's going to get suspicious—and, based on what he's already seen, if there's a problem with our submarine, he'll know it. So tell him I'm setting a restrictive EMCON condition and he is to use only passive sensors. That's at least got some basis in reality, and I won't have to change his station to keep him out of the way. Plus, his chances of detecting our submarine by passive means alone are pretty darn low." He glanced over at the submarine officer. "Aren't they?"

The submariner nodded vigorously. "Absolutely. If he's on passive only, he won't see us at all. But active—" he shook his head, "even with the special coating on our hull, he's going to get a return. And as sharp as those guys are, there's no way we're going to convince him it's a whale."

"So it might work," Coyote said.

"Might. But it's absolutely a violation of standard operating procedures. Admiral, with all due respect, there's not supposed to be *any* friendlies in that sub's area. None at all. Even if they don't find our boat, the possibilities for confusion and disaster are endless."

"I'll deal with briefing the sub CO," Coyote said. "All I want to know is that you're certain that the *Marshall P'eng* can't detect that boat on passive only."

"I'm certain."

"That's what I thought. So," he continued to the TAO, "Tell him now—passive only until I say otherwise. On second thought, get Major Ho in here. I don't want any misunderstanding about this, so have him make the call in their language. That way, there's no confusion."

Major Ho walked into TFCC, saluted immediately, and asked, "How can I assist the admiral?"

Coyote regarded him for a minute, still not certain what to make of this young man. "I want you to tell Captain Chang I'm setting a restrictive emissions condition, an EMCON. Passive sensors only subsurface. Do you understand? I don't mean the radars, of course. Keep those on-line. And he can stream his tail whenever he wants to. Just no active sonar transmissions. We have some people conducting special operations in the area," he embroidered on sudden inspiration, "and if active sonar blasted the wrong area it would kill them."

Major Ho bowed slightly. "Of course. I understand, and will convey that to Captain Chang." He glanced up at the display and the area marked off. "But I understand that Captain Chang is attempting to gain contact on the Chinese submarine at this moment. It would be natural for him to go active in order to maintain a perfect firing solution, should he gain contact."

Coyote glanced at the submarine officer, a movement that Ho did not miss. "Yes, it would. But so far, they have committed no hostile act. Let's keep tracking them passively and not give them any reason for assuming we're preparing to attack." He clapped Major Ho on the shoulder, as he would have one of his own officers. "Don't worry, Major. When there's a submarine to kill, your guys have first shot. I promise you."

Major Ho bowed again, then reached for the microphone connecting him to tactical. He made the call up, in English, then switched to Mandarin. "The American admiral, he asks me about your tracking solution," Major Ho said carefully. "He wonders whether you intend to use active sonar at this point?"

Captain Chang's answer came back, also in Mandarin. "I can if he wishes, but I had thought I would not spook the submarine if he is in the area. If I go active, he will know that he has been detected."

"The admiral thought that might be your decision," Ho said, choosing his words so as to convey the slightest disapproval. It was a subtle move, one that he was certain only Chang would understand.

"Of course, I can go active, if that is what the admiral desires," Chang responded immediately. "Here—I will demonstrate now."

USS **Seawolf**
0820 local (GMT +8)

The single, sharp sonar pulse blasted through the hull of the American submarine, and every man onboard flinched. Normally, this would be the precursor to a torpedo in the water, a final ranging ping to establish a precise firing solution before releasing weapons.

"What the bloody hell?" Captain Tran said, his voice soft with the slightest trace of a British accent in it. He turned to his XO. "Didn't that message get out changing our operating area?"

The XO nodded. "We got acknowledgement from the satellite that they picked it up, too. There's no question that they got our message."

"Then how come I'm getting blasted by some idiot?" the captain demanded. He reined in his legendary temper, and focused on the solution. "We're going to have to clear the area. How far how can I move off and still maintain some form of contact on the Chinese boat?"

"Maybe fifteen thousand yards, if we're lucky," the chief sonarman spoke up. "Captain, I can find him again for you, but I'd rather not."

The captain thought for a moment. The damage had already been done by the active ping. Their cover was blown. Furthermore, the Chinese sub would have heard it as well, and would be doing its best to clear the area.

At this point, he needed to destroy any firing solution that the pinging platform might have. "Who was it?" he asked the sonar chief.

"Had to be the Taiwanese," the chief answered. "We're not carrying that kind of sonar on our ships anymore."

"Then how come—never mind, doesn't matter." He'd address the coordination issues in a P4 to the admiral. What they had to do now was get the hell out of Dodge, try to maintain contact on a Chinese diesel doing the same thing, and then reacquire the contact if they lost him. A pain in the ass, but that's the way the game was played.

Marshall P'eng
0821 local (GMT + 8)

"Captain!" The sonarman's voice was slightly quieter than normal. "Captain, I have two subsurface contacts—*two*!" The sonarman looked up at him, confused. "But there is only one Chinese submarine in the area, Captain. I'm certain of it."

Chang thought for a moment, then his face cleared. Perhaps this was the admiral's way of expressing confidence in *Marshall P'eng*, of revealing to him secrets that he was not otherwise allowed to. The captain smiled slightly in pride. He had not thought the American admiral so subtle.

And if this was a test, then what was he expected to do now? As he paused, Major Ho's voice came over tac-

tical again. "The admiral asks if you would be so kind as
to secure your active sonar now. He is setting an emissions
condition, in which only passive tracking is allowed."

That confirmed Captain Chang's suspicion. It *had* been
a test, and one that they had passed satisfactorily. The admiral had intended them to know that there were two submarine contacts in the area, so that later, should attack be
necessary, Chang would know why certain precautions
were taken.

But now what was he expected to do? To report both
submarine contacts, or just one?

Just one, Chang decided. The admiral would not want
a U.S. submarine location transmitted over the circuit, for
the same reasons that he had not been permitted to tell
Captain Chang directly that the submarine was in the area.
And based on what he'd seen of the battle group's orders,
Chang had a pretty good idea which one was the American
and which one was the elusive Chinese diesel.

"Report the presence of only the one you believe to be
the Chinese submarine," he said, still quietly warmed by
the admiral's confidence. "But go back over the last hours
of data. See if now you see any acoustic evidence of an
American submarine in the area. For that is what the second contact is—of that I'm certain."

USS **United States**
0822 local (GMT+8)

"What the bloody hell!" Coyote roared, as the graphics
depicting an active sonar ping flashed on to the screen.
"What is he doing?!" Immediately, reports began pouring
in over the tactical circuit from the other surface ships.
The admiral sighed, then turned to Ho. "Okay, I guess
there are going to be some screw-ups. But you know what
I mean now—no active sonar, right?"

Ho bowed slightly. "Yes, Admiral. I made that very clear to Captain Chang Tso-Lin."

"Okay, then. What's done is done—no sense whining about it." Coyote paused as though he wanted to ask something else, then turned away. Just then, Captain Chang's watch officer's voice came over the circuit, giving the bearing and range to the Chinese submarine. Everyone in TFCC breathed a sigh of relief.

Coyote relaxed. However things had gotten screwed up, evidently the location of the American submarine had not been compromised. The *Marshall P'eng* had detected only the one she was supposed to, the Chinese one.

Good news in the short term, but perhaps not so good in the long run. He was hoping that *Marshall P'eng* could contribute to the ASW effort. However, given the ranges that were involved, she should have detected the American submarine as well. And if so, why had she not reported it? Perhaps Chang had realized something had gone wrong, and had decided not to report it. Or perhaps he hadn't detected the U.S. submarine. To ask about a second contact now would simply make a bigger deal out of it, and that was the one thing Coyote fervently didn't want to do.

So ignore it for now. Figure it was a screw-up, and go on. He knew what the submarine was doing—clearing the area, then returning along a different bearing to resume stalking her prey. If he could keep the Taiwanese frigate on passive now, she should be able to do that without interference, and without running the risk of being detected herself.

Suddenly, the Taiwanese frigate symbol on display changed course. It was moving away from the U.S. submarine, and toward the Chinese one. Captain Chang was moving his ship to the very edge of his operating box almost as though . . . almost as though . . . "Damn," Coyote said softly. "He's telling me something, isn't he?" He glanced over at the major, and saw no indication of understanding on his face. Then he looked back to tactical display. Either things were *really* screwed up, or he and

Captain Chang understood each other better than he thought they did.

It had been a long time since Lab Rat had popped tall for anyone, and he was really not enjoying it. Yet all it had taken was one glare from Captain Ganner to send him back into the braced salute of his midshipman days. He caught himself as he braced, and forced himself to relax.

"You have a problem, Commander?" Ganner demanded. "Because if you do, Mister, I want to hear about it."

"No, COS, I don't have a problem. Other than the one I've already pointed out to you."

"You're still on about the berthing assignments?" Ganner said, his face clouding over even darker. "I suppose your people are too good to live with the engineers?"

"Not at all, and you know it," Lab Rat said, his anger boiling over. "But my people are berthed all over the place. Come on, sir, you've been on a carrier before—you know how it is. It's just like on the . . ." He caught himself before he said "small boy," knowing the term wasn't a favorite among surface sailors, and continued with "a cruiser. You put part of your engineers together, another part somewhere else, so that if the missile hits, they won't all be destroyed at the same time, right? Then you spread them out so you have senior people in each compartment to take charge. It builds team unity, just like it does on a cruiser."

Ganner leaned back in his chair and tossed his pencil on the desk and glowered. "Well, I got the distinct impression your boys and girls already had this marvelous team unity—that's why the admiral brought you on board, isn't it? Because they were already a team? And now you're telling me that's not true?"

Lab Rat slammed his fist down on the chief of staff's

desk. He was aware that he probably looked silly—a short, blond, intell commander, barely weighing in at a hundred thirty pounds soaking wet, confronting a prototypical cruiser CO, tall, dark and strong. But he didn't care—this went beyond some stupid power-play. It was affecting his people, and he was going to put a stop to it.

"Sir, I don't know how and why you got so pissed off about all this," Lab Rat said. "And frankly, I don't really care. But the ship was built with berthing specifically designated for my department, and I want my people in it. It's closer to CVIC in case of general quarters. Now, if you want us to swap quarters with the engineers, we'll do that, too. That's if you think we're getting a special deal here. We'll swap completely, so I'll have two groups of men and a group of women berthed apart from each other. No more of this scattering us about at random between compartments. But if you tell us to do that, I imagine the engineer will have something to say about that, too. Because then his people will be just as far from their duty stations as mine are."

Ganner studied him warily. "And I suppose if I don't go along with it, you go to the admiral. And you aviators will stick together and you'll get what you want anyway, is that it?"

"Permission to speak frankly, sir?" Lab Rat asked.

"You haven't been?" Ganner sneered.

Lab Rat shook his head. "No, I haven't. But now I will. And I'll tell you what will happen if I go to the admiral. He'll agree with me. It won't take him any time at all to decide that I'm completely in the right and that you're jerking my chain for some reason. And then you know what he'll do? Hell tell me to get out of his office and deal with you. And he'll back you to the hilt, whatever you decide. Because that's the kind of man he is. You're next line in as his chief of staff, the man who will step in for him if something happened to him, and he's not going to undercut your authority. Oh, he won't agree—make no mistake about that. But he'll also back you up, right or wrong, unless you're actively putting people in danger."

The chief of staff's face took on a slightly surprised look, as though a mouse has really turned out to be a tiger.

Lab Rat continued. "And you know something else? Even knowing that in advance, even knowing I'm going to lose—I'll go anyway. Just like you would if our positions were reversed. Because that's the kind of man I am. You got some reason for doing what you're doing, but it doesn't have anything to do with me or my people. We just happen to be here."

There was a long moment of silence in the compartment. Lab Rat saw a range of emotions fly across the chief of staff's face. He wondered how long it had been since anyone had spoken that frankly to the man. And he wondered whether he'd just shot himself in the foot for the entire cruise.

Finally, Ganner burst out laughing. He pointed a finger at Lab Rat. "The admiral told me you were a pistol," he said, shaking his head. "I didn't believe him." He leaned forward and put his elbows on his desk and clasped his hands in front of him. "Okay. Sit down, Commander: Let's hash this out."

On impulse, Lab Rats stuck his hand out. After a moment, the chief of staff shook it. "We start over, sir? I'd like to introduce myself—I'm Commander Busby. But my friends call me Lab Rat."

Ganner nodded. "Okay, Lab Rat. Sit down and let's see what we can do to make this dog hunt."

FIFTEEN

AWACS One
Saturday, September 21
1200 local (GMT+9)

Air Force Major Frank Woods settled down in front of his
tactical console and shoved a small cooler under his seat.
It contained his lunch, a diet soda, and several candy bars.
Since the AWACS flew long missions, most of the crew
brought snacks along, even though it had a small, compact
galley on board.

The weather outside at Osaka Air Base was pleasant. It
was a clear, cool day, with the possibility of showers later
that afternoon, which was of no interest to Woods. The
AWACS was on a sixteen-hour mission in support of Cobra Dane and Cobra Judy, and the weather tomorrow
morning was the only report that Woods was really interested in. He had a soccer game scheduled with his seven-
year-old son.

"Going to be a long one," one of the other officers re-
marked. "Let's hope we have a home base to return to
when it's all over."

"Stow it, Harley." Harley Turks could find the dark side
to a rainbow, and right now the prospect of spending the

next sixteen hours in an aircraft with him was decidedly unpleasant.

"Come on, Frank. You got to have been thinking about it." Turks's voice was surly.

Woods nodded. The rumors were running wild all over the base, and had even made it into the preflight intell brief. Word on the street was that Japan would be terminating all landing rights for American aircraft, and that included any that were out of Osaka but airborne at the time. As mission commander, it would be Woods's job to select an alternate landing site and to deal with the worries and insecurities among the crew—as well as the logistics problems—should that happen.

"Okay, everybody, listen up," Woods said. The desultory chatter on the tactical interior circuit died down. "In all probability, this will be a long, boring flight with nothing to do. Just the way we like it, right? But like the intell weenies said at the briefing, there may be reason for concern, and I don't want to downplay that. So everybody, look sharp. Be flexible—we're dealing with the Navy. Harley will handle the communications, and try to keep it all working smoothly. Let's just hope we're bored out of our minds for the next sixteen hours, okay?"

Woods shoved his own worries aside as he ran through the remainder of the systems checks while he listened to the radio traffic piped into his right ear. So far, everything sounded normal, and his worries about missing tomorrow's soccer game receded. His crew sounded sharp, right on top of every checklist. There was no tension in the Japanese air controller's voice, nothing to indicate that this was anything other than a routine training operation.

But there wouldn't be, would there? After all, that's the reason they trained the way they fought, so that when the shit really hit the fan, it would be just another day in Uncle Sam's finest service. And under the circumstances, with one missile already launched and a cluster of naval ships milling about smartly off China's coast, it wasn't exactly routine, was it?

Cheyenne Mountain
U.S. Space Command Center
0100 local (GMT −7)

The AWACS had been on station for three hours when all hell started to break loose. It began with the most unobtrusive of the intelligence assets. A satellite relaying real time imagery to Space Command sent down a data packet that shattered the quiet static buzzing across an Air Force major's console, jolting the officer out of his quiet reflections on his possibilities of getting promoted.

The Air Force major bolted upright in his seat, staring aghast at his screen. The heat bloom on his screen was unmistakable. All around him, the information was being echoed on the other consoles, and the duty officer, an Army general, turned pale. There was no doubt that this was real—the question was, where it was headed.

"Space Command, this is USNS *Observation Island*. Be advised that we hold inbound antiship missiles along with probable missiles on long-range ballistic profile. Estimate TOT in approximately one hundred and sixty seconds." The voice from the ship was calm, if a bit tight.

The Army general grabbed his microphone. "USNS *Observation Island*, this is Space Command. Expect fighter support overhead immediately."

With that, the major began praying. Onboard *Observation Island*, they would be counting down the moments they had left to live.

USNS **Observation Island**
1105 local (GMT +8)

Waterson held two contacts, both of them definitely not artifacts or mistakes. It looked like a scenario straight out of training, with one missile headed for the AWACS overhead, the other one bound for yours truly.

Waterson glanced across at Vail, and wondered if the youngster knew just how serious the situation was. He had to—they had all talked about this possible scenario too many times for him not to get it. Yet the younger man sat quietly at his console, staring at the data, staring but apparently not seeing it.

"Bill—you okay?"

Vail nodded. "How long you think we have?"

Waterson shrugged. "Not long. Is there anything—I mean, do you . . . ?" He fell silent, knowing there was really nothing you could say at a time like this.

Vail shook his head. "They'll call away general quarters any time now. Those damage control teams—they'll handle it. I know they will."

Denial—it's one way to cope. Waterson couldn't bring himself to tell Vail just how unlikely it was that the ship could do anything at all to save itself.

So they sat, each lost in his own thoughts, each talking to his own God, as they waited for the end of their world.

USS **United States**
JIC
1106 local (GMT +8)

Lab Rat was just signing off a watch schedule when the red light on the side of his phone flashed and a buzzer went off. He grabbed for the handset and simultaneously, he punched the button to speak to TAO, and snapped out a quick, "Standby—urgent." Whatever was coming in was higher than flash precedence, and that meant only one thing—missiles inbound.

The voice coming to him from Cheyenne Mountain was cold and professional, not from lack of concern but because emotion was something they did not have time for. "Launch confirmation, Gungzho Facility. Number two, time on top six minutes. Request you launch fighter support and SAR assets in support of USNS *Observation Island*."

As the voice spelled out the launch details, Lab Rat was echoing them to the TAO. As soon as the first words were out of his mouth, he heard general quarters sounding. "*United States*, out," he snapped, as he started to replace the classified phone. As he was hanging it up, he heard, "Good luck, *United States*. Give 'em hell."

TFCC
1107 local (GMT+8)

Coyote stared at the screen as the missile symbols popped into being. In the background, he could hear the tense voice of the AWACS operator reeling off the details. "Home plate, picture. Missiles inbound, origin Gungzho station, number two." The information was immediately relayed to every station listening, including all the fighters.

"Orders, Admiral?" the TFCC TAO asked.

"Execute OPORD Ten," Coyote said, fighting for calm in his voice. "And get every spare SAR asset we can get headed for *Observation Island*."

Everything was in place now, the cruiser alerted, the fighters already forewarned. It was just a matter of everyone doing his job the way he'd trained, the way they'd planned.

USS Lake Champlain
1109 local (GMT+8)

Over the last three days, Norfolk had been alternating time in combat with his XO, each catching a few hours of sleep at a time. The watch section crews rotated more regularly, each of the three sections standing their normal four-hour watch, but general quarters had more than once interrupted their sleep as well. As a consequence, they were all starting to wear down, tempers growing short, and the effects of the pressure starting to show.

Oh, each one did his best not to show it, but there was the ever-present thought that every detail was critical, that anything they missed could kill them. When the call came from the carrier, arriving just as Space Command reached him via Navy Red, it was almost a relief to see the missile symbols pop into being. A relief, yet coupled with gut-wrenching terror. This was no drill, this was no simulation—it was the real thing, and if anyone screwed up, the crew of the cruiser as well as the aircraft carrier was done for.

The Aegis system was operating in semi-auto, and quickly identified the missile symbols as hostile targets. It assigned missile launch cells to each one, and paused on the verge of hurtling its weapons into the air. Both firing keys were already turned, to save those precious few seconds that might spell the difference between life and death.

The TAO's computer beeped incessantly, demanding action. With a quick glance at Norfolk, and a nod from him, the TAO acknowledged and authorized the firing. Seconds, only seconds—but was that fast enough? The ballistic missiles would launch, gain altitude, and cruise just outside the atmosphere before starting their final plunge back to their targets. The angle as they approached the cruiser would be particularly difficult, nose down, with no chance for a broader radar profile or larger target.

The Aegis radar system was capable of identifying a sparrow in flight. No, detection wouldn't be the problem—it was almost down to the vagaries of the wind, any slight stuttering in the solid fuel propellant driving the missile, or a glitch in programming or mechanical error.

The deck under his feet rumbled slightly, and he kept his gaze fixed on the camera focused on the forward deck. Missile hatches popped open, and a solid white antiair missile rose up from out of its cell, spouting fire from its tail.

It seemed to go slowly at first, almost hanging in the air, and made an awkward turn as it picked up speed. But within a few seconds of being airborne, the sheer raw power of its rocket motor overcame the forces of drag and gravity, and the missile steadied in flight and shot off to its target. It was visible for perhaps ten seconds, then lost in the clear blue sky.

As the first missile cleared the deck area, another one repeated the maneuver. Then there was a longer pause while the Aegis system tracked its own weapons, calculated the probability of kill, then decided whether another salvo was necessary.

It was. The TAO once again acknowledged the computer's recommendation, and the entire sequence of events was repeated.

During the launch, there was not a single sound in combat other than the standard reports made for a missile launch. Norfolk, who had one ear of his headset jacked into the weapons coordinator circuit, felt a rush of pride at their professionalism. Exhausted, ragged, at the edge of their capabilities, the crew rose to every challenge with superb professionalism.

The missile symbols, both hostile and friendly, were clearly identifiable. Norfolk studied the geometries for a moment. "Come left a bit, ten degrees," he ordered. That would put the ship bow on to the incoming missile, and thus present a smaller target. It would also clear the forward CIWS stations which might have a shot at taking out the missile if the standard missiles missed it.

"Sea skimmers!" one of the operations specialists shouted as he watched. "Captain, they've gone low!"

And as Norfolk watched the screen, the new missile contacts disappeared, indicating they were now flying just feet above the surface of the water. Where the hell was the AWACS picture, and why wasn't it showing them?

AWACS One
1209 local (GMT +9)

Woods watched in horror as the spiky missile symbols popped up on his screen. Just pixels arranged in a particular pattern, just glowing phosphors on an otherwise clear screen. Innocuous enough, if you didn't know what they meant to a thin-shelled aircraft.

The massive aircraft twisted in the air around him, the maneuvers more violent than he'd ever felt in an aircraft this size. It was as though the pilot was trying to conduct aerobatics in a nimble jet fighter instead of manhandling a 747 in the air. The deck dropped down hard under his feet as the aircraft dove, leaving Woods straining against his seatbelt. The aircraft went hard over to the right, standing virtually on wingtip as it desperately tried to shed altitude.

"He's got us! Come on, come on!" the other man shouted, his fear and panic instantly communicating itself to the rest of the flight crew. One part of Woods's mind, the part that wasn't devoted to coldly analyzing the situation, registered disapproval at the man's cowardice. He wasn't making it any easier for the rest of the crew.

Chaff and flares spewed out of the undercarriage, immediately creating a blanket of fire and radar reflecting strips of metal. The pilot twisted the aircraft again into an impossibly tight turn, straining to get the cloud of countermeasures between his aircraft and the incoming missiles. In the cockpit, the altimeter unwound at an alarming rate as the G-meter registered forces that the aircraft had never been intended to take.

Woods's weight increased suddenly as the floor of the compartment came hurtling up toward him. They pulled out of the steep dive only a few hundred feet above the wave tops, and the pilot immediately began a slower descent until they were virtually skimming the water like a massive hovercraft.

Chaff and flares weren't the only weapons of self-defense the aircraft possessed. Deep within its electronics, it possessed certain highly specialized circuits that were coupled to a small radar independent antenna. The circuits analyzed the incoming radar transmissions from the missile seeker head, made a few minor calculations, and then began transmitting a signal intended to mimic a radar return on the same frequency. In principle, the AWACS transmissions would spoof the missile into thinking that the aircraft was not where it was, fifteen feet to the left of where it actually was.

On his screen, Woods saw one missile veer suddenly to the left, increasing its altitude and climbing away from the aircraft. It streaked off into the distance, happily pursuing the illusion of the countermeasures cloud, and then finally detonated, briefly fuzzing his screen in that sector before the gain control circuitry kicked in.

One down, one to go.

The second missile was not nearly as gullible as its littermate. It blasted past the chaff and the flares, the tone of its seeker head a steady ping at the electronic warfare console and headed straight for the AWACS. At a range of five hundred yards, it turned slightly away, and Waterson had a moment of hope. Its new heading put it directly on course for the sun. Perhaps the heatseeker in its nose had decided that that brilliant heat source was the desired target, a problem many early generation heatseekers had had. Later generation U.S. missiles had discriminators that could distinguish between the sun and the exhaust from a jet engine, but it was possible they were using older models, wasn't it? In fact, it was more than possible—it was an absolute guarantee, it had to be. Woods knew a moment of hope, then blackness came crashing down on him as the missile immediately made a course correction and bore directly in on them.

The next four seconds of Woods's life were the longest he had ever known. Time stopped, seconds advancing at the speed of hours, the moments of life defined by a glowing green line on his screen that connected his aircraft with the missile. Figures immediately above and below the line read out the decreasing distance, clicking over at an incredible rate.

Every man and woman on the AWACS was so high on adrenaline, so completely stoked by the body's countermeasure to fear and panic, that the sudden flash of light and heat seemed like just one more problem to cope with. Each one had a momentary flash of: *I'm going to die. Now, here. No more.* It resounded on a deep emotional level, plucking at something more fundamental than any emotion they'd ever experienced. But the adrenaline surge kept it from mattering.

The shards of metal from the disintegrating engine penetrated the fuselage, passed through the crew compartment and left shattered flesh and bone in their wakes. Within seconds, the fuselage was no longer recognizable. Nor were the men and women who had inhabited it.

USNS **Observation Island**
1110 local (GMT +8)

"They're gone," Waterson said. In cold, clinical detail, the death of the AWACS and her crew had played out on the screen before him. The sensitive radar had lost track of the missiles as they descended in pursuit of the doomed aircraft, but the abrupt termination of the AWACS data feed ·and the small blur of static as parts of the wreckage were lofted back into the air at a high enough altitude for the radar to detect spelled out the details.

"We gotta do something," Vail said, his voice rising hysterically. He started unstrapping himself from his seat. "Get to the deck, launch the boats. We have time, we have time now!"

The retired master sergeant laid one hand on his compadre's shoulder. "We don't have time."

"But we—"

His friend's objection was terminated by the abrupt implosion of the side of the ship. The frags killed him immediately, but Waterson had time to watch the water pouring in, see the dark and hungry sea reaching for him before he died.

Viking 708
Overhead USNS Observation Island
1145 local (GMT +8)

Watching from above, it was like watching a turkey shoot. The massive ship made one futile attempt to maneuver and present a smaller aspect to the incoming missile, but it was more a demonstration of guts than of tactical superiority. The ship never stood a chance.

The missile impacted the hull just above the waterline, and for the merest second it looked like it might have been a dud. But it was designed to penetrate into the ship before detonating, thus ensuring much more damage.

Seconds after it pierced the hull, the steel after deck lifted slightly, a movement so unexpected as to be virtually unrecognizable. Then it lifted again, and large sections of it peeled back from the hull, leaving a fiery interior exposed. The flames spread quickly until fire was gouting out of every orifice of the ship.

Along the forward deck, the survivors swarmed around the self-deploying life boats, chopping through the restraining straps. Those with the presence of mind to do so simply triggered the deployment mechanism and the life rafts fell into the sea. The inflation devices triggered automatically when salt water hit them, and within seconds brilliant international orange inflatables were dotted around the ocean below the S-3. People plunged over the sides, making barely perceptible splashes in the water as they entered it, then struggled to paddle over to the nearest rafts. They faced large swells capped with whitecaps, and the wind was catching the life rafts and driving them away from the survivors. Those that did catch a life raft wielded the small paddles to try to return and help their ship mates, but more than one drowned before they could return to help them.

USS Jefferson
TFCC
1158 local (GMT+8)

As the reports from the Viking overhead the flaming wreckage of the *Observation Island* began coming in, a hush descended over the compartment. There was an occasional muttered curse as it became clear that few could have survived the attack, and in the background, the radio chattered as the air boss lofted every rescue helo he had into the air, sending most of them to the *Observation Island* and vectoring a few to the last known location of the AWACS.

Coyote cupped his face in his hands for a few moments. No one spoke to him. He needed no suggestions from his staff, no tentative outlines of a plan of action. It was to make the call in moments just like this that he had been placed in command of the battle group, and everyone instinctively knew that their advice and comments were neither required nor desired.

Finally, as the last of the helos lifted off the deck, Coyote looked up. His eyes were dark with unfathomable rage. There was no trace of anguish or sorrow on his face.

"They're going to pay for this," he said, his voice flat and cold. "And pay hard."

SIXTEEN

Wexler was working late. She had just finished going over the first response to China's petition to ban nuclear powered ships from territorial waters, addressing each ridiculous point as though it merited serious consideration, when the CNN headlines anchor said, "This just in." The secure, encrypted telephone line on her desk rang just as a map of Taiwan and China flashed up on the screen.

Wexler's head snapped up. Pamela Drake was neatly framed by the television screen. She was clearly made for this sort of work, and knew it. Large, intense green eyes seem to burn through the screen, framed by dark hair cut to chin level. Only the slightest touch of gray showed at the temples, and Wexler suspected that that would be soon eliminated.

"We have just learned," Drake began, her voice grave, "that China has been forced to respond to a U.S. incursion into her territorial waters' airspace. Earlier today, an

AWACS aircraft operating out of Japan ignored warnings of a Chinese naval exercise in progress and approached the ships maintaining, according to our sources, an 'aggressive posture.' The AWACS was accompanied by a surface vessel, the USNS *Observation Island*, a reconnaissance and intelligence platform. When the AWACS refused to turn back, Chinese aircraft fired upon her and the accompanying spy ship. The fate of the air crew and the crew of the ship is not known. Chinese forces are reporting no casualties."

Drake looked up from the notepad in her hand and stared directly into the camera, her face a mask of concern, her dark green eyes reproachful. "On the surface, it appears that this is another instance of America ignoring other nations' rights to their territorial sovereignty. The loss of life on board the AWACS and *Observation Island* is regrettable, but the true fault lies with the military commanders who insist on such aggressive posturing before all diplomatic measures are exhausted. China is not alone in the world in expressing grave concern about the presence of nuclear reactors just off her coast, and her concerns warrant serious consideration." She turned to a small monitor by her side and said, "With me now is General Herman Caring, who retired two years ago from the Air Force. General, what's your initial take on this?"

General Caring, USAF (retired) was the sort of senior officer who looked like a general. His features were strong, his voice confident as he spoke.

Caring. A fine person to ask. Cashiered for financial misconduct. They never should have let the bastard retire quietly—a court-martial, that would have kept him out of this cushy spot now. Wexler stared, as the general began to speak.

"Of course, our first thoughts must be with the crew of the AWACS," he said. "The crew carries parachutes, but in a combat situation, there is rarely time to use them."

"So you believe there's little chance they survived?" Drake asked.

"That would be my initial assessment." Although she had not thought it possible, Wexler saw Caring's face look even more concerned. "But as you say, the question about what the aircraft was doing there in the first place must be answered. I can tell you that during my days in command, all pilots were carefully briefed to observe international boundaries. But what practices are currently, I hesitate to say."

"But China does claim one thousand miles around her coastline as for own airspace, does she not?" Drake asked. "And neither the AWACS or the *Observation Island* carry offensive weapons, do they?"

Okay, give her credit. She's at least trying to put on a fair show. Maybe at least part of the people watching will understand.

"Yes, it's true that not all nations recognize China's territorial claims, the U.S. among them. And as to whether either American platform was carrying weapons, well—it wouldn't have been normal procedure," the general conceded. "Although with the portability of weapons platforms today, I could not state with any certainty that the ship was not carrying Harpoon antiship missiles. But Pamela, I think we have to look at the circumstances. This issue is still being addressed by a number of legal experts, and there are diplomatic ways to address this sort of thing. The use of force, in the aggressive testing of another nation's limits, should only be as a last resort. The consequences, as the families of the AWACS and *Observation Island* crews will tell you, are altogether too serious."

"I assume we can safely conclude that this is related to the rumors about a new ballistic missile that the Chinese have developed," Drake continued. "Can you put that in perspective for us, General?"

"Of course, Pamela." To Wexler's jaundiced eyes, General Caring appeared to enjoy addressing the reporter by her first name almost as much as he enjoyed taking pot shots at his former service. "You have to understand that many nations around the world engaged in ballistic missile development and testing. In China's case, her coastline does not primarily open on to open water, as ours does. The United States routinely conducts these sort of tests itself. But every report I've seen has shown that China has gone to extraordinary lengths to prevent any inadvertent problems from threatening the security of the world nations around her. Indeed, given the rise of anti-American sentiment in some regions, I would wonder that the other nations are not more supportive. After all, a strong China is the best defense against what they claim is American imperialism." Caring pointed one finger at the camera. "I must emphasize, that there is no evidence—none—that China is planning any ballistic missile test launch at this particular time. And even if they were, we have countless examples of how safely they have done that. There was no reason for American forces in the area to assume that aggressive posture, and certainly no reason to cut short the sea trials of an untested carrier. This sheer waste in terms of manpower and resources is absolutely mind-boggling." He leaned back, apparently confident that he had made his point.

But Wexler could see, to her credit, Pamela Drake was not fully convinced. Uncertainty furrowed her brow, and she looked as though she had several follow-up questions. That would have been in keeping with the Pamela Drake that Wexler knew.

But apparently in response to a question that she alone could hear, probably from the microphone in her ear, Drake simply said, "Thank you, General. I'm sure we all join you in wishing and hoping for the safety of the men and women on the AWACS."

I bet you are. Just drooling over the possibility of asking some grieving wife or husband how they feel about it, aren't you? Shoving the microphone in their faces just seconds after they've been told that someone is never, ever coming home again. And you people think diplomats are cold!

Suddenly, Wexler heard a scuffle in the outer office. At

first, it consisted of higher female voices raised in protest and indignation. Then, she heard Brad's deeper voice bark out, "Stop! You can't go in there." There was a crash as something hit the floor, and the door to her office flew open.

T'ing was framed in the doorway. Although he was not much taller than she was, the cold glare on his face and icy disdain in his eyes made him seem much more formidable.

Wexler stood, as much out of surprise as courtesy. "What's going on out there?"

Brad loomed immediately behind the ambassador from China. Wexler could tell he itched to grab T'ing and throw him bodily out, but she knew he wouldn't. Not under the circumstances.

T'ing drew himself up to his full height. "I apologize for barging in unannounced—but under the circumstances, it is clearly appropriate, if not practically demanded. Yesterday, the United States interfered with lawful, peaceful military operations conducted by my government. First, during a routine test over open ocean, your ships attacked and destroyed a missile. And now your commanders insist on deploying spy ships and aircraft into our territorial waters. Our response was immediate and proportionate, and only the greatest restraint on the part of our military commanders prevented the situation from escalating." She thought she saw something that looked like pain flit across his face. "And I am personally offended at your treachery. I thought that our working relationship precluded surprises such as this. But obviously I was mistaken."

"T'ing, please." She gestured to all of their subordinates. "Can we dispense with the formalities and sit down and have a civilized discussion about this?"

"Civilized? You speak of civilized conduct, after this?" He shook his head, and then renewed his glare. "No, Madame Ambassador. We will not speak alone. Before, that might have been possible. And I like to think that as representatives of two of the most powerful nations on this planet, you and I have managed to avert our share of crises. But this—no, this is far out of our hands. My government demands an immediate and complete apology, coupled with reparations. The president has twenty-four hours in which to comply. If not, whatever follows will be the sole and complete responsibility of the United States. You cannot treat other nations in the world like this. You cannot. It is time that someone demonstrated that to you conclusively and finally." With that, he turned, spoke sharply to an aide, and stalked out of the room.

Wexler sank back down in her chair, a feeling of loss pervading her soul. She could understand the Chinese position, oh, how well she could. And in one sense, T'ing was right. There should have been a way to resolve this before military action was required.

"That's it," Brad said with finality. "Madame Ambassador, I must insist that we upgrade security precautions immediately. I can't guarantee your safety otherwise."

"And just who's going to guarantee the safety of those men and women on our ships?" she said, her frustration boiling over into anger. "You heard the man—something terrible is afoot, Brad, and there's nothing I can do to stop it."

"If you're dead, there's nothing you can do at all," he said bluntly. "I've told you we need locked access to our suite, and you refuse to consider it. You're bull-headed, Sarah Wexler. Bull-headed and blind to the consequences of your actions." He crossed room and stood directly across from her. He pointed an accusing finger at her. "Just answer me this. If you're dead, who will sit in that chair? Can you guarantee me that it will be someone as capable?"

"The president will—" she began, and Brad cut her off.

"The president is a political creature. Yes, I know the two of you are friends. So even if you don't want to admit it to me, I know that you know he doesn't make his appointments based sheerly on ability. Name one potential candidate who would have been able to pull off the things that you've done in the last four years. Name one. And if you can convince me that there's anyone nearly as capable as you are, I'll stand aside. Be honest—I'm not asking you to brag or become an egomaniac. Just give me an honest assessment. Is it conceivable that he could appoint anyone with as much commitment to the process of diplomacy, who has as much understanding of international affairs, and who just all in all gives a shit about our military forces? Well? Is it?"

"You're out of your league, Brad. And way out of line," she said sharply.

"Am I?" He stood resolute, refusing to back down, and waited for answer. "Because if I am, and there is a great deal I have misunderstood about our working relationship."

And how had it come to this? First T'ing, now Brad. Was everyone in the world determined to have a showdown at the OK Corral this morning?

Brad had asked the one question that was almost impossible for Sarah Wexler to answer. She had deep streaks of both humility and pride running through her, and his question put them squarely at odds. Yes, she understood her role in the United Nations, understood in a way her predecessors never had. And, if she was forced to honesty, she would have had to say that most of them would not see her role as she saw it. It was something she had worked hard for, spent agonizing hours analyzing diplomacy and the art of it and now, at the culmination of her career, was able to bring every skill to bear on an increasingly precarious world.

At the same time, she was constitutionally incapable of admitting her own uniqueness. It went too hard against her grain to hold herself out as important, to claim to the world that indeed she was irreplaceable.

But a keen intellect such as hers could not long deny the truth of Brad's position. Yes, if she were replaced, in all probability it would be by someone less capable than she deemed herself. She thought the president would strive for someone he could count on the way he counted on her, but Brad was right about the role politics played as well. And she knew she was distinctly at odds with the rest of the diplomatic community in letting her concern for the American military factor into her decisions. Too often the State Department was foaming at the mouth: Send in the troops, send in the troops, constantly seeming to invalidate the very reason for their own existence. No one from State expressed concern over the American lives that might be lost, over the damage to countless families across the United States. No, when their best efforts failed, they immediately called for firepower, convinced that the failure lay in the intransigence of their opponents rather than in any shortcomings in their own capabilities.

"That missile was headed for Taiwan," she said slowly. "I'm certain of it." She let her thoughts roam over the probable scenarios, the massive loss of life, the consequences for the Taiwanese people of a return to the control of mainland China. Horrors raced before her eyes, countless atrocities and deprivation. As much as she admired— yes, and even liked—T'ing, she knew what his government was capable of. "And the AWACS and the ship were in international waters. There was no legal justification for attacking them."

Finally, she transferred her gaze to Brad's face. He was still waiting, and she saw that he must have an answer. Had to, for his own understanding and peace of mind.

"I will agree to certain additional precautions," she said slowly. "But not to making this an armed camp. Within what you have in mind, is there a way to accomplish that?"

She saw him immediately relax. He nodded, and said, "I know what you want and I know what I want. Let me give it some thought—I'll find a compromise that I think you can live with, okay?"

She leaned back in her chair, suddenly weary beyond measure. "I want to see the details before you implement it."

Brad nodded. He hesitated for moment, and said, "I meant what I said, Sarah. Right now, at this point in time, you are irreplaceable. And if I overstep my bounds occasionally, it's because I think I have a deeper understanding of that than you do."

She waved him off. "I don't want to talk about this anymore. It's been a long morning, and it promises to be a long week. But let me say this—one of the things I cherish about you is your bluntness. Now go on, get out of here before I change my mind."

SEVENTEEN

USS United States
TFCC
Saturday, September 21
1145 local (GMT +8)

Coyote was in a killing rage. The loss of the AWACS and the defenseless *Observation Island* ate at him, and the refusal of the National Command Authority to order an immediate retaliation almost drove him over the edge. On an intellectual level, he understood the reasoning. The United States was not prepared to go to war, not now. Forces had to be moved into place, the support of the public garnered, and every diplomatic avenue exhausted. When America fought, it fought with massive numbers of troops and assets, intending to win quickly and decisively, and there was no way the carrier and her escorts could pull that off—not yet.

But Coyote knew what the Chinese intended to do as surely as if he was sitting in on the Chinese staff meetings—and until they made the first move, there wasn't a damned thing he could do about it. Not actively—but he could get ready for them.

He turned to his operations officer. "Get us in an antiair formation," he ordered. "And that submarine—that worries the hell out of me." He pointed at the large symbol displayed on the screen. "Even with old gear, that Taiwanese frigate is the best asset we've got. I want her on the outer edge, with full authority to prosecute as her captain sees fit. And tell him I'm giving him two helos in addition to his Sea Sprite. He can use them any way he wants." Coyote glanced over at Major Ho. "If there are any communication problems, I want you on them immediately. Got it?"

Ho bowed slightly. "Of course, Admiral. There will be no problems."

A respectful answer, a competent one, but there was something in the Taiwanese Army officer's eyes that worried Coyote. What was it? Damn, these guys were hard to read sometimes, and it was a bitch getting them to speak up.

Despite his redneck origins, Coyote was an exceptionally astute observer of human nature. He knew that it was the cultural differences that made the Taiwanese officer sometimes seem deferential, when the Taiwanese officer thought he was making himself perfectly clear. He had debated several times on the best way to encourage the officer to speak up, and to make allowances for their lack of understanding, but nothing seemed to penetrate his reserve. Indeed, Coyote had the suspicion that the officer had taken his comments as criticism, rather than a plea for help. Because there was so much that they could do, so much that they could learn from each other. These people knew this water like no one else did, and that frigate—well, he hadn't seen a sailor do so much with so little since he worked with the Coast Guard on a few situations.

Damn it all, he tried. But the situation was getting too critical for niceties. He turned to Major Ho. "Is there anything on your mind?"

The Taiwanese officer's eyes were shuttered. "No, Admiral."

"Anything I have overlooked?" Coyote pressed.

A slight look of horror crossed the man's face, and quickly disappeared. "Of course not."

Coyote turned back to study the screen, frustrated at not being able to get the information he wanted. There was something on the Taiwanese officer's mind, but he couldn't get at it. Was it something in the formation? Coyote had the feeling the major was offended at something, but how could he possibly be offended at conveying primary responsibility for the submarine prosecution to his nation's ship, as well as giving the Taiwanese skipper operational control of two additional helicopters? If anything, it was Coyote's own DESRON Commander who was likely to get his panties in a knot over that.

"Your ship is well inside our antiair umbrella," he said, turning back to watch the officer's reaction. "She will be in no danger—or at least, no more than the American ships."

And now he really stepped on it, he could tell. Why? Had Ho taken it as an accusation of cowardice?

Inwardly, Coyote groaned, wondering how bad he'd screwed up this time with the man.

"I wish you to convey to your captain," he said to Ho, "my utmost respect and admiration for his abilities in ASW. It is for that reason that I ask them to take command of this problem."

The Taiwanese major bowed slightly again. "Of course. I'm certain he appreciates the honor."

Coyote gave up. The frigate's captain would either understand, or he wouldn't, and Coyote was betting that the more senior officer had spent more time working with the Americans and could see through any misinterpretations made by this young major.

"If he has any other requirements, please let my staff know immediately." Coyote gestured at his air operations officer. "Anything within reason."

•   •   •

Major Ho Kung-Sun picked up the microphone, inwardly raging. The blatant disrespect, for the admiral to refuse to communicate with his captain personally. And to add injury to insult by implying they were worried about an air attack. No, the admiral had tried to gloss it over, but Ho Kung-Sun understood very well what he'd meant. And he would make it plain to Captain Chang Tso-Lin as well.

The Marshall P'eng
1146 local (GMT +8)

Captain Chang listened as Major Ho detailed the admiral's plan. At first, he felt a rush of pride. Certainly it could not be often that a foreign ship was given such a substantial role in protecting the carrier battle group.

But then, as Ho continued, Chang began to frown. The voice coming over the speaker, speaking Mandarin, left no doubt as to Ho Kung-Sun's conclusions.

"They often refer to us in derogatory terms when they think I am not listening, Captain. Of course, I do not tell them what I hear—I wish for them to continue to think I do not understand, that I am a fool. But it is quite evident from this latest set of orders that they consider us far less capable." The major's voice was querulous.

Chang frowned. Ho Kung-Sun was a generally competent officer, although, of course, his primary background was in the Taiwanese Army. Still, he had been extensively trained at the nation's most prestigious military schools, and family connections had gotten him this sensitive position.

"Perhaps we should look at their actions rather than their words," Chang said mildly.

"Yes, perhaps we should. The admiral, he does not call you himself, does he? And look at our position within the screen. Our ship is exposed to the first wave of air attacks.

We will, in effect, be a missile sump for the American battle group."

"We are repositioned where we are in the best position to prosecute the submarine contact," Chang countered. "It is the same decision I would make myself."

"And you truly believe that is their intention? After all I have told you, my analysis of the dynamics here—you believe that? That with all of their advanced weaponry and sensors, the American Navy still needs the assistance of one broken-down frigate that they got rid of twenty years ago?"

Chang stiffened. Political pull or not, the major's tone was becoming unacceptable. "Our ship is—"

"—an antique. Ancient. Ming Dynasty," Ho finished, cutting him off.

The crew inside combat turned pale. Captain Chang, while he was not as well connected as Ho, was well-known throughout the Navy for his ability. For a junior officer to speak to him so was entirely out of order.

"Believe what you will, Captain," the major continued. "I will make the report. You'll see what the results will be. And in the meantime, do not be overly impressed by your interpretation of the admiral's reasoning. I can assure you that it is merely for public consumption. And this is just why I was placed here, was it not? To provide insight into the battle group's decisions."

Captain Chang, since he was treading on dangerous political ground, refrained from answering. Had he not been hesitant, his answer would have been, "No." He had been placed there to insure that there was a maximum degree of cooperation between United States Navy and our forces in defending Taiwan. Not for personal glory—not for political reasons. To make sure, just as their man here did, that we understood each other. That is all.

"I will keep your thoughts in mind," Captain Chang said out loud. "I thank you for your insight."

USS United States
JIC
1152 local (GMT+8)

Petty Officer Jim Lee, a cryptological technician (interpreter), or CTI, groaned as he listened to the conversation coming across his headset. He was taking notes, writing in Chinese characters, making an occasional English comment as a translator's note. Senior Chief Armstrong Brady stood to one side. On the other side was Commander Busby.

When the Chinese voices finally stopped, Wells leaned back in his chair and sighed. "They're pissed, sir. Real pissed. Major Ho Kung-Sun, he's telling that skipper that we're dissing him, disrespecting him. By the admiral not asking them directly to take care of that submarine, by assigning them to a station further away from the CV. That frigate captain, I'm not certain what he's thinking, but he's listening to the major. Doesn't sound like he's buying it one hundred percent, but he is listening. According to the background briefing, the major is connected back home. Real connected, I bet."

"That's right," Lab Rat said.

Lee nodded. "That's about the only thing that could account for the major taking that tone of voice with him. Talk about disrespect—it's not as much the words as the way he says it, the way he doesn't back off. I knew there was something else going on between them."

"Captain Chang Tso-Lin is a senior naval officer," the senior chief said. "That major—a ground pounder. I'm betting that the captain understands a lot more than the major does at this point."

Lab Rat nodded. "I wouldn't doubt it. But how is Captain Chang supposed handle this? I mean, Ho Kung-Sun is supposed to be his liaison. The Taiwanese would not have put him here if they didn't have some confidence in him."

"So we let them work it out themselves?" the senior chief asked.

"Yes, but—it's always 'yes, but,' isn't it?" Lab Rat said. "We can't afford to have any misunderstandings right now. Not when everything is about to break loose. So what do we do?"

The senior chief shrugged. "Above my pay grade, sir. But I'd sure as shit get in there with the admiral and tell him what's going on. Then try to figure out what set this whole thing off. There's got to be something." The senior chief turned to Lee. "How about you hang out in combat for a few days, kind of listen in on what's going on? I'll have someone else cover your watches. You keep an eye on this major. Maybe you can pick up some clues from how he's acting. Something's gone and pissed him off, and we need to figure out what it is before it gets any worse."

"Does Major Ho know you speak his language?" Lab Rat asked Lee.

Lee, who graduated first in his class from the Naval Language Institute, shook his head and smiled. Lee stood around six-foot-three and was a large black man. "No, he doesn't. And I'm betting I'm not going to be his first guess."

EIGHTEEN

T'ing had chosen traditional garb for the occasion, and the delicate silks with flowing lines were so much more natural on him that Wexler wondered he had ever worn a western suit at all. Behind him, his assistants and aides were similarly attired. There was a complete hush over the great hall as he stood.

"Mr. Secretary-General, members and delegates." He paused, and let his gaze roam over the entire assembly. Not a seat was vacant. Those who hadn't heard the rumors had obviously been alerted by his office. "I am deeply saddened to be here today under the circumstances. But the nature of this organization is such that these matters are often before us. Never, however, have I felt so personally distressed over what I must say today."

He turned slightly, facing directly toward the American delegation. "As most of you know, over the last two weeks, the United States has committed acts of war against my nation. We offered the United States the opportunity to apologize and pay reparations without further action.

That has been summarily rejected. Accordingly, we must now asked that the United Nations pass this resolution ordering sanctions against the United States, and condemning their action. The measures, I know, seem harsh. But they are no more harsh than the measures the United States has enforced against Iraq for the past ten years. Essentials would be permitted to enter the country, but nothing that could be converted to military use. All assets in China will be seized, and all American citizens and nationals expelled immediately.

"There is an American saying—what's sauce for the goose is sauce for the gander as well. I think that applies here as well." He paused for a moment as countless translators attempted to render the idiom into something meaningful in their own languages. "I apologize for difficulty to the translators."

Utter silence fell over the hall. Not a person moved, not even the Secretary-General. As the silence deepened, the Secretary-General finally broke it by asking, "Is there no hope of resolving this in another fashion? The United States has normally been amenable to compromises."

The delegate from Taiwan stood then, his face a mask of anger. "No—never!" He pointed an accusing finger at T'ing. "That missile was aimed at my country as are the ones sitting on those ships right now. All of you know it. Only the United States had the courage to step in and prevent this genocide. And now you dare to consider sanctions? If you do this, you'll completely destroy everything the United Nations stands for."

"That missile was in international airspace," T'ing said implacably. "We have conducted countless tests in the past, and there has never been any danger to your country."

"We both know that this time was different," the Taiwanese delegate shouted. "The beginning of the end—but we will not allow it. Oh no, we will not!" He slammed his hand down on his desk in frustration.

Wexler waited while the babble of voices around her crescendoed. Finally, she stood, and picked up her microphone. "We have no comment on this matter, Mr. Secretary-General. Everyone here knows the facts. I leave it to the sound judgment of the delegates to draw their own conclusions." With that, she sat down, and a strange sort of quiet crept into her heart. She and the president had decided on the strategy late last night, finally figuring that it was time to call the world to account for its actions. No more would the United States be the whipping boy for every politically correct movement. No more would they scrape and bow.

The matter was tabled for discussion, with a vote set for two days hence. There was really no need for that—she was certain that every nation had already made up its mind how to vote. And, she suspected, if it were put to a vote today, China would win.

She made her way back to her office flanked by her aides, Brad just behind her right elbow. The new security measures were already in place, and he reached past her and punched in the security code to unlock the door. She swept through the administrative spaces, past the locked reception area, and into her own office. She shut the door in Brad's startled face, and sank down on the couch. As with anything, waiting was the hardest part.

A knock on the door disturbed her. "What is it?" she snapped, wanting nothing more than to be left alone with her thoughts at this moment.

"Madam Ambassador—the Ambassador from Russia is here," Brad's carefully controlled voice said. In his tone she read the nuances of his thinking—that he knew she wished to be left alone, that the Ambassador had arrived suddenly, and that part of the plan she had hatched with Captain Hemingway was now coming to fruition. Cold dread coursed through her as the full implications of the situation sunk in.

"Tell him I'll be just a moment," she said. She took a deep, calming breath, and retreated to her private room behind her office for a moment to check her makeup and clothes. All in all, everything was in order. Another deep breath, and she crossed the room to open the door.

The Russian Ambassador was standing there, waiting for her, evidently not wanting to take advantage of the comfortable chairs in the waiting room. That would have implied that he was waiting to speak to her, when what he wanted to convey was some sort of immediate right or entitlement to her attention. It was a maneuver designed to intimidate her, to assert his power over her. In his eyes, she saw secret glee—glee, and determination.

"Please come in," she said quietly. She stepped back to allow him to enter. "Just you, Mr. Ambassador. I think our aides can all find something else to do." She saw the look of protest on Brad's face, and heard the Ambassador's aides start to protest. "Your English is certainly strong enough, and coupled with my meager Russian—" A lie; she spoke Russian quite fluently. "—we should be able to come to an understanding."

The Russian hesitated for a moment, then barked out an order to his people. They stepped back from the door, although they were clearly determined to wait right there until the ambassador emerged. The ambassador entered alone, and immediately walked over to her favorite couch.

"Understanding . . . an interesting phrase," the Russian Ambassador said. He settled himself into the couch, leaned back, and pulled out a cigar. "Do you mind?"

"Very much. I do not allow cigars in my office. Among other things," she said, going on the offensive. If what she believed was true, then he would understand what she meant.

He met her eyes with his, and just for a few moments it was the test of wills. Finally, he put the cigar away. "It may not always be so easy to have the world cater to your every whim, Madam."

"That applies to both of us, don't you think?" she asked pleasantly. "But then, the art of diplomacy includes understanding each other's strengths and weaknesses, and using a reasonable degree of civility in working out solutions, does it not?"

"Perhaps. And we all know that this is certainly the United States's position, this business of civility."

Wexler inclined her head ever so slightly. "As refreshing as it is to discuss diplomacy with you, sir, I wonder if we could dispense with the formalities and come straight to the point. After all, we understand each other all too well, and I will not think less of you for getting straight to the point."

He smiled and stretched his arms across the back of the couch, evidently completely at ease. That, Wexler hoped, would change shortly. "I treasure the friendship that makes such candor possible between us," he began, a cruel expression on his face. "And, as friends of the United States, I wish to tender a warning from our government—many would not understand, although we do, of course—about the United States's decision to deploy Patriot batteries in Taiwan." He waited, searching her face for an expression of surprise, and looking faintly disappointed when it was not forthcoming. "Of course, Russia understands the necessity, and we're willing to support the United States in this move."

"There has been no discussion of such a matter," Wexler said.

The Russian ambassador wagged a stubby finger at her. "Ah, there is no need to dissemble. Not with your few friends," he said. "Rest assured that we know the United States plans to do this. And, as I said, we're not opposed to such move. Certainly allowing China to repossess Taiwan would destabilize the region. Although," he continued, a look of longing on his face, "there's much to be said for the firm repatriation of wayward provinces." He seemed to reflect for a few moment on Russia's previous days of glory, then shook his head. "No, Taiwan and China—Hong Kong was bad enough, but this cannot be allowed."

"Then we can count on a contingent of Russian ships to assist us in defending Taiwan, I hope?" she asked.

He shook his head. "No, it would not be wise to be so

openly aggressive to our eastern neighbor. There are many issues to be worked out between Russia and China, you understand. Many issues." His eyes undressed her for a moment, and he said, "What Russia is willing to promise is her silence."

"I see. Russia's silence. And that would be in exchange for . . . ?" She let the question hang in the air.

He splayed out his hands in a gesture of openness. "Silence on the issue of the Kurile Islands. I think you must agree that our claim to them is far stronger than China's claim to Taiwan. Besides, it is a rocky, useless chain of islands. Of no import in the world economy."

"The Japanese don't think so," she said.

"The Japanese—bah."

"Yes, the Japanese. I believe they are currently in possession of the Kuriles and would probably object most strongly to a military action to retake the Islands. And I assume that is what you are proposing, since that is normally Russia's way. Or are you asking me to support the fair and democratic election in the Kuriles to allow the inhabitants to determine their own destiny? It is possible that they would choose to return to Russia's domination, I suppose."

It would be a cold day in hell before the Kuriles chose that indeed. The vast majority of the population have roots in Japan rather than Russia, and I suspect that taking the Islands from Japan would prove to be a difficult task.

But it would be less difficult if we don't interfere. Less difficult, less costly, and probably done quickly. Because we have assets in the area, we could divert them from Taiwan to the Kuriles. Whether or not we chose to do so would send a strong message to the rest of the world. And by the time we can get more carriers over there, it would be a done deal.

"But as I said, I suspect the issue is entirely moot," she said, bringing them back on track. "Because we have no plans to deploy the Patriot missiles in Taiwan. None at all." Now she leveled a hard glare of her own at the Russian Ambassador. "But I do think this little conversation has answered a number of questions in my mind. And perhaps some debate in your contingent as well." She stood, dismissing him. "I would not advise attempting any aggression toward the Kurile Islands or Japan," she said sternly. "Speaking as a friend, of course."

"But . . . but . . . you will regret this, Madam Ambassador. You will regret this."

"Ambassador! Such a tone to take with a friend. Before you go, please do me the favor of rendering me one final opinion. I would treasure your thoughts on the matter of redecorating my office."

"What nonsense is this?" he blustered. "Do you take me for a fool?"

"In particular, I am considering repainting my office. That red circle—it does not go well with the rest of the decor, does it?" She pointed to the red circle that covered a small portion of her wall and the molding around her door.

All the air seemed to rush out of the Russian Ambassador as he grasped her meaning. He turned on her, his expression ugly. "You tricked me!" he thundered.

"And you spied on me," she said calmly. "I wonder which action the world will find the more objectionable? I think I can guarantee, with some degree of certainty, that every delegate to the United Nations would be most interested in what we have discovered." Watching the emotions play across his face, she smiled brightly. "But, as originally proposed, we would be willing to remain silent. As a friend, of course. In exchange for Russia's full and complete support of our operations in Taiwan."

"Japan has denied you landing rights," he pointed out. "And yet you would choose them over us?

"We would, indeed," she said crisply. "But under the circumstances, I do not think we will have to choose at all."

NINETEEN

Coyote paced the bridge of the ship, dividing his attention between the impenetrable fog around them and the radar screen. Every two minutes, the ship sounded a prolonged blast on her whistle, warning others of her presence. From out on the bridge wing, although the fog had a sound-dampening effect, Coyote could hear a chorus of other small vessels sounding off as well. The other vessels' fog signals ranged from tinkling bells, and air horns, to an occasional voice shouting in panic.

"Nasty, isn't it?" the captain of the ship said as he walked up to Coyote. "And it's going to get worse, according to the weather reports."

"All these little boats are clearly insane," Coyote said. "They've got to know we're here, and have to know that we can't turn on a dime. If I were in a small boat, I'd stay well clear of us, you can bet your ass on that."

"We're in the middle of some good fishing grounds, Admiral," the captain said quietly. "It's the only source of income—and food—that some of these folks have. They

live on those boats, spend most of their days just searching
for enough fish to buy fuel and feed their families. They
can't afford a day off because of the fog."

"They'll be taking a lot of days off if we run into one
of them," Coyote muttered.

"I doubt it," the captain said, cynicism in his voice. "Because you know our government would pay reparations
immediately. Any family that we run into is set for life."

"So that's why they're so close, maybe?" Coyote asked.
"Hell of a way to play the lottery."

They both stared at the thick soup, trying to see what
lay before them. Visibility was reduced to a mere fifty feet
around them, far too little for them to even attempt evasive
maneuvers should it be required.

"It's going to get worse before it gets better," Coyote
said at last. "The president can't put up with this situation;
he just can't. I expect a message within the next eight
hours ordering us to conduct freedom of navigation operations. And the closer we get to shore, in the shallower,
warmer water, the heavier the fishing activity will be."

"Smaller boats, too," the captain agreed. "And more
desperate people."

Freedom of navigation operations were designed to exercise the provisions of international law that gave a ship
the right to sail into foreign territorial waters as long as it
did so expeditiously and did not stop to conduct military
operations. Although the Chinese claimed that their territorial waters were contiguous with their economic zone,
extending out to three hundred miles—and that their airspace extended a thousand miles off the coast as well—
and claimed the entire Yellow Sea as their own, they had
never before actively objected to freedom of navigation
operations. That, Coyote suspected, was about to change.

"Constrained waters—I know you're not going to like
it," he said, casting a glance over the captain. "Going to
play hell with the flight schedule as well."

"CAG is still complaining that not everybody has all

their traps," the captain said. "He wants to stay here in open water for at least another week."

"Not going to happen. It's a come-as-you-are game."

Just then, the USW tactical circuit crackled to life. It was the *Lake Champlain*'s TAO, reporting radar contact on a periscope. "But I don't want to send the helos out in this to continue localization," the TAO concluded after the formatted part of his report. "It's too nasty out there."

"God, no," Coyote said. "Nobody's launching anything until this clears up. Not as raw as most of our crew is."

"It's obviously a diesel," the *Lake Champlain*'s TAO continued. "We're picking up enough of the signature in the passive spectrum to say that. She's recharging her batteries, taking advantage of the fog."

"Great, just great," Coyote muttered. "Pass all your data to the *P'eng* and coordinate tracking with them. And pass on to Captain Chang that I don't want him getting gung-ho and launching that Sea Sprite of his. Tell Goforth to make that clear to him—we'll have at it when the weather lifts some, but for now maintain contact as well as you can, and a continuous firing solution to the best of your capabilities." Coyote glanced around the room, making sure Major Ho was not there. "And Captain, listen—you keep the *P'eng* out of the *Seawolf*'s box. I don't care what you tell them, but keep them out of there. If you're holding this contact, *Seawolf* has it, too, and she's going to be all over it. If it makes a run on the carrier, she'll be the first one to take it out."

Just then, a radioman approached Coyote, holding a clipboard in his hand. "Admiral?" He tendered the clipboard to Coyote.

Coyote glanced across to the captain, a smart-ass expression on his face. "You a betting man? I'm willing to give you two to one odds that this is the message ordering freedom of navigation operations."

The captain shook his head. "With all due respect, Admiral, not a chance in the world I'd take that bet."

Coyote scanned the message quickly then said, "Good

decision." He passed the clipboard to the captain. "Get your people ready—we're going in."

Probably the worst thing about freedom of navigation operations was that they were so close to the shore. It seemed like an obvious statement, but the real implication was that there would be far less warning should China launch an attack from her mainland. Shore-based antiship missiles, waves of fighter aircraft—all could be dealt with, given enough time to react. But the warning time during which they could expect to accomplish anything shrank from almost a minute down to mere seconds that close to land. It would be a Mexican standoff, Coyote thought, somewhat amused by the phrase. Yes, a Mexican stand-off—with China.

Jungwei
0631 local (GMT+8)

"Down periscope," the captain said. The rudimentary periscope sticking up above the surface of the water slipped smoothly back down into its pedestal. It was one of the few things aboard the submarine that worked all the time, primarily because it had so few moving parts.

"Shall I surface the ship, sir?" his officer of the deck asked.

The captain shook his head. "No. Not yet. I can't see any of their ships in this fog, but the radar shows the cruiser is nearby. Deploy the snorkel mast—it'll take longer that way, but will be safer."

There was a chance that the American radar would miss the snorkel mast, but not much of one. In all probability, their periscope had been detected the moment it was deployed. But under the current weather conditions, the captain was reasonably certain that no American officer would risk conducting flight operations. And without the specter of the dipping helos to contend with, the captain felt fairly confident that he could avoid prosecution by any surface ship. His submarine might be old, and the ancient diesel engines might be noisy, but when she was on battery-power, the submarine was virtually undetectable by anything other than active sonar. And active sonar would serve as a truly excellent homing beacon for any torpedo launched by the sub.

His operating orders verged on insanity. It was inconceivable that anyone familiar with submarine operations had even so much as looked at the plan. It called for his ship to operate down to thirty percent battery-power prior to surfacing to recharge. Thirty percent—a dangerous, foolhardy risk. In general, the captain preferred to go no lower than sixty percent, and even at that point he would be getting anxious.

But his commanders felt that the lower limit was necessary in order to allow the submarine to maintain contact on the carrier. It took a long time to slip in quietly, to calculate the carrier's probable speeding and course based on her operations, and to anticipate her position sufficiently in time to allow the submarine to cut her off. There was no way they could keep up with the carrier, not with the maximum surface speed at fourteen knots, and a markedly lower speed submerged.

Still, since they were not actively at war, it was absolute foolishness to allow battery power to drop so low. Indeed, the captain had considered several times disobeying his order, to surface and recharge, but that was a career-ending option as well. There was no telling how many officers and crewmen reported directly to an outside authority. If he chose to disregard his orders, armed guards would be waiting for him when he returned to port.

As a temporary measure, however, the captain had struck a deal with the engineer. The engineer was an old friend, their acquaintance spanning more than twenty-years, and the captain and he could count on him to some extent. Besides, he also knew that the engineer hated the orders they'd received, and truly despised being at very low battery power. They had agreed that should it come to it, the engineer would tinker with the gauges reporting their battery reserve until what was reported as thirty percent would actually be sixty percent. They would get caught if they ever truly had to run, as it would become quickly apparent that the submarine had far more reserve than indicated, but both of them were willing to take that chance. The captain also suspected that no one on the crew would not be in a position to object.

There was a grinding sound as the snorkel mast was extended. It sucked down great volumes of the damp, wet air, allowing the submarine to operate her diesel engines to recharge her battery. Thirty minutes, the captain decided. That should be enough to bring them up to the full charge, or perhaps a little less. And if the weather stayed as it was, he could even extend that in order to take on a full charge.

The pressure inside the submarine changed as the snorkel mast popped up. Then it dropped again, producing an ear-popping change, as the diesel engines lit off. The smoke and fumes from the engines were vented to another pipe located astern on the ship.

"Navigator, prepare an intercept course to the aircraft carrier," he ordered. He turned to the senior enlisted man standing immediately to his right. "I wish for you to supervise dry run torpedo approaches on the carrier. When the time comes, we will be ready."

The enlisted man looked on approvingly. "Yes, captain. A good plan, sir. An excellent plan." He went off to prepare the sonarmen and the weapons technicians, and personally check the readiness of each torpedo.

The captain turned back to the monitor that displayed the last picture his periscope had shown. His chief of the boat may have thought him a wise, aggressive captain, but he himself knew better. Their only hope of making a successful approach on the carrier lay in complete and absolute surprise. And that was going to be difficult to accomplish once the weather cleared. No, their best opportunity was right now. But his orders did not allow him that discretion, and there was no guarantee that matters would ever reach that stage.

And if it did, firing the torpedo at the aircraft carrier would be his last act of command. Of course, they practiced evasive maneuvers, studied the tactics, and most of the men were convinced that they would be able to easily evade and escape.

But the captain knew better. The carrier and surface ships, along with the aircraft, would immediately know where they were. There would be no escaping the onslaught of weapons, sonars, and assets brought to bear on them, not even by going deep and running silently on battery. No, the Americans would find them—find them and destroy them.

TWENTY

As soon as Tombstone landed, he was directed into a heated hanger, but his windscreen had already started to ice up. Tombstone slipped back the canopy, and started down the boarding ladder. Even a good day in Adak was brutal by anyone else's standards. The wind never seemed to stop, and the wind chill factor was always a consideration.

"Hold on, sir. You got some icing. Use this." A flight technician wheeled over a ladder stand to him.

"Icing already," Jason said happily. To him, it was just another challenge to overcome. "If you'd let me fly, we wouldn't have had a problem."

"Oh, I suppose your stick is so hot that it would keep ice from forming, right?"

"After you, the hottest stick this aircraft has ever seen," Jason said confidently. "And if I were you, I'd keep looking over my shoulder."

Despite his weariness, Tombstone laughed out loud. Jason Greene's brash, uninhibited approach to life never ceased to amaze him. "Any more guff out of you, boy, and I'll de-ice this aircraft just by letting you talk to it." The flight technician laughed at that.

"Good morning," a voice said. "I'm Commander Lawson, CO of the base." Tombstone turned to face a Navy officer in long-sleeved khakis approaching. "Welcome aboard." Tombstone noted the absence of the honorific "sir."

"Nice to meet you, Captain," Tombstone said. He resisted the impulse to salute, and glanced back to make sure Jason understood. "Appreciate your hospitality."

Lawson's face quirked into a grin. "My people are used to welcoming folks to our island paradise. Even people like you. You won't be asked any questions, and nobody's going to call you sir. Unless you actually need something, we'll pretend you don't exist. I hope that's okay with you."

"Sounds just right, Captain. Appreciate the consideration."

"Even if anyone recognizes you, they'll pretend they don't," Lawson said neutrally. "And some people will think that they do."

"Present company not excluded," Tombstone said softly.

Lawson nodded. "So if you don't mind, I'm going to escort you to your quarters myself. The fewer people in the loop, the better. Nobody will think it's unusual—it happens fairly often. Depending on the circumstances." He patted the side of Tombstone's Tomcat affectionately. "And we have the finest technicians in the world, si—" He cut off the word "sir" before he could finish it, and shook his head. "Sorry about that. Anyway, as I was saying, our technicians will take care of your bird. Between what we have onboard and those that flew in two days ago—"

"Flew in two days ago?" Tombstone asked, his voice incredulous. "But I didn't—never mind, Commander Lawson. Never mind."

As they followed Lawson off to a secluded corner of

the hanger, Greene said softly, "There's more to this cloak and dagger business than I thought."

"I should've worn a ski mask. Or let you do all the talking."

Jason turned to take one last look at the Tomcat. "We'll figure out how to handle it next time, Tombstone. I mean, Admir—I mean—uhhh . . ."

"Ah, what the hell," Tombstone said, disgusted. It had been foolish to think he could manage to stay unrecognized.

One corner of the hangar had been converted into a sleeping area, with additional sound-deadening materials lining the walls. Commander Lawson showed them to a sparsely furnished compartment which was more than adequately equipped for what they needed: sleep. The schedule allotted them twelve hours before they were due back in the air.

Tombstone stretched out on the rack furthest away from the door, and Jason settled down on the other. Within moments, the younger pilot was asleep, his breathing low and regular.

I remember when I could do that. You sleep, piss and eat when you can, because you don't know when you'll get another chance.

Nine and a half hours later, they were rousted by a mess cook knocking on the door. He bustled in carrying a large insulated pot of coffee and a number of covered plates. Delicious smells filled the room.

"Wasn't sure if you guys would be wanting breakfast, lunch, or dinner. So I settled on breakfast—pilots can always eat breakfast."

"Breakfast is fine."

With a flourish, the mess cook pulled off the silver tops from the dishes to reveal healthy portions of scrambled eggs, bacon, pancakes and sausage. Additional dishes contained fresh fruit, butter and syrup.

"Eat hearty, gents," he said serenely. Then he produced

a bag and held it out to them. "I packed you a little lunch, just in case you didn't have time to cook."

"Thank you," Tombstone said.

The mess cook grinned. "My pleasure, sir. And whatever you're up to—if you're up to anything, and I wouldn't know—you give 'em hell."

"Say, this is really good," Jason said around a mouthful of food. "You're quite a cook."

"Oh, I didn't make this," the man said. "The mess management specialist did. I'm just the delivery boy."

Tombstone and Jason exchanged a glance. "Then convey our compliments to the chef," Tombstone said. "How come he's not here himself?"

"It's a she, sir. And reason she isn't here is that she doesn't have a clearance. I do."

"So who the hell are you?" Jason asked, still wolfing down pancakes. "Pass the syrup, will you?"

"I'm the leading intelligence specialist here," he said. "And ten days ago, I saw some very interesting pictures." He caught himself, as though realizing he'd been presumptuous, and said, "Well, I'll let you eat in peace and quiet. Like I said, give 'em hell. I figure a couple of days from now, I'll know whether you did or not."

He left, with a victorious grin on his face.

"There's a lesson to be learned in this," Tombstone said. "He caught what was going on and he wants to feel a part of the solution. He wants to see how his work fits into the larger picture, wants to know that what he does matters. He's even willing to be a delivery boy to just get a look at us, and he's risking a lot just letting us know who he is. You keep that in mind, Jason. That's the sort of people we having backing us up, and with young men and women like that on our side, the Russians don't stand a chance."

Tombstone saw the reflective look on the younger pilot's face, and felt a rush of pride. His words had hit home—maybe, just maybe, Jason Greene would be a better man because Tombstone had reminded him about the little people in the world, the support troops that made everything else possible.

Jason cleared his throat, then looked away.

Touched—by damn, I got to him. His skipper in his squadron couldn't convince him to stay in the Navy, but maybe I've made a difference.

"What is it, son?" Tombstone asked gently, trying to encourage the younger man to voice his innermost thoughts. "What's on your mind?"

"Well, sir, I was just wondering . . ." Jason's voice trailed off.

"Go on," Tombstone said encouragingly.

"It's just that . . ."

"Whatever it is, I want to hear it."

"Are you going to eat your cinnamon roll?"

After allowing an hour for their food to settle and for the necessary bathroom visits, Tombstone and Greene started their preflight. As Lawson had promised, the aircraft had been fueled, serviced, and was in perfect shape. They ran through the preflight, talked to the maintenance technician who'd checked her out, and then climbed up the boarding ladder, still in the heated hangar.

"I don't have to tell you, you don't want to be hanging around down on the ground," the plane captain said. "You can ice up here in a heartbeat."

"Don't worry, we're out of here."

Tombstone slid the canopy forward and shut it, then checked to make sure the heat was working. The de-icers and the windscreen heaters worked perfectly. The temperature was actually quite comfortable inside the cockpit.

On signal, Tombstone started his engines, and then, after the doors slid back, commenced his taxi.

Once they cleared the hangar, the wind buffeted them. He could feel a chill radiating off the windscreen and he double-checked the heater.

"Tomcat, Tower, you're cleared for takeoff at your discretion, runway seventy right. After departure, ascend to ten thousand feet and check in with—well, who wants to hear from you." The controller continued with a quick weather brief, and then concluded with, "Good luck, gentlemen."

Even as the controller was speaking, Tombstone was taxiing to the staging area. As soon as he was released, he shoved the throttles forward into military power and felt the Tomcat surge underneath him. The cold air was exceptionally dense, and the Tomcat required only a small portion of the runway before they rotated and were airborne.

Tombstone checked out with the Adak tower and follow their flight plan as briefed. He continued west for a while, and then rolled out to the south. As Jason completed their post-launch checklist, Tombstone studied the radar picture on his HUD.

"Nothing around here now," he said. "Let's hope that doesn't change."

"I'm getting LINK feed from the *United States*," Jason announced. "Clear picture all around, Stoney. I think we might just pull this off."

"Keep an eye out for the tanker," Tombstone ordered. "Four hours out and that's only for the first one."

"Roger." Just then, a voice spoke over tactical. "Tomcat triple nickel, this is Big Eye. Do not acknowledge this transmission. I'm holding you southbound at four hundred and twenty knots, at location," and the voice reeled off lat and long coordinates. "Be advised I hold radar contact on both you and Texaco, and am available should you need a vector to the ten-yard line." The ten-yard line was the code word given to their first refueling point.

There was no more dangerous evolution, with the exception of perhaps a night carrier landing, than refueling. Refueling during short-notice operations with the Air Force in charge guaranteed that the pucker factor inside the cockpit was bound to be high.

In Tombstone's earliest days, coordination with the Air Force had not been particularly inspiring. There were misunderstandings, incompatible equipment, and a general morass of confusion surrounding the terminology. Over the decades that followed, the two services had finally managed to come to an accommodation, and refueling operations today were virtually seamless. Yet, in the back of his mind, Tombstone always retained the harsh early lessons.

As the time for their first rendezvous approached, Tombstone felt his tension increase. Jason seemed to sense the senior pilot's distraction and the flow of stories gradually trailed off.

"If there's a problem, the AWACS will let us know. I mean, hell, sir—it's their bird, right?" Greene's voice sounded distinctly uncomfortable with the idea of trying to reassure the more senior pilot. "He'll be there—he has to be there."

"Yeah, of course they will. We got comms with the AWACS if we need it."

But the only reason we'd need it is if something goes bad wrong. And if we punch out over these waters, the odds of surviving are pretty much nonexistent. If we don't freeze on the way down, we will within about thirty seconds of hitting the water.

But Tombstone kept his thoughts to himself. Jason knew the dangers as well as he did. "Be nice to have radar contact on the tanker, though," Tombstone said.

As though his radar were reading his mind, a small, fuzzy lozenge resolved out of the backscatter on the screen. Jason let out a yelp of glee. "Looks to me like a tanker, boss."

"You get any IFF?"

Jason fiddled with the IFF controls for a moment, then said, "Sure do. She's breaking for an Air Force KC-135. And I got a mode four IFF." Mode four was the encrypted mode signal that positively and indisputably identified an aircraft as a friendly military flight possessing the correct encryption gear for that particular day.

Tombstone felt himself relax slightly, and warned himself not to. In another thirty minutes, after it was all over, sure. He laid his hands on the controls. "I've got the aircraft."

Jason held his hands up momentarily. "You have the aircraft, sir," he said, acknowledging Tombstone's assumption of the controls. He'd been flying for the last two hours, and Tombstone had no doubt about his ability to execute the refueling. But Jason was in the back seat and his visibility from there wasn't nearly as good as it was up front.

"Next time, you can take front," Tombstone volunteered. "I don't want you getting rusty."

"Maybe, sir, we should make some practice runs refueling from the back seat. I mean, they sent us out in a two-seater for a reason, right?"

The reason is because we're going on long flights, not because something might happen to the guy up front. But you're right, kid. We got the capability, we need to train to it. Out loud, Tombstone said, "Put it on our list of things to do when we get back. Along with getting the name of that mess cook that made breakfast at Adak."

"Tomcat double nickel, this is Texaco. Do not acknowledge transmission unless there's a problem, gentlemen. I am on base course, base speed, awaiting your approach. Unless otherwise directed, I intend to pass ten thousand pounds to you." The cool, calm voice of the KC-135 pilot reassured them both.

"Nobody wants to talk to us," Jason muttered, although they both knew the reason for it. No transmissions meant they couldn't be triangulated by any passive sensors monitoring this part of the sky. "Okay, let's do it," Tombstone said. He had a visual on the tanker's lights now, and adjusted his altitude slightly. Tombstone always favored approaching from below, finding it somehow easier to control his attitude and altitude.

It was so familiar, this process. How many times over the last decade had he plugged the back of a tanker? A thousand, perhaps? So familiar, yet each time was a new experience, fraught with all the danger of the first one.

Time slowed as Tombstone made his approach slowly, carefully, until he had a perfect lineup on the basket. "Looking good, Tomcat. Come to Mama," the refueling technician said over tactical.

Tombstone nudged the power slightly, and slid forward for a perfect plug on the basket. The light on his enunciator panel lit up, indicating that the seal between the Tomcat probe and the tanker was airtight. "I got good flow," Tombstone said, as he watched the digits on his fuel status indicator click over. "Good flow."

"Ten thousand should do us," Jason said.

"Looking at the numbers, I don't think we could take more than one or two hundred more than that."

"Looking good on this end, folks," the tanker's voice said. "Speak up if you see any problems."

"You know, it occurs to me that there's not much use in maintaining radio silence," Jason said. "Any radar holding us knows that we're here, and can guess what the tanker is. So what's the big deal?"

"The big deal is that it keeps them guessing. Up until now, we could be an intelligence bird. They might be suspicious and they might not like it, but they won't get completely wound up unless they know this is a fighter."

"That's why I let somebody else do the thinking," Jason said.

Before long, they were done. The flow of fuel cut off precisely at ten thousand pounds, and Tombstone found the estimates were indeed correct. The tanker said, "That's it, folks. Disengage at will."

Tombstone eased back ever so slightly on the throttle and the Tomcat fell back gently from the tanker. He waited till he was well clear of the larger aircraft, then peeled off to the left, waggled his wings, and headed south.

"Good luck," the tanker said in parting.

"Luck's not what we need right now," Greene observed.

TWENTY-ONE

USS **Seawolf**
Due north of the carrier
0730 local (GMT +8)

"Solid firing solution, Captain," Jacobs said. He held his finger poised over the button that would unleash their AD-CAP torpedoes at the two contacts. "Request weapons free?"

"Weapons free, fire when ready," the captain ordered.

Jacobs took one last look at his solutions, and pressed the button.

There was a loud *whish* inside the submarine as well as a slight shudder and an ear-popping drop in interior pressure. The outer doors were already open, and the submarine's torpedoes were now given permission to launch. Compressed air blew them out of the tubes, their motors kicked in for a straight run for a short time and then they both arced off down a bearing heading for the two contacts.

Jacobs and Pencehaven maintained a continuous firing solution, double-checking their current contact information against the torpedoes' progress. Jacobs made one small correction with his joystick to one—the other needed no assistance in locating, identifying, and designating its target. Finally, at the one thousand yard mark, the guidance wires snapped and the torpedoes were on their own.

In addition to obscuring the enemy contacts, the U.S. torpedoes also dumped a substantial new amount of noise into the water, thus decreasing the other submarine's overall detection capabilities. However, it was clearly not sufficient to degrade them completely. Within moments, the hard, high-pitched pinging of torpedoes inbound was clearly audible over the speaker and visible on the sonar screen.

"Snapshot, Captain—they got us now," Jacobs said. And indeed that was not unexpected—the first consequence of launching torpedoes was to immediately rip off the "cloak of visibility" from the firing platform. If the other submarine had not know they were in the area, they had no doubts about it now.

"Officer of the deck, make your depth eighteen hundred feet," the captain said.

The officer of the deck repeated the order immediately, glancing at the captain to make sure that he had heard correctly.

The captain nodded, reassuring him. Yes, it was a risk. The stress on a submarine hull from the last attack could not be completely evaluated, and there was a chance that her structural integrity was compromised. But in every other category, the submarine had far outperformed the operating capabilities ascribed to her by her builders, and he was pretty certain that she was fully capable of withstanding that depth even with some minor structural damage.

Pretty sure. Confident enough, at least, to risk his life and that of his crew. Because from what they had seen of the Chinese torpedoes thus far, their best chance for evading it was to run below its operating depth. Like earlier Russian models, this torpedo could not go deep enough to catch her.

Around them, the hull creaked and groaned as the sub-

marine pitched bow down and headed for the depths. The
pressure of the seawater as she dove increased all around
her, increased to unimaginable levels, compressing the ten-
sile steel hull. It was a normal sound, one they had all
heard before, but when descending this quickly the noise
took on an eerie rhythm that threatened to spook them.

"She's singing to us, men," the captain said quietly.
"Telling us how safe we are in her. You hear it?" He
glanced around the control room and saw nods, a few expressions of relief.

And why wouldn't she sing? She talked to him in his
dreams, didn't she? And, in the end, there was nothing
odder about her singing to them than there was about her
talking.

Everyone fell silent, straining to hear the first sounds of
imminent danger. There wouldn't be time to react to it,
no, not at this depth. Even a pinhole leak would result in
an ice pick of water under such pressure that it could slash
through flesh as quickly as superheated steam. Were the
submarine to implode, there wouldn't be time to be frightened. There wouldn't be time to be anything.

All at once, the captain had an overwhelming, unbridled
sense of safety. This submarine had brought him through
too much already—there was no way she would let him
down now. He patted the bulkhead next to him, almost
absentmindedly, as though she were one of the horses on
his ranch in Montana. "Come on, old girl. You know you
got it in you," he said quietly, and his voice carried to
every corner of the compartment.

"Range, five thousand yards and closing, Captain. Bearing constant, range decreasing," Jacobs said, his voice
calm. The captain shot off a momentary prayer, thankful
for Jacobs's tone of voice. To hear one of their own reacting so calmly was even more reassuring than hearing it
from their captain. Because, after all, officers were supposed to be confident—everyone on the ship knew that.
And although they trusted the captain with their lives, they
trusted Jacobs to tell the truth.

"Descending, sir," Jacobs continued. "She has us, Captain." Everyone in the control room could hear that that was true, as the active sonar pings from the Chinese torpedo increased in frequency and speed, blasting acoustic energy off their anechoic-coated hull to further pinpoint their location.

"What do you think, Mannie?" the captain asked. "Wake homer or acoustic?"

"Tough call, Captain," Jacobs said, as though they were in a classroom discussing the latest advances in technology instead of putting it to a field test. "Could be a combination, since the wake homer is older technology. But then again, they have had some U.S. technology, haven't they? So I'd expect them to have some acoustics capability in it, if not as good as ours. I bet they're wishing right now they'd paid a little extra and gotten the right casing to hold it all." Jacobs laughed quietly. "Penny-wise and pound foolish, they say. They're screwed if we make it to eighteen hundred feet."

The captain groaned silently, and Jacobs immediately recognized his error. "When, I mean," he said, but the damage was already done. Everyone in the control room had heard Jacobs say "if."

"Oh, don't worry about that," the captain said offhandedly. "That's one thing we never skimp on, structural integrity. How's she sounding, acoustically?"

"Four thousand yards, Captain," Otter Pencehaven said, taking up Jacobs's duty of calling off the ranges.

"Sounds as solid as ever, Captain," Jacobs said. "The usual bitching as we descend, but nothing out of the ordinary. Heard it a thousand times already and I'll hear it a thousand more before I retire."

There was a moment of silence, broken only by Pencehaven's announcement. "Three thousand, Captain."

Just then the speaker picked up a new sound, and it took a moment for the captain, as focused as he was on incoming torpedoes, to realize what it was. It was just barely audible, as the submarine made her way down through the thermocline, decoys, noise makers and air bubble masses, corkscrewing violently.

And just before he could speak the words, Jacobs confirmed it.

"Torpedo, sir. But moving away from us. This one's headed for the carrier."

USS **United States**
TFCC
0825 local (GMT +8)

"*United States, Lake Champlain*—torpedo inbound! Recommend you commence evasive maneuvers immediately." As the destroyer continued to reel off locating data as they waited for the contact to appear in the LINK, Coyote felt a thrill of horror. Ballistic missiles, torpedoes—all the threats that couldn't be countered by the aircraft carrier herself, the ones that they had to depend on others to take care of. And the torpedo—if they were carrying the most advanced models, one exploding directly under the keel could crack a backbone of the carrier. Not only would thousands onboard the ship die, but all the aircraft airborne would have nowhere to land on the seriously damaged deck. And with Japan closed down, they would start running out of options fast.

"Hard right rudder!" the bitch box said, as the officer of the deck gave standard evasive maneuver orders. "Flank speed—now, engineer. I need it now!" It was odd to feel the deck of the carrier move under their feet. Normally she made slow, ponderous course and speed changes as she made allowances for the ships around her, the safety of personnel, and the security of the aircraft spotted on her deck. But this was no time for safety—not at all. Coyote swore softly, wondering why in the five hells he hadn't taken the submarine out the first time they had contact on her.

Because you were under orders not to—you know that's why it was. If it had been up to you or anybody out here, it would have been flotsam and jetsam by now. And to hell with international relations, walking the brink of diplomacy, all that shit. Because it allowed threats that we knew about to continue to exist, ones that could have been eliminated before they were allowed to jeopardize my entire battle group.

The terse commands continued over the bridge circuit as the officer of the deck ordered decoys and noise makers dumped over the side. The aircraft carrier herself had no torpedoes. *United States* depended on the other ships and aircraft in the battle group to keep the enemy submarines out of weapon's release range. The orders from higher authority had sabotaged all that, and allowed the submarine to get within range of the carrier. And there was little that the carrier could do, except use a few tricks of the trade and watch and wait.

USS Lake Champlain
0826 local (GMT +8)

Norfolk felt a moment of horror as he saw the torpedo symbol pop up on the monitor screen. It was coming in from the south, heading directly for the *United States*, and would pass about three thousand yards on the *Lake Champlain*'s starboard bow. He wished to hell he'd taken it out when he'd had the chance—dammit, it was always easier to ask forgiveness than permission, and he had known this moment was coming from the very second that the admiral had told him not to fire his ASROCs.

And now, it had come to this. Norfolk had known what he should do, had known and not acted. And now men and women would die by the thousands. Not only at sea, but on land, on the day that Taiwan was no longer under the sheltering protection of the U.S. airwing.

"All ahead flank," the captain ordered, barely even aware of the words as he spoke them. The TAO turn to look at him, his face a mask of doubt.

"Captain, the torpedo?"

"I gave you an order, mister," Norfolk snapped. He reached out to punch the button that connected the TAO to the bridge. "All ahead flank!"

"All ahead flank, aye-aye, sir," came the acknowledgement from his XO.

Maybe he doesn't know. If he's not watching the screen, if he doesn't see the geometry, he may not realize that we're going directly into harm's way.

Because that is the only way to prevent the greater tragedy—this situation should have never been allowed to develop like this, and I contributed by obeying orders.

And now, even though it required that he risk the ship and his entire crew, he would set it right. Set it right, if it was the last thing on earth that he did.

USS **United States**
TFCC
0824 local (GMT +8)

"What the hell is she doing?" the TAO said, his voice angry. "Dammit, the bitch is . . ." He fell silent abruptly as it sank in exactly what the *Lake Champlain* was doing.

"Damn, that man has balls," Coyote said. Whether or not he made it, he sure as hell was giving it the good old Navy try.

There was no mystery to what the *Lake Champlain*'s captain was attempting. It was clear that the torpedo would pass in front of the destroyer on its way to seek out its primary target, the aircraft carrier. What the *Lake Champlain* was trying to do was offer herself up as a sacrificial lamb, to take the shot to prevent it from reaching the carrier.

There were a hell of a lot of reasons that it might not work. First, if the torpedo was equipped with advanced acoustic analysis gear, it would immediately recognize that the destroyer was a smaller ship than the one it intended to hit, and would divert around to avoid the *Lake Champlain* and continue with its targeted mission. Second, the ranges and distances were such that it was extremely close. Indeed, the *Lake Champlain*'s captain's plan depended on the torpedo having acoustic ranging gear onboard, on being in active mode, on detecting a noisy mass of metal nearby and deciding that was a better target. The *Lake Champlain* would have no chance to decoy the weapon if it was simply a wake-homer, because the destroyer's wake was well out of the torpedo's detection range. But acoustically, the bow on aspect of the ship to the receiver was the most preferred target angle for detection.

Coyote picked up the mike. "*Lake Champlain, United States*. We're standing by with SAR assets." He nodded to the TAO, who gave the order to the air boss. More helicopters were moved into immediate launch status.

"Good luck," Coyote concluded, and replaced the mike, although he was not entirely certain what would constitute good luck for the *Lake Champlain*—achieving her mission and saving the carrier, or failing and saving her own skin at the expense of the carrier? He wondered which one *Lake Champlain* thought it was.

USS **Lake Champlain**
0829 local (GMT +8)

"One thousand yards," the TAO announced. "All stations report zebra set throughout the ship. Evacuated all unnecessary personnel from below the waterline." The last measure was a last-ditch effort to keep as many people as possible from being trapped below on a flooding ship.

All unnecessary personnel—that didn't translate into everyone. There would be perhaps fifteen people below the waterline.

Norfolk reached a decision. "All personnel—all of them," he ordered. "Get everybody out of there, TAO. I want every single body above the waterline."

Without questioning him, the TAO amended his order, and the captain could hear men and women running throughout the ship.

The hangar deck would be crowded, as would every passageway above the waterline. Few would seek safety on the open weather decks, because a hard explosion would rock the ship so violently that they might be thrown overboard. And even with the carrier's promise of SAR assistance, the odds of being rescued were not high.

Eight seconds now. Maybe ten. He had always wondered how he would act if he had known he was going to die. Whether he'd be who he wanted to be, the brave naval officer that by his own personal courage somehow made it easier for his men, who kept them so focused on the task and on duty as an overriding imperative that they barely even counted the personal cost? Or would he dissolve into the man his father thought he was, weak and screaming in terror?

He had always thought such a moment would be a watershed for him, and it seemed a profound shame that he would not know the answer until the very end of his life.

How long now, a few seconds? Oddly enough, the moment felt anticlimactic. He had thought that he would be frightened, reacting, but it was as though he had stepped outside himself and watched another man deal with the danger. A calm man, hard in some ways, one who could watch the closure between torpedo and ship impassively, as though it meant nothing to him personally whether the two symbols intersected on the screen or not.

Five seconds now. "Is everyone up from below decks?" he asked the TAO, still surprised to find out how calm and professional the stranger sounded. And why was he asking that, during these final moments? Shouldn't he be more worried about his own skin instead of the fate of some very junior sailors on the ship?

With an abrupt wrench, the captain felt himself back inside his own skin, and a sense of uncanny peace descended over him.

Because they are my men. I have trained them, I have worked with them, and they have trusted me—the Navy has entrusted me—with their very lives. And in the end, for every one of them that dies, a bit of me dies as well, no matter if I survive.

"Hard right rudder," he ordered, marveling at what he was about to do. How impossible was this, to try to calculate the exact point on the ship to take the hit?

Forward, and the missile launch cells might be irreparably damaged, not to mention the danger they would pose to firefighters. Completely astern, and there was a risk of fatal injury to the propeller itself, in which case the *Lake Champlain* would be a floating hole in the water completely at the mercy of waves and the sea. So where, if he had to take the hit, would he prefer it to be? It was like deciding whether to have a right or left hand amputated— or maybe whether to lose a hand or an eye. Every part of the ship was precious to him, just as every sailor was.

And yet the decision had to be made, even if it was a wildly improbable maneuver to attempt. Astern of amidships, he decided, but not all the way astern. Somewhere in the aft third quarter of the ship, where most of what would be damaged would be living quarters and support facilities. God help them, the propeller shaft ran all the way through there as well, but there was a chance that the shock bearings would be sufficient support. Along that last one-quarter of the ship, where his shafts were exposed to water, a hit would be more dangerous.

At times like this, no one questioned him. The *Lake Champlain*, a marvelously maneuverable beast, pivoted smartly as the officer of the deck wisely chose to use one shaft ahead full, and one shaft astern full in order to pivot the ship. She had just time for one maneuver before the first torpedo hit.

Everyone in combat was strapped into his or her chair, but he knew that the bridge crew and men and women crowding passageways above the waterline would not fare as well.

The ship slammed violently to the right, and Norfolk felt his harness cut hard into his gut, knocking his breath out of him. The strap itself seemed determined to cut through his midsection, and his head slammed into the side of the seat. In the next instant, the ship heeled back to the other side almost as violently, and he heard his neck creak and snap as he was flung to the other side. Combat was filled with muttered curses and a few cries of pain and surprise.

The cant on the deck increased alarmingly. She was five degrees down now, maybe ten. Oh God, how bad is it? The ship continued to rock back and forth, attempting to right herself, as the impact of the torpedo reverberated throughout her hull.

There were loud moans coming from some sections of combat now, and the captain could only imagine the damage the attack had done to the bridge. Even if they were braced, holding on for dear life to structural supports and stanchions, the impact must have flung them around the compartment like rag dolls.

And inside the ship—well, he would know soon enough. There was no time to worry, not if he was going to keep the ship afloat.

"Damage report!" he snapped at the TAO, marveling at his own voice. "Come on, mister—we're still afloat."

The sound-powered phone circuits sprung to life now, as weak, sometimes broken voices began summarizing the situation for them.

The torpedo had hit in the general area he'd hoped for, although not as forward as his best projection. It had penetrated in the lowest compartments, blasting a gaping hole open in them, and then continuing on through the ship before finally exploding. There was a massive fire in the ports stern sections of the ship, the investigator was reporting. No apparent casualties from the explosion, since everyone had been evacuated.

On the bridge, the situation was serious. The XO had been slammed against the hatch, and had slumped unconscious to the deck. The officer of the deck had not been able to ascertain his condition yet due to taking a fairly hard hit himself. There were no apparent fatalities, but numerous injuries. At that very moment, the officer of the deck was handling the helm himself, while the junior officer of the deck checked on everyone's condition. Did the captain have any orders?

"Not at the moment—we'll probably want to come right before long, to try to stabilize her. Give me a full steering gear check, including both rudders and both rudder cables. Tell me how much maneuverability we have left."

And then the reports began arriving in from engineering. The damage control teams were spreading out throughout the ship, fighting to contain the smoke, fire and flooding. Containing, then starting to push them back until they occupied the smallest possible area.

The chief engineer was in main control, which was co-located with damage control central. He was fully suited in his general quarters gear except for a firefighting ensemble and breathing apparatus.

Every alarm and telltale inside damage control was howling. Red lights flashed across all the status boards, indicating fires, flooding, and massive damage.

The chief engineer grabbed a sound-powered phone connected to the primary investigator. "As soon as they set smoke, fire, and flooding boundaries, I want a full report on shaft alley," he said, referring to the long compartment that crossed watertight bulkheads in the shaft's transit from the turbines to propellers. "Our first priority is to restore full maneuverability."

"Roger, sir. I can tell you that we probably lost the port shaft. It's still intact, but she looks like she's been badly warped. I'm not sure if we should even try to put any knots on her—it may just do more damage. The good news, though, is that the starboard shaft looks like it's okay."

The engineer breathed a sigh of relief. Even if both shafts had been damaged, they could have made slow forward speeds with the bow thrusters. But the small pump jets were designed for maneuvering, and for emergency propulsion, not for the long haul back across the Pacific to a shipyard. He wasn't even sure that they would stand up without burning out.

"The next question is steering. Can you get into aftersteering?"

"Hold on, sir. I'm going to move aft."

The primary investigator unplugged from a soundpowered phone jack and made his way aft. He came back on line, and said "I'm not so sure, sir. The hatch is still intact, but it's badly sprung. There may be a fair amount of flooding back there. What me to check the telltale?" The telltale was a small, independently operated access to allow personnel to check whether or not a compartment was flooded. It was easy to shut, where the massive hatch would not be if the full force of the water were against it. "What do the flooding indicators say?"

The chief engineer glanced at the enunciator board, then said, "It says flooding, but it says that about every compartment, even the ones we know are okay. I'm not inclined to trust it."

"Okay, sir, let me try the telltale." There was a moment of silence, then, "There's a little water in there on the deck, sir, but nothing that amounts to anything. I'd like people standing by, though, before I open the hatch."

"How deep?"

"From the little I can see, about six inches. I don't see any major change, but that could change when I open the hatch."

The engineer made his decision. "Stand by until I can get a team down there—we've got other things to take care of first, but they'll get there as soon as they can. We'll wait for the bridge to tell us whether or not they have maneuverability."

It was a risk, albeit a small one. Attempting to actuate a damaged component could result in further problems, up to and including fire. But if aftersteering did have major flooding problems, the last thing he wanted to do was create access to the rest of the ship. No, he would wait for the bridge to tell him whether or not they had adequate control of the rudders, then decide what to do after that.

"Aye-aye, sir. What next?"

"Check all compartments around, above, and below aftersteering. Then get me a follow-up report and double check the fire, smoke and flooding boundaries. I need to know what the status is on our valve lineup, as well—I think we'll have to pump fuel and water around in order to stabilize her."

As the engineer glanced back at the status board, he had a sense of being overwhelmed. The ship was so badly damaged—for a moment the details threatened to overwhelm them. How could one group possibly catch up with it all?

Then the hard-learned lessons came flooding back. One thing at a time—prioritize, prioritize, prioritize. No, you can't do everything at once. Keep her afloat for now, and the rest of it can be sorted out later.

USS **United States**
0845 local (GMT +8)

"It's bad, Admiral. But it could be worse." Norfolk's voice was tight and controlled. "We're still working to control the flooding. No fire, yet. One shaft very questionable, the propeller probably okay. No personnel killed, although we have a couple of injuries, broken bones, that sort of thing. One concussion, the corpsman thinks."

"What do you need from us?" the admiral asked.

"Medical evacuation, as soon as I can set flight quarters. We'll have to use the stretcher—I've got about ten degrees list on the deck."

Ten degrees—it didn't sound like much, but Coyote knew it was a hell of a lot of list. Ten degrees would make everything uphill, would knock all loose gear around in a compartment. That more than anything else *Lake Champlain*'s captain said told Coyote just how badly the destroyer was damaged.

"Combat systems?" Coyote asked.

"All operational," the captain said. "I'm not sure we can deploy the towed array, but sonar and all radars are on. As are our missiles and fire control."

Coyote paused for a moment, and said, "I know what you did, Captain. That last maneuver—I'm not sure I've ever seen such an outstanding if damned dangerous shiphandling maneuver. It looks like it worked, though."

"That it did, Admiral."

"Did you know it would?"

There was a long silence online, and for a moment Coyote thought they had lost communications. But then the captain spoke, his voice for the first time showing some of his pain. "No, Admiral, I didn't. But I had to try it—I pulled everyone up above the waterline before I did."

"Everyone?" Coyote was astounded.

"Everyone. My call, sir."

"Your call indeed, Captain," Coyote said promptly. He would not criticize, ever, a man who'd shown such courage. "Take care of your ship, captain—and your people. And tell me when you're ready to receive my helo. We'll use the frame and get them off immediately. When we can . . . it's going to get a little busy here in about five minutes."

"Roger that, Admiral. I'm watching inbound right now." The captain's voice was grim. "We're online, sir, and ready to fight."

USS Seawolf
0850 local (GMT +8)

"Oh, man," Jacobs said softly as he pulled his earphones away from his head. "Sounded like a direct hit, Captain," he finished. He glanced up at his skipper.

"God help them," the captain said. And although they had faced the same danger themselves not moments before, with far less possibility that they could recover from a hit, the captain felt a moment of profound sorrow for the surface ship. A direct hit, even for a ship as well-built as the *Lake Champlain* had to be dangerous.

"Thirteen hundred feet," the officer of the deck announced. "Continuing to descend to eighteen hundred."

The torpedoes were still clearly audible over the speaker, although the tone had a faintly fuzzy edge to it as the sound wound its way through the different layers of the ocean to reach them.

"Any problems?" the captain asked.

"None, sir."

"There won't be," Pencehaven said suddenly. It was the first time he had spoken in perhaps an hour, and his voice startled them both.

"You're awful certain, Otter," the captain said.

Pencehaven nodded. "Yes, Captain. I am. These stupid torpedoes are going to go for the noise makers—I guarantee it."

"Fourteen hundred feet."

"I have an idea, Captain," Pencehaven said. He held up a CD. "There's one way to make certain they think they've destroyed us."

"Absent actually taking a hit, I hope."

Pencehaven nodded. "Say we continue on down—two thousand feet isn't too much, Captain. They'll start to lose us at that depth and they may not be absolutely certain how deep we are and what kind of range they have on their torpedoes. So they're going to be listening very carefully. When the last torpedo goes for the decoy, we make them think it's us."

"With the recording?" the captain asked.

Pencehaven nodded. "I can ground out to the hull, Captain. The world's greatest speaker. Odds are that it'll sound exactly like we . . . like we . . . well, you know. At least I think it will."

The captain regarded him for a moment. There was no telling just how savvy the Chinese sonar operators were, not after what they'd seen. Still, this certainly wouldn't be anything they'd be expecting—hell, nobody but Otter would have thought of it to start with.

The captain nodded. "Get it ready. But we have to wait for exactly the right time."

"Sixteen hundred feet," the officer of the deck announced.

Otter slid the CD into the player and wound his patch cords and speaker outputs over to rest on metal brackets that were connected to the hull of the submarine. "I need the engineers to generate some sound shorts right here, sir. Or somewhere that I can reach with my speakers."

The captain made the arrangements, and Pencehaven had obviously talked this over with the engineer beforehand, because the arrangements went smoothly.

"Eighteen hundred feet." The noise of the two torpedoes had grown fuzzy, as the submarine passed through a shallow acoustic layer. But now it picked up again, as though they had finally located their quarry. Everyone in the submarine heard the seekerhead shift to a higher, more rapid ping as the torpedoes began to home in on them.

"Hear that?" Pencehaven asked. "Get ready, sir."

At first, the captain could hear nothing different coming over the speaker. But then he heard it—or thought he heard it—just at the edges of his perception. Then he knew he heard it—the faint growl of the torpedo's propeller.

"Any second, now, Captain," Pencehaven said.

It just might work . . . it's worth trying at least. At least I know that we can stay safely below their kill depth. But

*if they think they got us—well, the odds shift immeasurably
in our favor.*

Suddenly the regular motor noise exploded followed by
another explosion.

"Now!" Pencehaven pushed the play button.

The volume was cranked up to full, and sound filled the
submarine. It was eerie, an odd sound, of continuous explosions. The noise crescendoed until the individual com-
ponents were no longer distinguishable from the general
cacophony. It continued on for what seemed like hours,
days, months, and each person in the control room felt cold
sweep through him. The sounds translated too easily, too
immediately, into what they, too, would experience if the
torpedo found its mark. Finally, when each one thought
that the noise would drive him mad, it started to decrease.
The intermittent explosions and groans, continued for
some time, growing fainter and finally dying away completely.

The control room was utterly silent afterwards, as
though the crew were at a memorial service. They had just
listened to the death of a submarine and it was only sheer
luck and God's grace that it hadn't been them. But the
death of the other submarine, the recording they'd just
played, would serve a purpose—keeping the shipmates
they'd never known safe.

"I wonder if they bought it?" Jacobs said softly. "Man,
I'd give anything to hear what they're thinking."

Pencehaven smiled. "Oh, they bought it. You heard it—
wouldn't you?"

TWENTY-TWO

Tomcat 155
Monday, September 23
0200 local (GMT+7)

The second and third refueling passed uneventfully. Tombstone found his biggest problem was the boredom. The Tomcat's engines droned reassuringly around them, the low growl simply part of the background noise. His lower back ached from the hard curves of the ejection seat, and he made a mental note to see if his uncle could spring for an upgraded lumbar support device. There had to be a decent one around somewhere, there just had to be.

In the back seat, Jason, too, was fighting off the tedium. Finally, Tombstone said, "I wouldn't normally recommend this, but this is our first long flight, and we've got a learning curve. I'm thinking it might be a good idea for us to take turns catching a couple of winks."

"Go to sleep in a Tomcat?" Jason's voice was incredulous. "Man, that ranks high on the list of things I never thought I'd hear anyone say."

"Same place, on a list of things I never thought I'd say. I know tanker and surveillance aircraft pull longer flights, but they've got a full flight crew, can get up and stretch and we can't. I'm not embarrassed to admit I'm starting to dread the return haul."

"Yeah, well. It always takes more time on the way out, don't you think?"

"Anyway, let's give it a try," Tombstone said. "Go on, rack out for thirty minutes. I'll wake you up."

"Don't have to ask me twice." Within a few minutes, Jason's breathing was slow and regular. Tombstone wondered if he'd be able to nod off as easily when his turn came.

He glanced at the radar screen again, and saw a few commercial flights on their way across the ocean, but nothing out of the ordinary. The tactical circuit was silent, but he had no doubt that the AWACS was still monitoring their progress, so that must mean there were no problems. And it was another two hours to the next refueling.

That's the way it was, wasn't it? Hours of boredom leavened only by moments of sheer terror. Some things never changed.

When Jason's thirty minutes were up, Tombstone said, "Rise and shine, buddy."

No response from the back. He glanced in his mirror and saw the younger pilot's chest rising and falling.

Surely he didn't turn his radio off? He wouldn't—aw, hell. "Wake-up!" Tombstone shouted.

Still no response from Jason.

I don't believe this. What the hell is wrong with him? Food poisoning—something we both ate, maybe? Oh God, he can't be dead. No.

"Jason, wake-up!" Tombstone shouted, after he'd jerked his own 02 mask off. "You asshole—wake up!" Tombstone followed with a string of curses that he hadn't used in quite some time, and was rewarded by the slightest movement from the unconscious figure in his back seat.

"Mom?" a sleepy voice croaked. "Is it time for school?"

Oh, this is priceless. If I have anything to say about it, Jason Greene will never live this down.

"You listen to me, young man. You get up right this

second," Tombstone said in high-pitched voice, his gaze locked on the mirror.

Jason bolted upright, a look of confusion on his face. Then a red flush crept up his cheeks.

In the front seat, Tombstone howled. "Oh, man, what I wouldn't give to be in a squadron right now," Tombstone chortled. "But since we're a squadron of two, I'm going to assume responsibility. I don't care what your call sign was before, you're now Schoolboy."

Jason muttered something too low to be heard, and Tombstone said, "What's that? Speak up, Schoolboy."

"If I'm Schoolboy, guess that that makes you Mommy dearest." Jason sniggered. "Yeah, I like that. No more Tombstone—you're Mommy from now on."

"Oh, no you don't," Tombstone retorted. "Not if you ever want a shot at the front seat."

"Funny, that's exactly what my mom used to say."

"Triple nickels, this is Big Eyes," the AWACS said suddenly over tactical. They both jumped. "Be advised that there's additional activity taking place at Six Flags. No launches, just warnings and indications." Six Flags was the code word for the nearest Russian air base.

Jason groaned. "Just what we need."

"Doesn't necessarily have anything to do with us," Tombstone said. But it did—someone on the ground somewhere had taken note of a tanker in the air, and the small, virtually insignificant radar speck headed south and west. Taken note of it, and decided to do something about it. And while there might not be Russian fighters airborne right now, there would be if Tombstone continued heading south.

"I've got a few tricks up my sleeve," Big Eyes continued. "And I'm about to pull one of them out now. You're going to get degradation on all your comm circuits, radars, and ECM indicators. If you got anything to tell me, make it snappy. I'll give you ten seconds."

"We have anything to tell them, Mommy?"

"Shut the hell up. No, I don't. You?"

"The right engine is running a little hot," Jason said. "Nothing to worry about now—well within specs. It's just that the temperature started to rise slowly over the last two hours."

"Yeah, I know. But there's nothing to tell Big Eyes about yet. It's not like he can do anything about it, anyway."

"Roger, concur."

"Five seconds," Big Eyes said. He continued counting down, and just as he reached zero, Tombstone had a flash of insight. "Turn down your radio volume—way low," he ordered. He reached out and switched his down.

USS **United States**
TFCC
0800 local (GMT +8)

"What the hell is that contact?" Coyote asked. He pointed out the offending radar blip, marked as a neutral aircraft, but headed toward the Russian Islands. "Anybody know?"

Bird Dog shook his head. "No answer to a call up on distress frequencies, sir. But by its flight profile, it looks like a fighter."

"I'm not taking any chances right now," Coyote snapped. "Break off two Tomcats to fly CAP directly over *Marshall P'eng*."

"What about that Chinese surface action group?" Bird Dog asked.

"They moved yet?"

"No, sir. But they're within missile range now."

"Watch 'em. The second one of those bastards so much as sneezes, I want missiles on them like stink on shit, and I don't give a damn what the United Nations says," Coyote said.

Suddenly, the radio came to life. Goforth, the liaison on the *P'eng*, was calling. "TAO, Captain Chang has a few questions about what he's just heard over sonar. Evidently he believes he heard a submarine breaking up after that torpedo shot. He's wondering if there's anything you need to tell him, TAO. Like can he assume that the contact that was sunk was the Chinese diesel he's been after? And if it was, does the admiral want his helos back?"

Suddenly, the tactical screen flared into life. The seemingly random disposition of Chinese surface ships resolved into a classic amphibious operations and antiair formation. At the same time, the airspace along the coast of China was suddenly lousy with air contacts. The staff stared in horror as wave upon wave of Chinese fighters went feet wet. Half of the formation turned slightly north and headed for the island of Taiwan. The others bore down directly on the USS *United States*.

Goforth's questions hung in the air, as the majority of the staff concentrated on the incoming waves of Chinese fighter aircraft. The speaker was a cacophony of voices as the E-2 directed fighters to individual engagements and maintained the overall picture on the fur ball now developing to the east.

Ho glanced around desperately, aware that no one was answering. Why not? The answer was clear to him—the lives of the people onboard *Marshall P'eng* were not nearly as important to them as their precious fighter aircraft.

Ho approached the admiral, anger surging under the calm he forced on his face. He waited to be recognized, as would be appropriate in his own culture, but no one even acknowledged his presence.

He cleared his throat. No one even looked in his direction.

Finally, he spoke, his voice coming out harsh. "Admiral, my captain—he has asked for instructions." He waited.

Coyote was still deep in conversation with the commanding officer of the Viking squadron. "Get two more tankers ready to launch—and no, I don't want to see Rabies on the flight schedule for that. You know what we're up against—put him on the submarine. He's the best we've got."

Ho Kung-Sun tried again. "Admiral. The *Marshall P'eng*."

Coyote was turning to his air operations officer. "You have to cover for the AWACS. I don't want to lose another one. Gas in the air is going to be the limiting factor. Refueling is our top priority."

"Admiral!" Surprising even himself, but his fury knowing no bounds, Ho Kung-Sun reached out to touch Coyote on the arm.

On a ship from his own country, such disrespect would have ended his career immediately. Yet the American admiral turned to look at him with no more than minor annoyance on his face. "What is it?"

"Captain Chang—he wishes to know whether you want him to continue to attempt to locate the Chinese submarine, under the circumstances. Or should he move closer to the carrier and return the helos to your operational command?"

"Keep the helos and keep them looking for a submarine," Coyote said. He noticed the look of concern on the young Taiwanese major's face. "Look, he's well within our air umbrella. I know he heard one sub breaking up, but there's no guarantee there's not another one out there." Coyote said a silent prayer that it had been the Chinese diesel that had taken the hit, not the *Seawolf*. But until *Seawolf* checked in, the admiral couldn't be entirely sure. "*P'eng* is in no more danger than the rest of the surface ships are, and getting that submarine is a major priority right now. Ask him what he needs—set up the second separate coordination circuit if you need to."

Ho turned to study the plot, Coyote's dismissive words ringing in his ears. Was *Marshall P'eng* really within the air umbrella protection? How could that be?—she was so much further away than the other ships. No, the admiral was keeping his own ships in closer, risking *Marshall P'eng* for some purpose of his own. Perhaps as a decoy to

draw Chinese fighters away from the carrier—yes, that
would make sense. A missile sump—that's all they were.

A radioman touched Ho on the arm, and he drew back,
seriously affronted. For an enlisted man to touch him—
that was what came of his touching the American admiral.
Now a very junior man felt free to do the same to him.
"You want a separate circuit, sir?" the radioman asked, his
voice urgent but polite. "I got to know now, Major."

A separate circuit, even. More evidence—they were relegated to the sidelines, not part of the main battle. Yet
still, this could be turned to his advantage as well.

"Yes—a separate circuit. That will be good."

"Five minutes, sir. Maybe less." The radioman turned
and picked up a telephone and spoke with the communications center. He hung up, and began setting dial switches
to the appropriate channels. "You need a speaker, sir? Or
just a mike and a headset?"

"A headset will be fine, thank you. After all, this is just
to speak to one ship on one issue."

The radioman nodded, as much as admitting it was true.

Moments later, Ho heard the circuit come to life. The
radioman handed him a headset. "It's all yours, sir," he
said.

Ho slipped the headset on. It was, indeed, all his now.
And the Americans would understand—if they survived
this—that they could not treat the Taiwanese nation in
such a cavalier fashion.

Marshall P'eng
0830 local (GMT+8)

Captain Chang listened to the words coming over the
speaker with a growing sense of unreality. After the first
sentence, he clicked off the feed to the speaker and listened
to the call on a headset. His astonishment grew with every
sentence that came out of Ho's mouth.

"I have told you repeatedly, my captain, that these people are not to be trusted entirely. It is good I am on the scene, because had I not heard the derogatory remarks and seen the disrespect toward our forces, I would not have believed it myself. Even you can have no doubts at this point. We have been removed from the main battle circuit, Captain, removed and relegated to this link. And as you can see from your screen, you are further away from the American carrier and the cruiser than any other ship. It is the admiral's intent to use you to draw off fighters from his carrier, knowing how much the Chinese hate us. He believes that they will attack you first, giving his forces a chance to follow-up to prevent damage to the American ships."

"He said that?" the captain asked, still not believing what he was hearing. It was so inconsistent with everything he had seen from the Americans so far, completely inconsistent.

And yet it was possible, wasn't it? American support for Taiwan had always been difficult for the Taiwanese to understand. In their mind, there should have been a massive retaliatory strike against China at the first offense. But the Americans temporized, talking about free trade, the need to maintain relationships with those nations. Taiwan, in the end, could count it as nothing more than a betrayal.

"You know how they speak," Ho said. "With the Americans, it is better to watch what they do instead of listen to what they say. And can you have any doubts yourself at this point? Look how exposed the ship is—and all because of the submarine that poses the primary threat to the Americans."

"And to us as well," Chang pointed out. "And I am using American helicopters to pin her down as well, do not forget."

"And what of the American fighters that he sent for defense? If you're truly within his cruiser's protection envelope, why would he send fighters at all?" Ho Kung-Sun asked.

Why, indeed? Chang pondered this for moment, a

sinking feeling in his gut. Had he so misjudged the admiral, this Coyote? A slip of information from his cross-cultural studies class came back to mind. In the Native American culture, the Coyote was considered the trickster, the one who was always pulling a sly prank on a trusting person. Could it be that this admiral, this Coyote, was very correctly named?

"If you go further north, you risk more," Ho said. "Captain, it makes sense to break off prosecution and return close to the carrier. You can take the submarine just as easily from here as from there."

"And risk her coming in closer," Chang said quietly. "Additionally, the water to the south is not as favorable as these conditions. We would lose in terms of our detection capabilities from the noise generated by the American ships alone. No, it is better to prosecute here. If that is the only factor considered."

"But it is not, is it?" Ho said, now certain that he had Chang worried.

"No, it is not. Are you absolutely certain that this is the American admiral's intention? Certain?"

"Yes. I am, sir."

Just then, Chang Tso-Lin saw the fighters inbound on his ship. Why fighters? Hadn't the admiral assured him that *Marshall P'eng* was within the antiair protection envelope? If that was true, then there was no need for fighter cover.

Unless Ho is right. The admiral wishes to destroy us, but he dare not risk antiship missiles at this range. He may need them for dealing with the Chinese ships, and using the fighters prevents him from putting his own ships at risk?

But why? We are allies! Or at least I believed that we were.

Perhaps he will try to claim China did this, and use that as an excuse to establish firmer control of the region. There are political forces at work here that I do not un-

*derstand, will never understand. But I do know when
someone is trying to kill me.*

"Then we must avenge this act of war," Chang said
firmly. He was certain that Ho did not know what he was
starting. If indeed they had been betrayed by the Americans, then the only honorable path was to avenge that betrayal by the Americans. And it would begin with *Marshall
P'eng*. Now and here.

But instead of the righteous light of anger in his soul,
he felt dishonorable and incompetent. How could he have
so misjudged the American admiral? He thought he knew
the man, had seen the spirit of ancient warriors in his soul.
But to be betrayed like this, well, there could be no doubt.

"You will tell the people how we died," Chang said.
"Tell them my men served bravely, and in defense of a
free and glorious Taiwan."

He replaced the mike in the holder, and clicked off the
circuit. There was nothing else discussed—while Ho
Kung-Sun may not have intended this reaction, Chang
Tso-Lin had no choice. He turned to his watch officer.
"Break the helicopters off—have them return to us. And
as they do, target them with our antiair missiles."

The watch officer's jaw dropped, but true to his training,
he did as he was told.

USS **United States**
TFCC
0835 local (GMT+8)

The speed leader on the *Marshall P'eng* suddenly changed
directions and length, as did those of the helicopters in
support of the antisubmarine engagement. Coyote watched
for a moment, wondering whether it was a computer glitch
of some sort, then turned to Ho Kung-Sun. "What is your
captain doing?"

"What he should have done a long time ago," the Tai-

wanese major answered, savage glee in his voice. "Perhaps
I will survive, perhaps not. But it makes no difference. I
will die in defense of my country."

"What?!" Coyote's head snapped back and forth between the screen and the major. "What are you babbling
about? What did you tell him?"

"I do not babble. I merely speak the truth. And I have
so informed my captain." His voice was proud. "No longer
will we be subject to your treachery."

"Treachery? What the hell are you talking about?"

Just then, the first missile left the rails of the frigate,
headed toward a helicopter.

Seahunter 601
0855 local (GMT+8)

The SH-60 helicopter pilot was puzzled as he headed back
for the carrier. He clicked on its ICS mike. "I just don't
get it. We were getting close, we had her. And they break
us off?"

"Why the hell do they do anything?" his copilot answered. "Another five minutes, and we would have had
her solid."

The sensor operator spoke up from the back. "I figure
we have her pinned down, so the frigate wants to go in
for the kill. Take all the credit for it, you know? That
would make them look like the big guys around here, even
though we really did all the work."

"You think? Well, it's not like we were the only ones,
though. That little Sea Sprite driver is a tenacious little
fellow. You give him enough time, and I think he may
have gotten the sub off alone. And that frigate's no slouch,
either. Face it, guys. They could have handled it without
us."

"But not as quickly." the sensor operator said.

"Yeah, that's true." The pilot clicked over to call the

carrier and request a green deck. Just as he did so, he saw
a long, white con trail streaming out from the deck of the
frigate. For a moment, he couldn't believe his eyes. Then
training and reflex took over, and he put the helicopter into
a hard bank and headed for the surface of the ocean. "We
got incoming!" he yelled over tactical. "What the hell is
going on around here? They shot at us—the *Marshall
P'eng* just shot at us!"

Marshall P'eng
0900 local (GMT+8)

Chang studied the display, then listened to a report from
his lookout. The missile had missed, but not by much. A
second one was off the rails, headed for the other helicopter. "Retarget the lead helo," he ordered. "And continue in
toward the carrier."

USS United States
0903 local (GMT+8)

"What's the loadout on the helo?" Coyote demanded. "I
can't believe this is happening."

"Strictly antisub, sir," the air operations officer said.

"Guns, though," Bird Dog noted. "That could do a lot
of damage to a frigate, sir."

"Get those helos back on board," Coyote answered. "I
want to talk to the captain—there's something screwy going on here, and I have a feeling our little major is behind
it."

Major Ho drew himself up to his full height. "You are
behind it, Admiral. Not me."

Marshall P'eng
0904 local (GMT+8)

Lieutenant Goforth stared in horror at the picture unfolding on the screen. He had not followed all of the conversation between Chang Tso-Lin and Ho Kung-Sun, although he found something in their tone definitely disturbing. Now, everything was becoming unreal—break off from the prosecution of the submarine when they almost had it? And shooting at the American helos? He felt the blood drain from his face and a cold chill sweep over him. What next? Would they execute him as a spy?

He turned to face Captain Chang, trying to frame the question. But the words simply wouldn't come, although the captain watched him carefully. Finally, he managed to say, "Captain, sir, there has been a serious misunderstanding. I must speak to my admiral immediately, sir."

The captain shook his head. In remarkably clear and precise English, he said, "Talk is cheap, Lieutenant." He pointed at the tactical display. "Your admiral has betrayed us. Perhaps losing his helicopters will teach him not to kill all gooks."

Goforth's jaw dropped. Captain Chang smiled bitterly. "Surprised that I speak your language? I thought so."

"No, sir—yes, sir, I mean but—but, sir—what makes you think that's what he's trying to do?"

"Major Ho Kung-Sun explained." Captain Chang Tso-Lin turned his back on him, evidently through with the conversation. "I had thought better of your admiral. I thought we understood each other in a very special sort of way. After he revealed the U.S. submarine to me . . ."

"He *what*?!"

"It does not matter now," Chang continued.

Goforth turned back to the screen and saw the missiles headed directly for the two helicopters. Then, forgetting everything he had had drummed into his head about the Taiwanese culture, as well as every bit of military protocol from his own service, he grabbed Chang by the arm.

"Look—those Tomcats. They are here to protect us, sir. Watch—you see what they do."

The captain shook his head, although Goforth thought he saw a trace of sorrow on his face. The translator turned back to the American. "I cannot take the chance."

Goforth took a deep breath. "You say it matters what we do, not what we say." He pointed to the screen again. "Then watch what they do, sir. They're here to protect you—not to attack. Just watch for a few seconds before you decide. Please, sir."

Chinese Fencer 101
0910 local (GMT +8)

The order came from a nervous ground controller who obviously had brass standing behind him. "I am directed to tell you to disengage two flights of fighters from the first wave and prosecute the treasonous Chinese vessel *Marshall P'eng* located just to the north of the main battle group. You will use all means at your disposal to ensure that the frigate is destroyed."

All means—the pilot knew what that meant. If necessary, he was required to make a suicidal dive on her, if he could not reach her with his antisurface missiles.

"Acknowledged," he said, and clicked over to the short range channel with his wingman. "You are ready?"

"Of course."

The two aircraft turned in unison, breaking apart slightly for loose formation as they headed for the Taiwanese frigate.

Tomcat 309
0945 local (GMT+8)

The pilot studied the display, and saw that the rest of their wing was now heavily engaged in a fur ball to the south. It was ranging over a wide area of ocean, but drifting gradually to the east, bringing it to the edge of the area that the cruiser was designated to handle with its missiles. It was always a risk, making sure you're outside the missile engagement sound. Even though the sensitive Aegis missile system would not attack target radiating friendly IFF, there was not a single pilot he'd ever talked to who was willing to bet his life on it.

"We're way out of it," his wingman groused. "Just burning fuel and wasting time when we could be—"

"Knock it off," the lead pilot ordered. "We got our orders, we follow them. You understand?"

"Yeah, I got it. But they're not coming up here—that would be crazy. Even the Chinese aren't stupid enough to take on the Aegis cruiser."

Something shifted on the pilot's HUD and adrenaline rushed into his system. "You seeing what I'm seeing?"

"Yeah. About time."

As he watched, two Chinese fighters broke off from the pack, and headed directly for them. "Go high," the pilot ordered. "And make sure the E-2 has a handle on what's going on." He stroked his stick, his fingers playing over the weapon selection toggle. "You got it yet, RIO?"

"Got it, sir," the RIO answered.

"Your dot."

The first missile dropped off the Tomcat's wing, and shot unerringly for the lead of the two Chinese fighters.

In short succession, lead and his wing fired off another three missiles. If that didn't do it, they were prepared to get serious.

Marshall P'eng
0950 local (GMT +8)

"You see?" Goforth shouted, almost jumping up and down
to get Chang Tso-Lin's attention. "They're taking on the
Chinese fighters—not you! They turned as soon as the
fighters were inbound!" He stepped two respectful paces
back, kept his eyes lowered, trying desperately to sound
like a respectful officer conscious of the power of his captain. "Captain, I'm simply asking permission to contact my
admiral. He has inadvertently created a misunderstanding
that I know he would be most sorrowful about. He said,
watch what we do, not what we say." He pointed to the
screen. "That's who we are, sir. And that's how we value
our alliance with your nation."

Chinese Fencer 101
0952 local (GMT +8)

"Break right! break right!" the lead howled, throwing his
own aircraft to the left in a nose-down attitude. His altimeter wound down as he peeled off altitude.

The missile zoomed between them, traveling too fast to
make a turn and come back on them. When it tried to
search the area for another target, it confronted a snowstorm of chaff and decoys in the air, including two infrared
flares. It paused, unable to find the sweet hot target it had
been following before, then picked the most probable location and detonated. Its bundle of expanding rods ripped
through the air, shredding the chaff into even smaller
pieces and further confusing the second missile coming.

"Get by the chaff, get by the chaff!" the lead shouted,
doing just that as he snapped the aircraft back up into a
hard drive, kicking in the afterburners. The afterburners
were a risk, providing an enticingly clear target should the
Americans fire the heat seeker, but it was a risk he had to

take. It was more dangerous to remain alone in the air without the sheltering fog of chaff.

His wingman, however, was not so lucky. As the second missile turned, catching a glimpse of them with its seeker head, he panicked. He turned away from it and ran, kicking in full afterburners, making it an even more attractive target. The missile had no doubt about what it should do. It homed in unerringly, and, moving at twice the maximum speed of the aircraft, caught it within seconds. The result was a blinding fireball of orange, red, and metal sparking off into the air.

The lead felt a rush of pain, as his wingman was an old friend, but there was no time for sentiment, not if he was going to get out of this alive. He pumped out more chaff, making a trail back to where the fireball was, hoping that would distract the subsequent missile. He jockeyed to stay behind it as long as it was burning, and popped up more chaff and flares to create an additional distraction. On his heads-up display, he saw two more missiles inbound.

All measures—they said all measures. He screwed up his courage, shot up above the sheltering cloud of chaff, and bore directly down on the missiles.

Tomcat 309
0953 local (GMT+8)

"What's that crazy bastard doing?" the RIO asked. "He's heading right for us. Doesn't he know he's outnumbered?"

"He couldn't miss his wing going down," the pilot answered. "He's a gutsy bastard, I'll give him that."

As they watched, the Chinese fighter headed directly for the two missiles. Then the pilot felt a creeping sensation of uneasiness. "Head-to-head—the closure rate of Mach 5. If he—"

Just then, his HUD anticipated his next words. The Chinese pilot let the missiles get so close he could almost

touch them, then jerked violently upward, then down, por-
poising around them. The missiles tried to make the turn,
but the first one nicked the second, and both exploded.

"Okay, we'll have to do this the hard way," the pilot
said. He punched in the afterburners, and headed for the
MiG.

The wingman circled around, coming in at an angle, and
intended to trap the Chinese fighter and take him out with
guns. But before he could get in position, the Chinese
fighter took a shot at him, and a missile found its mark.

The wingman saw the missile inbound and did his best
to avoid it. But in the last seconds, he could see that it was
in vain. Just before the missile reached them, his hand
closed on the ejection seat, and he and the RIO left the
aircraft to the mercy of the missile.

TWENTY-THREE

Marshall P'eng
Monday, September 24
1000 local (GMT +8)

Without a word, Captain Chang reached up and turned the speaker to tactical back on as well as the circuit he shared with Ho on board the carrier. Combat was immediately flooded with a babble of American voices, which sounded particularly like music to Goforth's ears.

But one voice booming out over both circuits cut through everything else. Captain Chang recognized it as that of Coyote.

"*Marshall P'eng, Marshall P'eng*, this is the *United States*. Over." The call up was repeated three times, then the circuit cleared for the battle group to take care of other business.

Captain Chang picked up the mike, then turned to face the American officer. "Courage—yes, you have courage."

"*United States*, this is *Marshall P'eng*," the captain said, his voice clear and his English accented. "Be advised I am initiating a SAR mission with the two helos—three helos—under my control. I am close—I will get pilots, Admiral."

Coyote's voice came back over the circuit. "Roger, sir.

But would you care to explain what just happened? I've got two helos damn near the wave tops who are a little bit reluctant to return to your command and control, Captain."

"A great error on my part, Admiral," Chang said, his voice deadly serious. "I will explain later—but you'll forgive me if I concentrate my attention on getting your men out of the water right now. The explanations can wait, sir. I assure you, I will pay for my mistake later."

"Roger, then, Captain," Coyote's voice said. "You coordinate the SAR—I may have some matters to take care of down here. And as for the submarine—"

"Pardon, Admiral," Chang interrupted, and everyone stared aghast at the rudeness. "Consider the submarine gone."

He turned back to his watch section, and began giving orders again. Goforth felt the ship heel over hard as the nimble frigate turned. "The SAR—shall I talk to them?" he asked.

Chang handed him the mike. "Major Ho Kung-Sun has made a very grave mistake as well," he said. "Extend my apologies—I am deeply sorry. But it is imperative, whatever their feelings, that they obey my orders immediately. We must get these men out of the water within the next three minutes."

"Roger, sir—but to be blunt, what's the hurry? They have survival gear and the water is relatively warm."

The captain shook his head. "You do not understand. I have been patrolling this area for about a week now, in my home waters. I know everything about this part of the ocean, and know it well. I have watched this over countless missions. The problem is not the temperature of the water. It is what follows in our wake." His face reflected his concern. "Sharks. Great white. And after feasting on our trash for several weeks, they will find the morsels such as your pilots quite tasty. Now, tell your helos to obey me or be prepared to bear responsibility for what follows."

It took only thirty seconds for the American officer to explain the situation to the helo pilots, and after the first ten seconds, they were already turning and heading for the SAR location. When it became apparent they had located the men, Captain Chang broke one off to join his Sea Sprite and head north. There was plenty of fuel on board, and he had one last piece of business to take care of before he dealt with his own conscience.

The submarine.

The voice of Chang's senior enlisted man came over the speaker, firm and competent. "I have an initial detection on the diesel submarine, sir. Her range is eight thousand yards, bearing zero one zero."

Dead ahead. Captain Chang stepped over to the bitch box. "Hard right rudder—Combat, I want a recommended intercept course *now*. I will notify the carrier—this time we will make good use of the helos."

The sailors on deck sprang into action at the announcement. Chang gazed at the water ahead of the replenishment ship with malice in his eyes. So a submarine was trying to take out the replenishment ship, was she? This far from friendly ports, that would do far more damage to the American battle group than attacking any other ship.

Well, that was not going to have to happen. Not if *Marshall P'eng* had anything to say about it.

Captain Chang Tso-Lin picked up the mike to call the carrier. This was one conversation that he intended to have directly with the admiral.

USS **United States**
TFCC
1010 local (GMT+8)

Coyote had just sat down to supper when the buzzer next to his seat sounded. He picked up the handset and said, "Admiral." He listened for a moment, then shoved himself back from the table, reaching out to grab a sandwich as he did so. "You'll excuse me, gentlemen. That was my

TAO. That little Taiwanese frigate is about to kick some
serious ass and I want to be there to see it."

In TFCC, Coyote hovered over the TAO's shoulder as
he watched the action unfold. The American liaison officer
onboard the frigate was reading off the datum, his voice
excited. A few words were spoken in firm Mandarin, and
he paused for a moment, then continued. "Captain Chang
Tso-Lin wishes me to convey his utmost respect, Admiral,
and we'd be pleased to eliminate this submarine from the
ocean if that comports with your desires. He also told me,"
the officer continued, his voice slightly embarrassed, "to
calm down and not look so excited. He said it is not appropriate."

"I agree," the admiral said gravely. "Please tell the captain that I appreciate his courtesy in correcting one of my
officers, and I regret any inconvenience or embarrassment
it may cause."

"Admiral?" Now the officer sounded uncertain.

"Tell him what I said." The admiral's voice was low
and courteous. He listened as the officer translated his remarks. Finally, he heard the line go quiet for a moment,
then click back on as a new voice came on.

"It is my honor, Admiral," a heavily accented voice said
carefully. "I shall take the submarine, yes?"

So you do speak some English! "Yes, please, take the
submarine," the admiral said. "Would it be of any assistance to have my helicopter standing by?" There was a
brief pause and a flurry of translation.

"Yes. Please to send two—we do this quickly, yes?"

"Yes. Quickly." The admiral paused for moment, uncertain as to how to continue, then took the plunge. "Captain, if there have been any misunderstandings, I deeply
apologize for them. You should know your ship and your
command have my utmost confidence, and we consider it
an honor to serve with such a ship, officers, and crew."

This time there was a longer conversation, and then the
American officer came back on with a horrified note in his
voice. "Admiral, the captain has given me permission to

add my own remarks as necessary to clarify for his esteemed American colleagues. He says that he believes that there have been some misunderstandings, but perhaps they were not necessary. And sir, I think I can clear up a lot of this in just a few minutes here—the captain has asked me to explain to him the difference between a gook and a geek."

The watch officer sitting in front of Coyote slapped his forehead. "Oh, man—that was it, wasn't it?" He turned to Bird Dog. "Remember that day—two days ago. Ho Kung-Sun was standing behind us and you were shouting for the geeks. He must have thought you said—"

"Shit," Bird Dog said softly. "Don't repeat it now . . . come on, please."

Coyote turned to Lab Rat. "Find Major Ho Kung-Sun. Take Lee with you. Explain it to him. Dammit, man, move!"

TWENTY-FOUR

USS Lake Champlain
Monday, September 23
1050 local (GMT +8)

Norfolk stared at the screen, swearing quietly. He turned to his TAO. "Dammit, get on the horn to the E-2—they have to keep those fighters out of my airspace. Right now, it's so clobbered I can't risk taking a shot."

The TAO relayed the captain's orders to the Hawkeye, then listened as the response came. The fighters were all too closely engaged for the E-2 to risk breaking any of them off. Consequently, the Hawkeye was recommending truncating the missile engagement envelope along that bearing.

"*United States*, this is *Lake Champlain*," the captain said on tactical. "Admiral, I can solve this problem if you can get your boys out of the way. This is what I recommend." Norfolk continued for twenty seconds, explaining his plan, and when he finished, he concluded with, "I'm pretty sure it'll work, sir. But you'll have to do your part with the airwing."

Coyote's voice came booming back. "You got it, Skipper. Stand by—I'll give the order in fifteen seconds." He switched immediately to an airwing call-up. "All flights, this is Coyote. On my mark, disengage, and buster for angels three one. Get as high as you can, boys and girls, and we'll let the Aegis make your job a little bit easier for you."

Tomcat 102
1055 local (GMT+8)

The pilot heard the call, but couldn't spare any attention to count down the seconds. He turned it over to his RIO as he fought desperately to keep out of the clutches of the MiG on his ass. With his wingman gone, it was becoming increasingly difficult, as the smaller aircraft cut them off with every maneuver. The rest of his flight was engaged with their own bogeys, and the HUD display showed that a second wave was just taking off from the mainland.

"Ten seconds," his RIO shouted, his voice audible in the cockpit even without the ICS. "Bruce, pay attention—you can't screw this up."

But the pilot had just cut hard to the left, hoping to drop back in behind the MiG for a killing shot, when the nimble MiG flipped wing over wing, circled above him, and dropped back in behind him. The pilot cut hard right, saw that bought him a few seconds, then dropped his speed breaks down to peel off airspeed like a ripe banana.

"Five seconds!" the RIO said. "Come on, you can do it."

The pilot hoped to hell he could. If he couldn't get out of the way, there was every chance that one of the Aegis missiles would decide that his massive metal airframe was just as good a target as a Chinese Craft. But to break off now and simply head for altitude, even though he could do it more quickly than the MiG, would be to expose his warm and tasty tailpipes to Chinese heat seeker missiles. It would be over quickly, too quickly, and he wouldn't have to wait for the Aegis missiles to pepper this guy with deadly expanding-rod antiair missiles.

There was a chance, just one chance—they could keep this game up forever until one of them got lucky or the other ran out of gas. But the Aegis plan had just put limitations on that as well.

The words of his military science instructor from ROTC came back to him: "Consider the terrain, the fatal terrain."

But what terrain? The answer flashed into his mind, wonderful in its brilliant simplicity and elegance.

The terrain here was empty air. Granted, there were different electromagnetic transmission zones. Peppering it like mountain ranges were the fur balls in progress, just as much terrain as a mountain has. If you could just . . . yes, there was an opportunity. It was a slim chance, but the only one he had.

The pilot cut back hard then kicked in his afterburners. He cut back immediately in the other direction, hoping to tighten his turn enough to come up behind the MiG—or at least force the MiG to conduct the same maneuver that he had on previous occasions.

Every time before, when he tried to circle back on the MiG, the MiG executed a wingover, almost a roll, and came in over him to get back in position. Every time, Bruce had responded with a hard turn to the right to shake the MiG.

But this time it would be different. He started to make his normal maneuver, and punched in the afterburners hard. Instead of coming around to try to close on the MiG again, the Tomcat shot straight up in the air, shoving the pilot and the RIO both back into the seat with a hard slam. Bruce felt his vision start to go gray, and he grunted and tensed his muscles in order to keep blood flowing to his brain.

And there it was, just ahead. A fur ball of two Tomcats and MiGs, both punching chaff and flares into the air like they had unlimited quantities, the Tomcats covering for each other as they broke off and headed for altitude.

Bruce zoomed in behind the MiGs, turning only slightly to stitch the wing assembly of one of them with gunfire and continuing on for altitude.

"Passing through angels thirty," his RIO announced. "It's going to be close."

"Yeah, but not as close as it was before."

USS **United States**
TFCC
1104 local (GMT+8)

"All clear except two," the TAO announced, as his assistant counted down the seconds. Coyote nodded, mentally working through the time-distance problem. It would be close, too close. He felt a moment of intense pain as he contemplated the possibility that he might take out his own pilots. Blue on blue engagements—there was no more painful moment for any commander.

"I'm out of choices—we have to get this engagement back on track before the second wave reaches us," he snapped. "On my mark—mark!"

The TAO relayed the information to the pilots, and watched the two laggards desperately claw for altitude.

USS **Lake Champlain**
1105 local (GMT+8)

"Mark!" Coyote's voice came across the circuit clearly.

"Full auto," the captain snapped. "Everything below angels thirty is a target. Now, let's see if we can even up the odds."

With the fire control system in full auto, the Aegis cruiser was capable of rippling off missiles in one-second intervals. The next thirty seconds, the deck under their feet rumbled and shook with deadly intensity as the missiles rippled out of their vertical launch cells. On the bridge, the crew turned away, the smoke and fire from the missile launch blinding them and burning their retinas with sharp afterimages.

Then, it was over. The light southern breeze cleared the smoke away from the cruiser. The missiles were still in flight.

Tomcat 102
1106 local (GMT +8)

"Incoming!" the RIO shouted, twisting around to watch behind them as long white telephone poles invaded the airspace they just left. "Approaching thirty-thousand feet— come on, we can do it. We can do it."

The pilot felt a strange calm come over him. He had done everything he could, had fought his aircraft to the best of his ability. Now it was up to luck, chance, and whatever god watched over fighter pilots. A few hundred feet would make all the difference in the world to the flurry of missiles behind them. He just hoped that it would be enough.

USS **Lake Champlain**
1107 local (GMT +8)

Lieutenant Ackwurst floated his cursor between the two aircraft that were still within the Aegis firing envelope. He clicked on one, then the other, watching as the altitude figures on each rolled over, more quickly than normal, but far too slow for comfort. No, the missiles wouldn't intentionally target friendly aircraft, but even smart missiles were pretty dumb. There was every chance that the two aircraft would be damaged in the fireballs or debris as the missiles found their true targets.

The lead aircraft kicked over 30,000 feet, and then only one remained. They watched, the altitude slowly increasing. As the aircraft reached 29,000 feet, the first standard missile found its target. Not that it was a particularly dramatic event by tactical data display—merely a blip, the change to a different symbol to indicate a kill, and a line of text rolling across the monitor: CONFIRMED KILL.

On the raw video and radar consoles, it was at least a bit more dramatic. The discrete green lozenge of the enemy aircraft and sharper image of the missile intersecting. The computer watched it, then re-evaluated its display, and the two sharp images dissolved into a myriad of spatters before the computer decided there was no longer a discrete target there.

A flurry of MiGs were behind the last Tomcat, the reason behind his desperate gyrations as he tried to prevent any one of them from dropping into perfect firing position. But then, modern missiles didn't need perfect firing conditions. As the team watched, four antiair missiles sprang out from the Chinese horde and headed straight for the hapless American aircraft.

The captain had been holding the mike in his hand, his thumb hoisted over the key. He pressed down hard, and snapped, "Punch out! punch out!" shouting as he did so, knowing that the few microseconds the computer had taken to process data meant that he was already too late.

Tomcat 102
1108 local (GMT +8)

"Eject! eject!" the RIO shouted, his hand closing over the ejection handle. He'd seen the smoke and fire as the missiles were launched, even from almost a mile away.

But there was a reason the guy in front was a pilot, and

that became quickly evident. His reflexes were faster, his motor skills honed to a lightning edge. He reached for the handle, jerked down, and pressed his back into the ejection seat. The canopy blasted off. Then the pilot, followed four seconds later by his RIO, punched out of the aircraft.

They shot out at a 45 degree angle from the doomed airframe, each one to a different side, the flames under their ejection seat from the rocket igniters the smaller cousins of their afterburner fire. The Tomcat spun in the air. It seemed to try to catch itself and continue on upward. But then, as they fell back down through 29,000 feet toward the ocean, three missiles caught the aircraft almost simultaneously.

The air above them exploded into an ugly orange mass, black smoke whirling implacably across the sky. The pilot shouted his protest, anger and frustration but also fear in his voice.

When they were well clear, the ejection seats separated from them, and their parachutes deployed. As the billowing fabric above them caught in the air, the pilot was jerked upward with a strong force. Not actually upward, but such a sudden decrease in his rate of descent that it felt as though he were being lifted up through the air.

The pilot saw his RIO's chute, although he couldn't tell if the man dangling underneath it was injured. And the Tomcats safely at altitude, they'd see the chutes—they'd let the carrier know.

For an aviator, the air around him was filthy. It seemed that every two hundred feet held another MiG. Most of the aircraft swerved away to avoid them, relying instinctively on international principles of military law, leaving them to descend in the clear blue sky alone.

But one didn't. It circled around him, the jet wash blasting him sideways under the chute. For a moment, the pilot thought that the jet wash would spill the air out of his chute, sending him plummeting down to the sea like a rock. He touched his auxiliary chute, praying that whoever packed it had been damned good.

But whether or not they were, he would never have a chance to find out. The aircraft turned and came back once again, and for just a flash, the Tomcat pilot could see the pilot in the cockpit turning to look at them. Although the man's face was masked, he felt like they made eye contact. Then the MiG rolled out overhead, came back down, and the American pilot saw a line of tracers spit out from its nose gun. His chute twisted him around to face the other way, but he twisted, shouting and screaming at the heavens, to get back in position. When he made it back, he could see that the RIO's parachute wasn't far below him. The man was already falling so fast that in a few moments he would be almost invisible.

And what of his RIO? The pilot started to curse. Had the bullets killed the RIO, or had the MiG pilot intentionally shredded the chute and left the RIO to the living hell of plummeting the remaining 20,000 feet, knowing that any second he would hit the ocean, watching it come up to meet him, the waves growing larger and larger, until he smashed into it like a watermelon dropped from 50 stories onto concrete?

The pilot prayed that his RIO was dead. Dead, or still conscious enough to rip off his oxygen mask and let the lack of oxygen render him unconscious.

The pilot was just swearing vengeance when the MiG came back for him.

USS **United States**
TFCC
1106 local (GMT +8)

The Taiwanese officer was standing against the back bulkhead, a look of horror on his face. "What the hell happened out there?" the admiral demanded of the terrified officer. "What did you say to him?"

"I . . . I explained your decisions and your position," the

major started, visions of his eventual execution flashing
into his mind. He would die for this, of that he was certain.

"Did you tell him to go active?" Coyote demanded.
"And did you tell him to break off prosecution of that
submarine?"

"I . . . I . . ." the major stopped, aware that his silence
gave his answer.

Lab Rat stepped forward, his face a grim mask. "Yes.
He did." Coyote had never seen the intelligence officer so
coldly furious. "My linguistic team monitored his transmissions." He held out a sheet of paper. "Here is the tran-
script."

Marshall P'eng
1115 local (GMT +8)

"We got them! We got them!" the SAR helo pilot shouted,
his voice exultant. "Both of them are breathing and conscious, although I think a pilot might have a broken leg.
It looks bad, anyway. We're headed to the carrier, Cricket.
We'll be back once we drop these guys off."

"Do not be too long," the captain said grimly. "Indeed,
I hope to finish this game before you can even return."
The captain switched to his own language and said,
"Break, Grasshopper One—initial datum three miles west
of your current location. Commence search pattern. I will
run the path perpendicular, tail wet."

The helo pilot's voice came back, distinctive in the
whop-whop effect from the vibrations the small helicopter
had on his voice. He evidently acknowledged the transmission, and a translator confirmed that, murmuring in the
American officer's ear so as not to disturb the captain.

The captain then directed the second SH-60 to a point
just north of that, and she spit out a pattern of sonobuoys
as well.

"Captain, sonar," the translator said. "Initial contact, subsurface contact, classified as possible Chinese diesel submarine." There was no change in the captain's expression as he said, "Localize and destroy. Immediately."

Grasshopper One
1108 local (GMT+8)

The pilot stared down at the surface of the ocean. Somewhere below him, at approximately 300 feet, was the Chinese diesel submarine. "Cricket, this is Grasshopper One. I'm in firing position. I await your instructions." He clicked the mike off, then turned to the copilot. "The three of us are all in firing position. It's up to the captain."

The copilot sighed. "Our submarine, but he will probably give that kill to the Americans. Perhaps it will make up for what he tried earlier."

"Perhaps he will. Be ready." The pilot glanced over and saw the copilot's finger was poised above his weapons switch.

A booming American voice came through on tactical, effectively ending the discussion. "Captain of *Marshall P'eng*, this is Admiral Grant. I would be pleased, sir, if your helicopter would eliminate that submarine from this world."

The pilot glanced over at the copilot, a rare smile stretching across his face. Almost immediately, they heard their captain's response. "Acknowledged, Admiral. It will be our pleasure." The captain's voice switched to their own language, and said, "Do it now. Both weapons—let there be no need for a second engagement."

"Yes, Captain. Immediately." Even as the pilot spoke, the copilot was toggling off both torpedoes.

Jungwei
1110 local (GMT +8)

The hard, shimmering ping of the active sonar cut through
the still compartment like a knife. The captain sucked in
a hard breath, and his face turned pale. Every man on the
ship knew it immediately—the most deadly foe of a submarine was a dipping helo. Two of them working together,
or one working with a surface ship, was the most fearful
adversary any of them ever faced.

A second active sonar shimmered in the water, this one
higher pitched and more insistent. The captain's guts felt
as though they were about to explode. An active sonobuoy,
operating on a different bearing from the dipping sonar.
With those two sources, the helos undoubtedly had them
localized.

"All forward flank, hard right rudder. Make your depth
six hundred feet." With that maneuver, he hoped to create
a mass of air bubbles in the water that would distract the
torpedoes that must surely be ready to launch. Six hundred
feet was near the maximum of the ancient diesel's capabilities, but there was no choice now. Even more dangerous, operating at that depth would make escaping the
submarine, should they be hit, virtually impossible.

In theory, at least, the submarine would create a second
target in the water that would distract the torpedoes, giving
the submarine a chance to disappear in the thermocline.
Then, if the sonars were unable to relocate them, the submarine would creep away stealthily, putting distance between itself and the attackers, before resuming transit
speed.

In theory, at least. As a practical matter, both the dipping
sonar and the sonobuoys were capable of being set at different depths, and both pilots would undoubtedly attempt
that. Additionally, the depth of the Taiwanese frigate's
towed array could be varied, and it could be repositioned
in deeper water, although it would take longer to settle
down and generate stable bearings.

Even with those disadvantages, the situation was absolutely critical. Escaping a dipping sonar was no mean feat, and the captain had done it only a couple times in the simulator.

A third active sonobuoy joined into the cacophony. The submarine's hull was bombarded with acoustic energy, each sonar refining the submarine's location further until it was practically a pinpoint in the ocean.

The deck heeled underneath them as the submarine made its hard turn. Any could tell without looking at the sonar display that they were generating massive amounts of acoustic energy on their own. "Decoys, noise makers," he ordered, dumping the countermeasures into the water around his air bubble.

The deck tilted down as she dove at her top speed for the bottom of the ocean. The old hull creaked and groaned around them, and just for one fearful moment he wondered if that would be their fate rather than a torpedo. The noise around them was increasing, almost deafening them, and he could see the stark terror on everyone's face.

Suddenly, every noise stopped. The water around them was silent, punctuated only by the noise of their decoys and their own propeller. A young helmsman, on his first cruise aboard a submarine, let out a stifled yelp of joy. He turned to his captain, his eyes shining, relief on his face. The relief turned to puzzlement when no one else joined in. Stark fear crept back in.

In those final moments, the captain did not have the heart to tell the young man that the reason the noise had stopped was to avoid distracting the torpedoes that were surely on their way into the water now.

Staring at the young man's face, the captain made an instant, irrevocable decision. "Emergency blow—emergency blow!"

The officer of the deck hit the valve that would immediately blast compressed air into every ballast tank. The captain felt the momentum change immediately, as the deck seemed to rise up under him. They lost the depth they'd just gained in seconds and rocketed up toward the surface of the water.

He could hear them now, the hard, grinding whine of the small torpedo propellers as they bore in on his boat. At least if they were hit now, perhaps they would have enough momentum to reach the surface and give the crew a chance to survive. And at that moment, that was all the captain cared about—not politics, not Taiwan, not the court-martial or certain disgrace and instant execution that would await him if he returned home. All he cared about was that his crew would have a chance to live.

The first torpedo encountered the noise makers and the mass of air bubbles simultaneously, and its tiny electronic brain froze in a moment of indecision. It ran nose-first into one of the noise makers, fatally jarring a critical component. It continued on, executing a wide turn to the right, until it ran out of fuel.

The second torpedo was luckier. It entered the water well to the north of the noise makers and cavitation and began its search circle. Almost immediately, it acquired the enticing sounds of the submarine heading away from it. It changed course, locked on, and bore in steadily.

Another round of noise makers failed to distract it. It simply brushed passed them, driving unwaveringly toward the delectable sounds of the submarine's machinery.

As the submarine heard it approaching, bearing constant and range decreasing, her captain tried one last series of desperate measures. He threw the submarine into another tight turn—tight at least by submarine standards—hoping desperately to generate another knuckle in the water. But as he did so, the torpedo adjusted its course, and impacted the submarine just aft of the control room.

The immediate force of the explosion buckled the old hull and frigid seawater came pouring in. The submarine was at two hundred feet, still rising, and it took several moments for the incoming rush of water to overcome her negative buoyancy.

The water blasted through the compartment with the force of a sledgehammer, pulverizing three crewman against the bullhead. The watertight door between the passageway and a control room buckled almost immediately. The first few streams of water were ice pick-hard as they hammered into the control room, finding their targets in the electronics panel and immediately shorting out electrical power. The submarine plunged into blackness for a moment, and then battery-operated emergency red lights came on. In a way, it would have been better if they had not.

The captain shouted out orders, urging the crew toward the emergency egress hatch, but panic and confusion ruled. Most knew what to do for emergency escape, and they grabbed emergency escape breathing devices and tried to wade through the increasingly deep water to the escape trunk. Three made it up the ladder into the tower safely, but the rising flow of water caught the rest of them.

Ten seconds after the hatch buckled, it gave way completely. Seawater flooded through, a solid tidal wave immediately capturing those few who were still struggling for the ladder. The three men inside the escape hatch had time to pull it shut, gazing down on the stricken faces below them as they were swept away, and dog it shut. They donned their breathing devices, listening to the awful screaming beneath them. They could feel the submarine already starting to settle lower in the water, heading back down for the depths. They opened the valves full, to flood the compartment as quickly as possible.

The minutes ticked over, and each one knew despair. Finally, the trunk was flooded sufficiently to equalize the pressure and allow them to leave the dying submarine. By that time, the bottom of the hull was approaching four hundred feet in depth.

The three left, and the buoyancy of their breathing devices pulled them toward the surface. As they ascended, they exhaled continuously, trying desperately to keep the change in pressure from rupturing their lungs. The other denizens of the sea happening by stared at them in mild astonishment, then turned to follow them up.

Below them, the remaining crew members' deaths were just as terrible, if far less graphic. The middle section of the submarine was immediately flooded and then the forward one-third. But the aft section retained, through some miracle of engineering, its watertight integrity. The submarine was bow down so hard that the forward bulkheads became the deck, and crippled and wounded men piled up there like rag dolls. Several were still able to move, and tried desperately to reach the aft egress trunk against the force of gravity, with no success. That did not keep them from trying, even as the submarine sank deeper into the water.

In the meantime, the bank of batteries broke free and ruptured. One smashed into a sailor, crushing him instantly. The others came in contact with water, generating chlorine gas, killing the men before they could drown.

The submarine headed for the bottom quickly now, and reached it three minutes later. Along the way, the remainder of the compartments flooded, forcing the deadly gas out into the sea.

Above the crushed hull that held their shipmates, the three men in the water waited in silent horror as they stared at the circling fins.

USS **United States**
TFCC
1200 local (GMT +8)

"They . . . they shot them out of the air!" the pilot shouted, his voice stark with horror. "I had two chutes, then the MiG—damn them all, kill them all!"

Coyote stared at the screen, horror on his face. Every aviator in the room could feel his blood turn to ice as well. To punch out, to take that risk, watch the aircraft that had been so much a part of you destroyed, looking frantically for your wingman, and praying he would survive the ejection and eventually be picked up . . . well, that was hard enough without facing the possibility of being strafed.

In quiet moments, they had all had discussions, had made those quiet decisions about what they would do. Most, when they would speak at all about it, agreed that the preferred course of action would be to strip off one's oxygen mask and pass out from hypoxia on the way down. But there was always the chance that at lower altitude the oxygen might revive you, and what would that be like, to wake to the sensation of falling?

No, this action was completely indefensible. Coyote would make sure the Chinese paid for it, and paid dearly.

"I want them destroyed," he said evenly, his voice a deadly threat. "Destroyed completely."

TWENTY-FIVE

Tomcat 155
Monday, September 23
1600 local (GMT +8)

Just as they were approaching their fourth tanker rendezvous, a voice came over tactical. "Triple nickels, this is
Big Eyes. Be advised that the tribal council meets tonight
on CBS in minutes three. Do not acknowledge this transmission." The jamming resumed as soon as the AWACS
finished transmission.

"Break it," Tombstone ordered. Every trace of weariness
was instantly swept out of his body.

"Tribal council—air activity, on the ground. CBS is the
airfield, and it started three minutes ago."

"No launches then, yet."

"No. That would be 'You're voted off the island.' "

"Well, then, no time like the present." Tombstone
boosted the aircraft into afterburner and felt the G-forces
push him back against the seat. "The tanker should be
waiting for us. We'll just make the rendezvous a bit earlier.
If we need more gas, we'll just ask for it." The rendezvous
point had been preplanned using a given speed of advance,
but there was some leeway in the schedule to allow for

headwinds, tailwinds, and other vagaries of flight.

"Tombstone, that right engine—are you watching it?"

"Yes. Still well within normal parameters." Even as he spoke, Tombstone knew what Jason's point was. The outlet temperature on the right engine had been increasing steadily over the last two hours. Not alarmingly, and not outside of normal operating range, but still increasing. The left temperature data showed no change.

"Shouldn't Big Eyes know about that?" Jason asked.

"I thought about that. But there's not much he can do about it, is there?" Tombstone said gently, counting on Jason's experience and general levelheadedness to keep him from panic.

"No, I guess not. If we have to, we can always bingo to Japan. They won't refuse us landing rights."

At least right now, they won't. But there's no telling, not if we're outbound from a bombing mission. But Tombstone did not voice the thought and instead agreed, "Yeah, and the *United States* is in the area as well."

"There's the tanker." Greene said. "One o'clock, low."

I remember when my eyes were that sharp. "Got him," Tombstone said, when he finally saw the tiny speck in the air. He corrected his course slightly.

Due to the jamming, the final refueling was conducted without radio communications. Tombstone had practiced the procedure many times before, and the tanker was obviously prepared for them.

"Eight minutes," Tombstone said. He concentrated his attention ahead of them for the island. If their inertia navigation system was operating correctly, it should be dead ahead.

"They've got to know something is happening," Jason said. "I mean, you don't get your entire electromagnetic spectrum blanked out for nothing."

"They might know something, but they won't be able to find us. Not unless they get real lucky and get a visual. And mind you, I'm not ruling that out—they've got to be worried about this operation going down."

"There it is," Greene announced, peering around Tomb-stone's ejection seat to look out of the windscreen. "I got it."

"Roger, I got the island." Tombstone's radar screen was still a massive static. "Commencing final. Let's hope those ships haven't moved."

He tipped the Tomcat over into a steep dive, and felt the acceleration shove him back into his seat. He tensed his muscles and grunted, performing the M1 maneuver designed to keep blood flowing to the brain during high G-force situations. He could hear Jason's breathing over the ICS, and knew he was performing the same maneuver. His G-suit automatically inflated as it sensed the increase in G-forces, forcing blood of out of his legs and into his torso. The bands around his arms constricted as well, but any discomfort was quickly washed away by the adrenaline.

"There they are," Tombstone said, and he made a slight course correction. Ahead of him, just to the right, were three tiny specs of flat gray on the ocean. At altitude, they had appeared to be simply wave tops, but as he descended, their outlines became more and more distinct.

"They're on-loading!" Jason said. "Look, small boats!"

On closer examination, Tombstone could see the small craft cutting wakes perpendicular to the whitecaps as the landing craft ferried men and equipment from shore to the transports.

"They're not approaching—the coastline must be too rugged here. Maybe rocks, maybe something else. But you can be damned sure that they know where the good beaches are to the south. They'll have to, so they can move so fast that the Japanese won't have a clue what hit them."

"No fire control radar, Tombstone," Greene said unhappily. "Big Eye's cutting it close."

"He knows the schedule—he's checking on us," Tomb-stone said with more confidence than he felt.

The antiship missiles under his wings were virtually useless without his radar to guide them in on their targets.

Oh, sure, he could try a manual line of bearing shot, but the probability of kill went way down.

"Three minutes," Jason called out.

Now Tombstone could see the activity on the rocky shore. There was a mass of movement, both of troop formations and individuals straggling about singly. Nearest to the beach, there was an orderly queue, as men and equipment waited their turn on the landing craft. Further inland, there was still confusion, as the troops tried to find their proper place in line.

Although amphibious assault looked like a sudden, violent disgorging of everything at once, in truth it was as carefully orchestrated as flight deck operations. The details of who went ashore first—and thus, who was embarked last—occupied the nightmares of more than one amphibious operations planner. There was nothing worse than having your ground troops off first, followed by your long-range artillery. The enemy forces would simply decimate the men first without the artillery there to make them keep their heads down.

"Two minutes, Tombstone—Mom, I mean." Jason's joke was an attempt to break the tension. If the radar didn't clear, then they would have to make a pass and come around again. And every second that they remained overhead increased the chances of a mobile antiair installation or other weapon getting off a lucky shot.

Tombstone heard a sharp *plink*. "Small arms fire." The Tomcat could take a lot of damage, as long as the rounds missed the hydraulic signs and fuel tanks.

"Let's get the hell out of here," Jason said. "I don't want to be around when they . . ." Just then, a sharp *crack* echoed to the cockpit, and a shudder ran through the Tomcat. Jason screamed.

"Jason!" Tombstone shouted. "Where are you hit?"

"Arm. Straight through," Jason said through clenched teeth. "Right through the bicep."

"How bad is it?" Tombstone asked, a sick feeling starting in his gut.

"Lots of blood, but it punched straight through the muscle." Tombstone could hear the strain in his voice. "Damned small cockpit. I'm putting on a direct pressure bandage. That will slow it down some. It hurts like hell, but it ain't going to kill me."

"Descending on final," Tombstone said calmly. At some point during any mission, you simply had to decide whether or not you were going to trust everyone else to do their jobs as well as you were doing yours. If you guessed wrong, you wound up dead.

In a normal operation, that trust was normally built up by repeated training and constant familiarity with each other's operations. By the end of battle group workups, everyone in the battle group pretty much knew who the weak sisters were and who could be counted on to do what they were supposed to be doing. Even such minor details as a ship's station-keeping ability was factored into the equation.

But now, there was no experience to fall back on. It was just a matter of trust. Trust in the Air Force, and trust in his uncle.

So far, everything had gone right. That alone was enough to worry him.

"Ninety seconds," Jason announced. "Sir, we've got to consider the possibility of an abort."

"No abort," Tombstone said. "Worst-case, we come around for another pass." *And I hope to hell it doesn't come down to that. Because I've got a very, very bad feeling about this.*

"Roger, copy," Jason said, his voice taking on the impassive tone of a man who has decided to place his life in the hands of his pilot. "Based on visual, recommend you come right two degrees for better alignment."

"Roger, concur." Tombstone made the minor course correction, his eyes moving rapidly over his instruments, back out to the beach in front of him, and then to check the sky around him for contacts.

The transports were now clearly visible, and he could

make out the details of their superstructure. The flat flight decks had movement all over them, and he thought he could see people turning to stare and point at him. They must hear the Tomcat by now, and the more experienced among them would immediately recognize the throaty growl of the Navy's most potent fighter.

"Sixty seconds," Jason announced. "On altitude, on speed. Looking good, sir."

Just as Jason finished speaking, the radar screen fuzzed out completely, then went dead. He could hear Jason swearing in the back seat.

"Circuit breaker," Tombstone said, just as Jason restored power to the screen. Solid green fuzz for a few seconds, but then the static quickly resolved into individual contacts. He could hear buzz of chatter over tactical as well, and then heard a familiar voice.

Batman, is that you? I hope so, old friend. Because if I'm in trouble, at least I know you're in the area and you'll do everything you can to get to me.

"All right, triple nickels, you got sixty seconds of clear air. Get in, get out, because the picture's going to shit again after that. You want to be long gone before anybody's in a position to . . . ah, shit. Triple nickel, you are voted off the island, estimated departure in ten miles."

Tombstone groaned. It had all gone too smoothly so far, entirely too smoothly. There was always going to be a screwup, and you just hoped and prayed that it occurred early enough that you could take it into consideration before you committed on target.

"Thirty seconds. Your dot, sir," Jason said.

"Take it, Jason. I need to keep my eyes on what's going on around us."

"My dot, aye." Jason selected and released the antiship weapons, and Tombstone felt the Tomcat jolt up as first one and then the other of the heavy antiship missiles left his wings. "New target to you, sir."

"Your dot, Jason," Tombstone said. He kept his gaze moving around horizon, searching for the first faint trace

of a contrail or jet exhaust that would indicate an enemy
fighter. But there was nothing on radar and nothing in the
sky, either, as far as he could tell. The greatest threat was
from the ground troops. "IP in five seconds ... four ...
three ... two ... one," Jason said, and then he toggled off
the antipersonnel weapons. That left Tombstone with only
three AMRAAM antiair missiles left on his wings.

"Break left, break left," Jason said. "We're out of here."

Tombstone swung the now-lighter Tomcat around the
left, kicking in the afterburners as he did so. With enemy
fighters just fifteen minutes out, he was in complete agreement with Big Eyes. He wanted to be long gone before
they were in range for a visual.

"Say goodnight, Gracie," Big Eyes announced, and
again their communication circuits, radar screens, and
everything else that operated in the electromagnetic spectrum was overwhelmed with static.

"Man, I never thought I'd be so relieved to have no
radar," Jason said.

"Yes, me too. Now let's get the hell out of Dodge, find
Texaco, and head for home.

"Yes, I think that's a—shit!"

"I see it," Tombstone said, and stared down at the offending temperature gauge. With all his attention focused
on the sky, he had committed the first major sin of any
naval aviator. He had not kept up his scan, and while he
wasn't looking, the exhaust temperature indicator for the
right engine had crept steadily upward. Now the needle
quivered just below the red area, as though undecided as
to whether to creep up even higher.

"Don't do it, please, don't do it," Jason said quietly, as
though through sheer force of will power he could force
the engine to cool down.

"They're built to a heavy tolerance factor," Tombstone
said. "At least fifty percent over normal temps before you
even have to start sweating, and another twenty-five percent after that before the engine is in danger."

"You certain about that, sir?"

"Oh yes, I'm certain." With a pang, he remembered just how he had come to learn that particular fact about the Tomcat. It had been during Tomboy's early days as a test pilot, when her time was consumed by memorizing the facts and figures that constituted the normal operating envelope for the Tomcat. She had to know every fuel consumption curve, every speed versus angle of attack diagram and then every safety margin built in, just so she could try to push the envelope out just a little bit.

Tombstone's decades of experience in compartmentalizing his thoughts kicked in. He shoved away the thoughts of Tomboy, feeling not the slightest bit of regret as he did so, and concentrated on trying to stay alive. She would have understood, if anyone would.

"Options?" Tombstone asked, although they both knew exactly what the choices were.

"Japan or the *United States*," Greene said. They were both within range—but both had problems, as well. Getting to Iceland meant heading directly back toward the fighters that had launched, and Japan . . . well, Japan was an entirely different set of problems.

Will Japan even let us land? I'm not so certain, not if they find out what we've been up to. Because the last thing Japan wants is a one-on-one confrontation with China, and that's what she's going to get once the Russians figure out what happened.

"Our first mission and we blow our cover," Tombstone said. "Not a good deal."

"Very much not a good deal. But I'm not sure that that engine's going to make it all the way back up to Adak, are you?"

"Maybe . . . no. No, it won't," Tombstone admitted.

Suddenly, a thought occurred to him. The *United States* wasn't the only aircraft carrier around. He had heard Batman's voice on tactical, and now he stared at his HUD and mentally reconstructed the last picture he'd seen there. Yes, *Jefferson* was within range, and a good deal closer that either of their other bingo options.

"*Jefferson*," he said, and the moment he spoke the ship's name he knew that she was the answer. "You got a frequency for her on your kneeboard?"

"Yes, sure, but she's a supply depot, not an operational carrier," Jason protested. Even as he spoke, he was thumbing through the laminated plastic cards, looking for the communications index.

"Oh, I'm willing to bet she's a good deal more than that," Tombstone said fiercely. "Batman's in command, and you can bet your ass whatever capabilities she had when she left port, she's exceeded them by now. He's put her through her paces, fixed everything that could be fixed, and I'm willing to bet that his first priority was restoring at least some of her flight deck capabilities."

"Here it is." Green reeled off the frequency and Tombstone punched them into the communications panel.

Then, with intense feeling of fierce pride, he said, "Homeplate, this is Stoney. I got a problem. Over."

TWENTY-SIX

USS **Jefferson**
Monday, September 23
2200 local (GMT +8)

Batman paced the compartment, an angry, fearsome presence. TFCC was minimally manned, little more than a radio watch. Yet he could not avoid the compulsion to be here when anything was happening. He paced the small compartment just as he had in the old days, agitated, trying to think of some way he could help, something he could do.

But there was nothing. After all, what was *Jefferson* now except a spare parts depot? Oh sure, he understood the importance of spare parts in supporting the mission, and knew that he wasn't just out here killing time. After all, not everybody could be on the front lines, could they? The tooth to kill ratio was always about ten to one, meaning that the fighting forces were always outnumbered by their own support forces by a factor of ten.

Still, why did it have to be *Jefferson*? Hell, he didn't even have a normal complement of communication gear—they had cannibalized his crypto to supply other ships, and he was left with just one secure circuit. He listened to the battle going on over it, longing with all of his soul to be part of it, if not in the air, at least in command of the forces.

Suddenly, a new voice came over. "Homeplate, meet me on . . ." and the voice reeled off a frequency, asking him to reconfigure his secure gear to listen on that channel.

Batman turn to his TAO, or what passed for one on the *Jefferson* now. "What the hell?"

"New channel assignment, I guess?"

Batman felt the overwhelming sense of frustration. Not only was he not permitted to be in the conflict, he was now not even allowed to listen to it. "Do it," he snarled.

"Roger, sir." The TAO made the arrangements for the frequency change, and then turned to him, a puzzled look on his face. "Admiral, that voice sound familiar to you?"

Batman played it back in his mind. A smile started across his face. "Yes. Yes, it sure as hell did."

As a light went on indicating that the channel assignment had been changed, Batman picked up the mike, and said, "Stoney, this is Homeplate. Go ahead. Over."

Tomcat 155
2203 local (GMT +8)

Tombstone smiled at the sound of his old wingman's voice. There would never need to be call signs or recognition codes between the two of them, not when they recognized each other's voice so easily. He imagined the look of surprise on Batman's face, could almost see that shit-eating grin spread from ear to ear. Well, there'd be time enough to explain when he got onboard—and that was the first problem.

"You doing okay back there?" he asked over ICS. He glanced in the mirror and saw Jason's pale, strained face.

"I'm fine. It's not serious, I swear. Hurts like hell, but it isn't going to kill me."

"Yeah, I know. I'm not worried about that." Tombstone tried for more confidence in his voice than he felt. "It's just that you're getting my cockpit all fouled up."

"Yeah." Jason tried to smile, but was unable to quite pull it off. Tombstone switched back to tactical. "Homeplate, I got a situation up here. You got any deck space?"

"That's about all I got, as you well know," Batman answered. "How come you're not heading for big brother?"

"The circumstances are . . . ah . . . a bit difficult," Tombstone said, not wanting to go into detail over the circuit. No matter how highly classified any radio circuit was, he wasn't sure enough about any system in the U.S. inventory to make him comfortable discussing this. "How about an arresting wire and catapult? Are those operational?"

"Yes. We just use them for post-maintenance flight checks. You're serious about this?"

"Dead serious, Batman. Clear me out a spot, will you? I can't head for big brother for very good reasons. I'll explain it all what I get down on deck, okay?"

"How do you know they're not listening in?" Batman asked.

"You remember that radio installed just before you left? Well, if you check with your communications officer, you'll find Pete has some very special instructions that you know nothing about. Just for situations like this. Now, are we going to stand here talking about old times or are you going to get me some deck space?"

"Give us fifteen minutes—hell, I have to wake up half the civilians. But we'll be ready for you, Tombstone. We'll be ready."

As Tombstone signed off, he glanced again in the back seat. Jason appeared to have nodded off. Before he ended the transmission, he said, "And Homeplate? I'll need medical assistance right after we get down. My backseater."

"Roger, Tombstone. We'll be waiting for you. And unless you lost your touch, you won't need the safety barrier."

TWENTY-SEVEN

Cruiser officers and crew were usually known to be fairly tight-assed, cold professionals when it came to their jobs. But as they watched the number of confirmed kills building on their screens, the captain could hear an undercurrent of muted exclamations and cheers breaking out around the compartment. One of the electronic warfare technicians, commonly known as earthworms, even ran over to give the air tracks supervisor a high five. They both broke away immediately after, looking a bit ashamed of their emotional outbreak, but neither was able to completely hide the grin on his face.

Oh, hell. Let them celebrate. It's not often that you know you're going to be painting twenty fighter profiles on your superstructure within the next week.

For indeed, the computer had awarded confirmed kills for every missile they'd launched. A second shot on any one target had not been necessary, and all the shots had been well inside parameters. Even the destroyer, with her six missiles total, had each downed the target.

Yes, overall, an impressive record. But even as he joined in the muted celebration, the captain felt a sense of uneasiness sweep over him. Twenty missiles, twenty kills? No misses, no mechanical problems? Sure, maybe—but that hadn't been his experience with technology. Parts rub, seals go bad, a stray electron hits the wrong beam of light—shit happens. And while he'd be glad to take the twenty missiles–twenty kills record if warranted, something deep inside of him worried.

"Lead aircraft inside their engagement zone," the TAO announced. "Captain, we have time for four more shots on the far edge of the MEZ, if you want them?"

"Hell, yes, I want them," the captain said, and this time the cheers in combat rose to audible levels. He watched what had quickly become such a smooth operation as four more missiles were launched.

"Captain—I have aircraft inbound from the north."

"The north! What the hell?" He listened as his TAO called out the data and began an initial query of the aircraft.

"Looks like one of our fighters, sir. And it's breaking IFF Mode Four. Whoever it is, it is definitely a friendly. No way I can target."

"Call the carrier. Ask them if one of their boys is lost. Because he came out of nowhere as far as I could see— down from the Kurile Islands. And," the TAO continued, a look of worry growing on his face, "he's headed for the *Jefferson.*" Now worry dominated his expression. "Captain, the *Jefferson* doesn't have air protection right now— and if we're going to do something, we need to do it now. Should be within weapons range of the *Jefferson* in approximately five minutes."

"Call the carrier, ask him what else is going on. And stand by to take it out."

USS **United States**
2235 local (GMT +8)

Coyote listened to the request for information coming over the circuit, and then turned to his TAO, a puzzled look on his face. "Who the hell is that? Some tanker or something? The Air Force get lost again?"

"I don't know, sir—but if it's squawking Mode Four, it's definitely a friendly."

Coyote swore quietly. "I'm going to kill some son of a bitch when I get back Stateside. What the hell are they doing, flying in this area without letting me know?"

Suddenly, a familiar voice came over an open, nonencrypted circuit, using designated code names instead of their real identities. "Big Brother, this is Homeplate. Be advised I have a friendly inbound for recovery—no time to generate message traffic or SPINS on it. But we're taking her on board. I can't explain anything else, Big Brother—just trust me on this one. Home plate out."

"Batman!" Coyote roared. "Damn it, tell me what's going on here."

But there was silence on the circuit. Coyote turned to his communications officer, frustrated. "Where is he?"

The communications officer shook his head. "*Jefferson* only has one classified circuit. If he has a contact inbound, he's probably talking to him on that. He can't do both at the same time, sir. He just came on this frequency to let us know not to shoot."

USS **United States**
TFCC
Monday, September 23
2250 local (GMT +8)

Coyote paced the compartment, barely able to contain himself. The roar inside TFCC was continuous as the air boss and the flight deck crew raced to launch every fighter in the inventory. There was so little time, so little.

As the wave of Chinese aircraft rolled in toward the carrier, the cruiser would attempt to eliminate as many of them as possible. Even the destroyer, operating under the cruiser's guidance, could attempt to get off a couple of shots with her shorter range missiles while the enemy was inside the missile engagement zone, or MEZ.

But MEZ was a painfully small window of opportunity and within minutes the Chinese aircraft would be in the FEZ, or fighter engagement zone, and that was where the true test of skill, training, equipment and people would take place. American lives would then be on the line as the fighters took them on one by one.

"How many in the first wave?" Coyote asked.

"It looks like about seventy, sir," the TAO said. "Using the cruiser's data."

And the cruiser's data would be better than most, given the powerful SPY-1 radar. Still, there was a chance she could be mistaken—there might be fewer. Some processing error, human or machine, could lead to false contacts.

No. Don't even consider that. Go with the numbers your people can give you, don't depend on false hope. Because if seventy aircraft are inbound now, you can bet that there are another seventy behind them somewhere, already starting to launch. We'll have to go for maximum damage from the very first, no quarter given or expected, in order to avoid being overwhelmed in very short order.

He clicked the mike on. "Weapons free, all Chinese forces declared hostile. Good luck people—let's make them pay for this."

Batman and Tombstone had known this, he knew now. The complete and utter frustration of sitting in TFCC, watching the intense engagement take place without your participation. There could be no more frustrating feeling, your fingers clenching, moving involuntarily as though you were in the lead aircraft yourself. Why hadn't they told him it was this difficult?

"First engagement, sir. The cruiser's targeted ten of them—we have a launch, we have a launch."

On the tactical display, a series of ten missile symbols rippled into being, all barreling straight up from the cruiser and toward the incoming flight. The destroyer added another three long-range missiles to the pack. Although her slower fire control system was not able to process as many immediately, the Aegis was able to provide targeting data directly to her.

"Seventy minus thirteen, what's that leave?" Coyote asked.

"Fifty-seven, sir," the TAO answered, leaving unspoken the words that everyone was thinking.

Fifty-seven if all the missiles found their marks. And if, in the process of shooting them down, our own people don't screw up badly enough to get in the path of the incoming. Because we can't afford to lose even one of our own, particularly not to friendly fire. Not with the odds the way they are now.

And how many waves of seventy fighters will the Chinese send out? We don't even have an accurate count of their air inventory, damn it.

Doesn't matter. Right now, if it flies, it dies, and that's all there is to it.

Hornet 106
2251 local (GMT +8)

Thor was totally focused, and was ignoring the quick thrill of adrenaline in his blood. Discipline, that's what it was about—the ability to control the blood lust that rose up in you as you contemplated what was to come, to control the fear that lay right behind it. Because this was the moment you trained for, dreamed about, you knew everything about in the world except how it would actually feel when you went into combat for the first time.

But this wasn't Thor's first time. Oh, no, not by a long shot.

"Packer flight, picture," the monotone voice of the Hawkeye broke it. "Inbound on radial two seven zero, three waves of twenty units and one of ten. Composition fighters, supported by Mainstay command and control aircraft as well. Hornet one zero six, target lead," and the Hawkeye continued, doling out assignments to maintain air clearance between the units. "All flights, observe missile engagement zone safety restrictions. Launch from cruiser is going down on your three o'clock at this time. Stand well clear, guys—it's going to get messy."

Thor throttled back slightly, and felt the Hornet sink gently beneath him. He'd get his chance—no point making the problem any more complicated than it had to be.

"All flights, Hawkeye. Cruiser has launched another ten missiles. Stay well clear of missile engagement zone."

Twenty-three total? Well, we appreciate all the help we can get, boys and girls, but it's going to come down to knife fighting. And that's my business.

USS Lake Champlain
2251 local (GMT +8)

Norfolk watched the missiles arrow out on virtually identical paths, then break apart as a shotgun load would do. Each missile was assigned to a different target, but the computer was instantaneously calculating the probability of a kill and whether or not a second weapon was needed on any one aircraft. Each missile took its guidance originally from the computer on board the cruiser, with initial course and target location fed into it just microseconds before it launched.

During the first few moments of flight, the picture inside the missile's tiny brain was updated. Right now, combat was as busy as it ever would be, monitoring the initial stages of the flight and preparing any instantaneous corrections that needed to be done. As each missile continued on toward its target, it would finally acquire the enemy aircraft with its own seeker head, and at that point use its own illumination to guide it to the final kill.

"At least the fighters are staying out of the way," the TAO said. "Good thing, too."

Norfolk just grinned. He knew that many members of the cruiser community felt that aircraft were virtually obsolete, that a cruiser could completely protect a carrier from every possible air threat. But he wasn't of that school, having seen far too many fights in too many parts of the world to believe that the ship was as invulnerable as most people thought. It was the low-tech stuff that screwed you up the worst, he had learned. Mines, small boats with handheld launchers, the stuff you didn't see until it was right on you.

"Reporting target acquisition, missiles one through twelve," the TAO announced. "On terminal—*bingo*." He turned excitedly to the captain. "Ten kills, sir."

"Ten kills assigned by the computer," the captain corrected. A computer's decision that a missile had intercepted its target, detonated successfully, and eliminated a threat was a good deal different from seeing the fireball yourself. "Let's wait for the air crew confirmation."

The TAO looked slightly taken aback, but he was too busy with his duties to worry about it.

Nonfolk turned his attention back to the screen. *I hope you're ready to go, boys and girls. Because this is going to get very nasty before very long. I don't know how many fighters they have in their inventory, but they're certain to have more aircraft than I have missiles onboard. Even with the* United States*'s help, even with perfect targeting, there's no way I can take them all. Not in time.*

Tomcat 203
2254 local (GMT +8)

"Whoa!" Bird Dog hollered. "You see that, Music? Did you ever see such a beautiful thing in your life?"

Music craned his head around to look out past Bird Dog's ejection seat. In the air ahead, there were nine small fireballs, ugly and obscene against the blue sky.

But it wasn't nine fireballs—it was eighteen men. Sure, Chinese, sure—but aviators just like he was. For a moment, Music felt his stomach curl into a hard knot. Was he the only one who felt this way, who realized that the people they were blasting out of the air were just regular guys? He had to be—no one else was worried. And if there's one thing that Music was at this point, it was very, very worried.

"Looks great, sir," he agreed heartily, wishing to hell he was anywhere else except in the back seat of this Tomcat.

"You're damn right it looks great." Bird Dog shouted. "What you're looking at is a better chance of us going home in one piece with our aircraft around us!"

Music looked down at his console. The computer was reporting ten direct hits, and then it added another three to the total as the destroyer's missiles found their targets. Music glanced back up at the sky and counted again. Nine, ten, eleven, twelve—no, there were only twelve fireballs, not thirteen.

"I count twelve, sir," Music said.

"Yes, twelve—that's what I've got. Hold on, Music—it's almost our turn."

"But sir . . . the computer shows thirteen kills. I don't get it. What about the other aircraft?"

"Don't worry, kid. There'll be enough for all of us."

"But sir, if they say it's thirteen, but it's really only twelve, they might miss one."

"Give me a vector, Music," Bird Dog ordered. "Forget it, just worry about what you see. Save it for another twenty years until you're an admiral, OK? For now, give me a target."

"Not yet, sir. Another wave of missiles is outbound."

Bird Dog swore quietly. "I burn more fuel up here than I do weapons."

As Music listened to his pilot bitch, he tried to keep track of the fireballs. But with Bird Dog wheeling around in the sky, staying clear of the missile engagements while still ready to pounce in the second, it was difficult to stay oriented. Sometimes he thought he counted ten, other times thirteen. There was no way to tell for sure. Maybe the computer was right—maybe a few fireballs were hidden behind the others. But somehow, he didn't think so.

"Fastball, you watching this?" Bird Dog said over tactical. "You stay in place, buddy. None of that bullshit from before."

"Roger, Lead," Bird Dog heard Rat acknowledge, and knew she got his message. Fastball might be a hothead, but Rat seemed to have some degree of control over him. She was simply reminding him of that fact.

"That Rat, she's something else," Bird Dog said admiringly. "If it were me, I'd never climb back in the cockpit with that cowboy. She's got all the right stuff. She even saved Fastball's ass last cruise—you remember, when she punched them out when they were in that flame-out on final?"

"Yes, Bird Dog." So that was the ideal, was it? To be bloodthirsty? And even Rat was managing to show all the right stuff, was she? Even a woman. Music felt his own personal failings more strongly than he ever had before. And the worst of it was, there was no one he could talk to about it.

Tomcat 209
2255 local (GMT +8)

"I don't know why you're so pleasant to them," Fastball snapped. "The way everybody acts, you'd think Bird Dog was some sort of god."

Rat bit back the comments she longed to make. Sure, Bird Dog was . . . well, Bird Dog. Abrasive, arrogant and sometimes downright infuriating. But outside of the admiral, through a weird combination of events, Bird Dog probably had more combat time than any other pilot on the ship, including the CAG. Okay, so he punched out more times than anyone had a right to expect in a career, but he brought his RIO back safe and sound. And that's not something you could say about every pilot, now, was it?

So what are you doing back in this cockpit? This idiot almost got you killed twice, and you still fly with him? Are you out of your mind?

It was me or a nugget, a colder part of her mind responded. *And a nugget, he stands no chance of coming back—somebody has to keep his ass out of trouble.*

And that someone would be you?

Yes.

Stupid idea. But in that last furious conversation in the ready room, when they'd almost come to blows, she thought she had straightened him out. There would be no more of this pilot attitude, no more ignoring her and never giving her the dot. They would fight the aircraft as equals, and he would listen to her opinion. Even on matters involving flying, although she acknowledged she would have to defer to him on those.

"Music, picture," the E-2 said. "You copied my last?"

"Roger. Give me a target, hot guy," she heard Bird Dog answer for his RIO. A vector to a target followed, and then the E-2 Hawkeye coordinating the air battle jumped in on the circuit.

"Tomcat two zero niner, come right to course 000 to rejoin your lead. Acknowledge."

"What?!" Fastball started swearing.

"You heard the man, Fastball," Rat said crisply. "Now move your ass. Let's get going."

"But the fight's back here," Fastball whined. "It's not fair, it's not fair, I'm going to—"

Rat cut him off. "You're going to do exactly as you were told," she said crisply. "Because if you don't, you will be explaining to the CAG and the admiral why you're back on board without your canopy or your RIO. I told you, I've had it with your attitude. A professional follows orders, Fastball—follows orders, whether they involve the opportunity for personal glory or not. So you may not like getting broken off to fly CAP for the destroyer, but the fact is that she puts her ass on the line to keep your airfield float. The least you can do is return the favor. Now, if I don't see this aircraft turning in approximately five seconds, I'm out of here."

"Okay, okay. But I'm going to have a talk about this with the CAG when we get back on board," he muttered. He yanked the Tomcat into a violent turn, slamming Rat into the side of her ejection seat, and building up Gs to the point of forcing her into an M1 maneuver to counteract the effects.

You're not the only one who's going to be talking to people when we get back aboard, she swore silently, fighting to remain conscious. *XO, CO, then CAG, then the admiral if I have to. One way or another, you idiot, I'm going to do my best to see that you're grounded.*

Hornet 106
2257 local (GMT +8)

"Raiders, picture. Bogies now FEZ, follow indicated vectors and take targets at will. Good hunting. See you back on the boat." With that, the Hawkeye slipped back into a monitor mode as the individual flights of aircraft broke out to seek out their targets.

Thor had been following his target on his HUD since the initial call, and was already mentally fighting the battle. He would come in high, with Archer taking the low slot, and let Archer draw a bogie off to the south. As soon as the MiG turned, Thor would drop in behind into the killing position. He clicked on his mike. "You ready, Archer?"

"As ready as ever, boss," the other Marine's voice came back. "Inbound now!"

Archer slammed his wing over, rolled out of position, and bore down on their designated target. Thor kicked in his afterburners, gained altitude, and headed in the same direction although slightly offset, hoping he could circle back slightly and be in the perfect position.

He looked down and saw that Archer was already in afterburner, and called out a warning. "Watch your fuel consumption, Wayne. We don't have time to tank."

A single click on the mike acknowledged his transmission. As he watched, Archer cut back out of afterburner.

But the Fencer had figured out what was happening, and was kicking butt and heading for the sky. The bogie pilot clearly understood the need to gain altitude to avoid being trapped in a pincer maneuver, and Thor swore quietly. He had hoped it would work first time out, but evidently that was not to be.

"Take low, Archer. Watch my six—I'm going to try to shoo him back down toward you."

"Roger, sir. Take him out as soon as you can. Don't worry about me."

Thor laughed out loud. "Oh, don't worry about that— you'll get your chance." Thor kicked in the afterburner for a moment as well, getting a head start on his climb. It was important not to let the Fencer gain too much altitude on him. While the aircraft were relatively equally matched in terms of endurance and performance, there was no time for a long drawn-out game as each one sought the advantage. No, this needed to be fast and brutal. There were simply too many Chinese to waste time.

As the Fencer headed for altitude, Thor backed off slightly and let him get ahead, then converted his upward motion into a sharp, gut-wrenching turn. Then he continued to ascend, staying on the outside of the Fencer's path and waiting for the breakaway. "Go north of us, Archer," Thor called out, already figuring out the geometries in his mind. "Cut him off if he tries to break out of this."

The old laws of gravity applied to fighters just as surely as they did to the apple that fell on Sir Isaac Newton's head. What goes up, must come down, and an aircraft was no exception to the inevitable rule. Oh, sure, she might go up faster than usual, but coming down was going to be a bitch.

"Thor, I got a Fitter on my ass—he's got me locked." Archer's voice was a little higher than normal, betraying worries. "I'm heading back toward you. Pull him off if you can!"

"Roger—I'll keep an eye on his buddy as well." Thor broadened the arc of his turn slightly, gained a visual on Archer, and saw the Fitter on his tail. As they closed range on him, he was immediately faced with a decision: wait for his designated contact to come back down within range or turn away from this engagement and chase the Fitter on Archer's tale.

There was a good chance that Archer could handle the other aircraft himself; it was simply a matter of driving him into the vertical game, then waiting for him to make a mistake. But if Thor broke off from his current target, there was every chance the Fencer would slide back in behind the MiG and reverse exactly the scenario Thor had had in mind for him.

But I know what I'm doing. Archer's the new kid on the block. I better buster down after him.

"Let's give him a little taste of metal to keep him honest," Thor muttered. He designated the target, waited for tone, and toggled off a missile at it. He felt the Hornet jolt slightly as the massive weapons leaped off his wing and headed for altitude. "That'll keep him busy for awhile."

As Thor shed some altitude, he kept a visual on Archer. His wingman's situation was clearly becoming increasingly desperate. Archer was weaving and bobbing around in the sky, but the Fitter seemed to anticipate his every move. Archer had him slightly off angle now, and Thor knew that the other pilot was waiting for the perfect shot up Archer's tailpipes. That was the advantage of having numbers in your favor—you could afford to wait to take the shot, gang up on a poor defenseless Hornet. Well, it wasn't going to happen that way, not on Thor's watch.

Thor peeled off altitude quickly now, descending like a plummeting rock, the sleek, aerodynamic lines of the Hornet adding to his acceleration. He aimed directly for the Fitter, not wasting any time on the niceties of aerodynamics. To an outsider, it would look as though Thor intended to simply forget the missiles and ram the other aircraft out of the sky.

"He's got me, he's got me," Archer howled, his voice anguished. "Jesus, Thor, I can't shake him."

"On my mark, break hard to the left," Thor said. "Three seconds, now. Two, one, *mark!* Break left, break left!"

Archer kicked his Hornet into a steep left turn, so hard and sudden it seemed that he would surely stall. He immediately dropped his nose down to allow the aircraft to gain speed. Thor engaged his nose gun, and stitched a line of rounds down the Fitter's side. Fluid spurted immediately, whether from hydraulics lines or fuel tanks, Thor couldn't tell. The Fitter departed controlled flight for a moment and lost the advantage of position he'd had on Archer. Archer whipped his Hornet over and around, falling neatly in behind the Fitter in a textbook demonstration of aerial combat tactics.

"All yours, buddy," Thor sang out as he pulled away from them and grabbed for altitude. "I got some unfinished business up above."

A short touch of afterburner quickly eased the Hornet's

objection to simultaneously turning, ascending and maintaining airspeed. The throaty roar sounded like the purr of a hungry lion.

Just as the Hornet reached sixty degrees nose up, silver and black flashed below Thor, a streak of aircraft moving past him in afterburner. The Fencer, the one who'd evaded the trap he and Archer had in mind. As soon as the Fencer cleared Thor's gun engagement range, it pulled up into a hard climb, darting ahead of Thor.

"So you want it like that, huh?" Thor kicked the afterburner back in and executed a corkscrewing maneuver that danced the Hornet across the sky until it was directly below the climbing Fencer. He then converted all of his motion into a climb, and kept pace, watching for the Fencer to heel over at the top of his arc or to peel out of the climb and entice him into a horizontal game.

"Splash one Fitter!" he heard Archer cry over tactical. "Hang on, Thor, I'm on my way!"

"Roger." *What's the big hurry, junior? I think I can manage to—*

Suddenly, Thor saw the reason for Archer's concern. Three Fencers had broken away from the fur ball and had evidently decided that Thor's Hornet would be their next project.

Shit! I fell for it! The lead Fencer above him had been no more than a distracter, and while Thor's attention was focused on it and Archer's situation, the air immediately to his south had filled up with bogies. Above him, the lead Fencer, its diversionary role over, rolled out of the climb and streaked off to the north.

"Got tone, got tone—break right!" Archer's voice snapped. Without hesitating, Thor slammed his Hornet into a hard roll to the right, holding the roll as he lost altitude and tried to swing in high on Archer. Two AMRAAMS cluttered the air around him, and for one heart-stopping moment, Thor thought they'd locked on him. He was now at the same altitude as the pursuing Fencers, but descending, while the Fencers were just now rolling out to follow.

Their orderly pursuit shattered into chaos as they realized that there were missiles inbound, and they muddied the air with chaff and flares.

Too late. The AMRAAM knew better. After wild, last-ditch spirals in an attempt to shake the missiles' locks, two of the Fencers exploded into flames.

"That's better," Archer said, hot satisfaction in his voice. "That's *lots* better."

"One on one," Thor said. "Our friend in high station is headed back down." The original Fencer seemed brighter on Thor's HUD than any of the other targets. *That bastard's mine.*

"I'm on him!" Archer shouted, giving chase on the remaining Fencer. Archer snapped hard to the right and caught the last of the group of three with a short burst from his nose gun. The Fencer spouted long streamers of red hydraulic fluid and oil from the forward part of its fuselage. The volatile fluids snaked into the screaming turbines, and it was all over. They immediately ignited, and within moments, the aircraft exploded into shards of metal and gobbets of flesh.

"Mine!" shouted Thor, and peeled off toward his target. The remaining Fencer evidently had reassessed his tactical position and had come to the same conclusion that Thor had: it sucked. Without the other three Fencers to provide a diversion and killing force, facing two pissed off Hornets, discretion was the better part of valor. The Fencer turned and tried to run.

"Not so fast, you bastard!" Thor said. He tucked his Hornet in behind the now desperately weaving and bobbing Fencer. It was as though he could read the other pilot's mind and anticipate his every move. It was an equal match of skill and capabilities, and for just a second Thor was tempted to let it play out, to harry the now-panicked Fencer like a cat playing with a mouse.

Too many other targets. Thor toggled off a Sidewinder and watched the heat-seeker slide up to kiss the Fencer's exhaust. He cut hard to the left, just in time to clear the resulting explosion.

As he turned back into the fray, waiting for his next target, Thor felt a momentary flash of . . . what? Embarrassment? Shame? There was no point in playing with another pilot who was as good as dead. It was Thor's job to kill them, not to like killing them. He should take personal satisfaction in his own skill, not in the death of another. Because that's what he hoped he'd get from a bogie if their positions were ever reversed: a quick kill.

"Hornet one zero six, bogies at your three o'clock, high," the AWACS rapped out, identifying Thor's next targets. "Number, three. Engage at will."

Archer glided in to form up on Thor's wing, and the two turned to meet their next set of foolhardy Fencers and Fitters who thought they could mess with the United States Marine Corps.

Tomcat 203
2301 local (GMT +8)

Even though he would never admit it, Bird Dog's greatest strength as a fighter pilot was his ability to do math. Not simple addition and subtraction, although Bird Dog himself would have pointed out that his sole purpose in life was to subtract enemy aircraft from the correlation of forces. And while that was indeed the end result, it was not what kept him alive.

Bird Dog's ability to do math had very little to do with numbers and everything to do with spatial relationships. Some part of his cerebrum was able to instantly calculate vectors, angles and even do the calculus necessary to determine exactly where a given aircraft with X amount of acceleration and Y amount of increasing drag would end up in relation to his own aircraft. It also measured with incredible precision the distance between objects, and that ability had allowed him to slide in between two objects—say, a rock and a hard place, or a cliff and another aircraft—when other pilots might have thought twice about it. Bird Dog's mathematical ability was coupled directly to his eyes and bypassed his consciousness.

Now, that part of Bird Dog's mind was assessing the air in front of him and correlating it with his HUD as well as the actual count of enemy aircraft downed as tallied by the exultant cries of the other pilots over tactical. It processed the data, compared it with the briefing he'd had just as he launched, and came to an ominous conclusion: there was an aircraft missing. Not an American aircraft, no. He knew where all those were, and he didn't question the fact that he did. No, the conclusion that surfaced in his mind, supported by a host of highly analytical processes that Bird Dog was never conscious of was that there was a Chinese aircraft missing from the tally.

Could someone have splashed it and been squelched on tactical? No, he hadn't heard a partial report cut off by static or any other indication that someone had gotten down and dirty and not been able to tell anyone about it.

Maybe the missile barrage took out an additional aircraft early on and someone had screwed up the count? No. While he couldn't have told anyone why he knew that was not so, he knew that was not the answer. He'd seen the distant specks of black that indicated an aircraft and a missile simultaneously trying to occupy the same airspace, and the registers in his mind had automatically toted up the numbers.

But if there was one missing, where was it? Why wasn't it on his radar? And why wasn't anyone else worried about it?

Bird Dog toggled his ICS. "Music, what were you saying about the count? You know, what the cruiser said and how many fireballs you saw?"

"It's off. Or at least I think it is. The cruiser reported thirteen kills and there—well, I could have been mistaken I guess."

"No. What?"

"I only counted twelve fireballs."

Bird Dog thought for just a second, then said, "We gotta find that other aircraft, Music. It's out there somewhere. I don't know why nobody else sees it or is worried about it, but for whatever reason, we're the only ones who know something's wrong."

"Why don't we see it?" Music asked, his words coming in hard grunts as Bird Dog kicked the Tomcat into a steep climb, ignoring the Hawkeye's vector guidance. "They don't have stealth, do they?"

"Naw, not that we know about. They could, I guess. But then we wouldn't have the original count right, would we?"

"So where is it?"

The answer to most problems and questions in the air is: altitude. Altitude buys a pilot time, time to sort out exactly what's gone wrong, time to find some configuration of speed and control surfaces that will convince an aircraft to keep flying, and, in the very worst of circumstances, time to make sure somebody knows exactly where he's punching out. So, faced with the problem of a missing enemy fighter, Bird Dog figured that altitude was the least likely thing to hurt him.

"How can you lose a fighter?" Bird Dog asked, trying to list the options. "Outside of range, maybe. If it's not stealth and nobody's holding it, then where is it? Turned tail and gone home? No, we would have seen it depart the pattern. It can't be out of range of every Tomcat and the Hawkeye. So it's in range somewhere. If we were over land, it'd be behind a hill or something, but we're—*shit!* Music, that's it! It's on the deck somewhere, down so low we're losing it in the sea state! That's got to be it!"

"He's crazy, then," Music said flatly. "Not in sea state five."

"Yeah, crazy. Or very, very good." Bird Dog flipped over to tactical. "U.S., you got a problem. You got a sea-skimming Fencer or Fitter inbound, somebody heading in for you just barely clearing the waves. You got anything that would correlate with that?"

"Bird Dog, you gotta be kidding," the Hawkeye broke in. "There's nobody down that low."

"Yeah? Count it again, buddy. Add up what came in, what's gone down, and what's in the air now. Then you tell me." Bird Dog waited impatiently for a few seconds, then rolled the Tomcat over inverted to get a better look at the surface of the ocean. "You watching for him, Music?"

"I'm trying not to puke, Bird Dog."

"You puke on the canopy now and I'll punch you out," Bird Dog threatened. "I swear to god I will."

"Wait!" Music said, forgetting his nausea in the rush of adrenaline spiking through his veins. "There—your dot, Bird Dog!"

"That ain't a dot, that's a—*shit, there it is*! U.S., I got a visual. Engaging. Fastball, you're on your own for a few miles while I nail this Fencer playing hovercraft."

Rat spoke up then. "Bird Dog, we should take high station on you."

"Leave him alone," Fastball snapped. "He knows what he's doing."

"I just think—"

"Then don't. Not about flying."

Music listened to the argument between pilot and RIO spill over the airwaves, desperately hoping that Rat would win this one. But Fastball had the ultimate veto authority over any plan about where the aircraft should go. It wasn't like Rat had controls in the back seat.

"Talley-ho!" Bird Dog shouted, putting the Tomcat into a steep dive, so steep that Music felt the gray creep in around the edges of his vision. "Come on, Music, let's nail this bastard!"

Tomcat 209
2305 local (GMT +8)

"He's your *lead*, Fastball. You don't let your lead wander off on his own," Rat said coldly.

"It ever occur to you that we're a little outnumbered up here, Rat?" Fastball shot back. "Bird Dog knows what he's doing. We can do more good up here, taking out a few more of these Fencers while he's cleaning up that little mess down below. By the time he gets back up to altitude, we'll probably have another six kills under our belt."

"Is that what this is about? Getting more kills than Bird Dog?"

"No! That's not it at all! What, you think you're not good enough to get us six more kills with the gas we've got left?"

"Bullshit. That's not the point."

"He doesn't *want* backup," Fastball snapped.

"Like you don't want an RIO?" she asked.

There was a moment of silence. Rat listened to the progress of the air battle around them, to the other pilots calling out their kill counts, their next targets—and, occasionally, a curse, followed by a Mayday as an American was overwhelmed by the attackers. She knew Fastball wanted to be in the thick of it, knew how hard it was for him to turn away from the fun ball and do what was right. It was a choice she couldn't force him to make.

The aircraft suddenly dropped out from under her, throwing her hard against her ejection harness. "Okay, okay," Fastball said. "He shouldn't be going down on his own, should he? I know that, you know that. But it's Bird Dog, Rat, and he's going to be one pissed-off pilot when we get back to the boat, us heading down to back him up when he says he doesn't need it. You know how he is."

"Yeah, I do. He's a whole lot like you," Rat said softly.

Tomcat 203
2310 local (GMT +8)

"He's only four miles from the carrier," Music said, his face buried in the radar hood. If he could just get the right resolution, maybe, just maybe, he'd be able to get a radar lock on the target. Without radar contact, he had no way to target the missile.

"A little more than that," Bird Dog said, not really consciously marking off the miles, but knowing it was true anyway. "We got time."

"Not much." *Hell, where is he? He's got to be in here somewhere. But it's all static, all reflections off the waves—he must be suicidal to be that low in this sea state! But they all are, aren't they? Their pilots, ours. Bird Dog's going down there to find him, as much to prove that he can do anything a Fencer can do better, longer and harder than anything else. And I'm not going to like it one little bit—no, I'm not.*

As Music tried every trick he knew to pull the contact out of the clutter, he suddenly realized with a gut-wrenching sense of relief that this was his last combat flight. He knew how RIOs felt about pilots, how they all bitched about the maniacs sitting in the front seat, and he'd chimed in, trying to sound exactly like them, but knowing at some level that he was far more serious about it. RIOs bitched to let off steam, to hide the fear. But for Music, it went far deeper than that.

He understood the importance of what they were doing out here, of the necessity for fighters and fighter pilots and for strong military forces. In the interest of their national security, America had to be able to be the biggest kid on the block. And it wasn't that he was afraid of doing his part. He'd volunteered, hadn't he?

It was just that he thought there ought to be another way—that there *had* to be another way—of resolving conflicts. You go out and beat somebody up, they're going to wait until they're strong enough to beat you up. Not a question of being afraid, not that at all. No, it was a question of choice.

The last time I'll fly. So I better do a damned good job of it.

Just then, two bits of sea return merged, stabilized and turned into a target. "Your dot, Bird Dog," Music said. "Definitely your dot."

Tomcat 209
2311 local (GMT +8)

"I got a visual on him," Fastball announced. "Looks like it's going to be a wasted trip, Rat."

Rat gritted her teeth. Fastball would always rub it in, wouldn't he? She knew how the story would be replayed on the carrier when they got back.

"See, he's already got a missile on him," Fastball said. "I don't know why I ever listen to you, Rat. You're such a—"

The surface of the ocean exploded into a fireball. A hot wave of expanding gases rushed over them, buffeting the Tomcat violently. Fastball swore as he fought for control, then finally pulled the Tomcat out into level flight.

"What the hell??!!" he shouted, adrenaline pumping through his system.

Rat stared down at the ocean, numb. "Suicide mission. Like the one that nailed the USS *Cole*," she said. "That was no normal explosion—man, that thing had to be packed with explosives."

"Bird Dog—where is he?"

Rat stared down at her radar screen, searching for the contact that the system would label as a friendly Tomcat. Static stared back at her, the superheated air along the surface of the ocean wreaking havoc with waveforms and transmission paths. "No joy," she said softly.

"He's gotta be down there somewhere!" Fastball insisted. "That was Bird Dog!"

Over tactical, a chatter of reports streamed in as the carrier insisted on asking what the hell was going on while the air boss vectored helos into the area. The explosion had flung shrapnel toward the carrier, and several pieces of metal traveling at supersonic speeds had skewered both aircraft and personnel in the hangar bay and on the flight deck. Damage control teams were fighting one small fire and the yellow gear was moving in to shove the burning aircraft over the side, the only way to control a Class Delta metal fire.

"Somebody want to come get me?" a familiar voice said irritably over the air distress frequency.

"Bird Dog!" Fastball shouted. "He's alive!"

"I'm over on the starboard side, just after your wake, Big Boy. Call it four hundred feet and opening," Bird Dog's voice continued. "Let's make it snappy, okay? And get me another aircraft ready."

"How'd you get over there?" the air boss asked, after he'd relayed vectors to the SAR helo.

"I figured it out right before I took the shot, so I did a bunny hop over the carrier. Timed it so the bulk of the carrier would shield us from most of the blast, but we ended up in the drink anyway," Bird Dog said, his voice seriously aggrieved. "I almost had it, but there was a hell of a lot more explosives on it than I figured."

"And he had time to punch out," Fastball said, awed at the speed at which Bird Dog had deciphered the situation and gotten himself clear. "Time to figure out when to shoot, kick in afterburner and clear the carrier, then get back down low enough to be shielded. The blast must have nailed him through the open hangar bay. And *then*, on top of that, he manages to roll enough to avoid punching out into the carrier and time it so that they stay clear of the stern."

Evidently the air boss made the same conclusions, because when he spoke again, his voice was filled with gruff respect. "Roger, Bird Dog, we're on our way."

"Medical for my RIO," Bird Dog said, his voice starting to mirror the strain now. "I think he's hurt bad. I want to . . ."

As Bird Dog's voice trailed off, the circuit was filled with a flurry of orders. Within the next fifteen seconds, the rescue helo had a swimmer in the water holding the pilot and RIO's faces out of the water as a rescue basket was lowered to them. Bird Dog regained consciousness just long enough to insist that Music take the first ride up.

Bird Dog watched Music being hoisted up to the helo, then turned his attention to staying alive. The large waves were alternately lifting him to their peaks and then tossing him into the valleys, and the spray was so heavy that it was hard to draw a deep breath. The life jacket was doing a good job of keeping him afloat, but it was up to him to keep his head out of the water and time his breaths so he wouldn't take in a lungful of water.

Finally, it was his turn. The rescue carry basket descended, and he swam over to it, cursing when it swung out of reach. Finally, he managed to hook one hand around the bottom of it and pulled it toward him. He pulled himself inside, strapped in, and raised a thumbs-up at the hoist operator. With a hard jerk, the rescue basket began its ascent.

As it came level with the side hatch of the helo, Bird Dog was already struggling with the strap, trying to undo it even before he was inside. "Stop that!" a crew member snapped, and swung the basket inside the helo. He motioned to the other man to shut the hatch, and then glared at Bird Dog. "What do you think you're trying to do, you idiot?" He grabbed for a hand hold as the helo banked sharply away from the area and back toward the carrier. "I go to all the trouble to pull you out of the water, and you're trying to get thrown back in. If you fall out, I'm leaving you there."

"How is he?" Bird Dog asked, letting them undo the straps. Music was stretched out on his back, pale and only semi-conscious. A corpsman was already ripping apart the flight suit to take a look at the wound.

"He'll live," the corpsman said. "Didn't even break the bone. Once it heals up, there's no reason he can't be back in a flight status after some physical therapy."

At that, Music groaned and opened his eyes. "No more flying. That's it for me."

Bird Dog stared at him, disbelief in his eyes. "What do you mean, no more flying? Come on, Music, I wouldn't have let anything happen to you."

Music shook his head weakly. "It's not for me, Bird Dog. It's just not. As soon as we get back on deck, I'm turning in my wings."

"Back to the fight?" Rat said, and then she noticed that the Tomcat was already ascending again.

"Back to the fight," Fastball said grimly. "Watch my ass, Rat. We're going to kill us some Fencers."

Fifteen minutes later, it was all over. Fastball hadn't gotten six kills, but he sounded fairly content with the three he'd managed to rack up. The last had been a real son of a bitch, stitching a line of bullets down his vertical control surfaces before finally wandering into Fastball's own guns.

As the American forces headed for the tanker, then lined up for a shot at the deck, the few remaining Chinese aircraft were already facing the consequences of failure as they landed.

Marshall P'eng

Captain Chang was seated in his stateroom, his back to the door. He heard his second in command announce Major Ho, but, as they'd planned, he did not answer.

The door opened and hesitant footsteps sounded on the spotless white tile. Still Chang did not turn. This was the first test.

Five minutes passed, and there was no sound behind him.

Not an impatient throat clearing, not a scuffle, not even a sniff. Finally, Chang wheeled around to stare directly at the top of Ho's head. The younger man's bow was as deep as Chang had ever seen, and Ho was waiting to be acknowledged with a patience and submissiveness that Chang would not have expected from him.

Good. He understands that much about respect. Perhaps there is hope.

"Sit," Chang said flatly. "Sit, and listen."

Ho unbent and slipped into the chair in front of Chang's desk. He perched on the very edge of it, his back straight, his eyes staring at the floor. At that moment, Chang's plan changed.

"There is no need to review your conduct and your decisions," Chang began. "By now, you have understood what you did wrong, correct? And how your own pride and ego led to mistakes that almost cost men's lives. There is no shame in misunderstanding another culture—there *is* shame in failing to admit to your misunderstanding. As a rule, you must assume that others are honorable until they prove otherwise. You did not allow the Americans that opportunity. Is this a correct summary of your understanding?"

"Yes, Captain." Ho's gaze was still fixed on the deck.

Chang leaned back in his chair and studied the man. Certainly he had the family connections and the education to go far in the military—indeed, he could walk the line between the ancient sources of power and authority in Taiwan and the emerging technocracy that was so at odds with tradition. If he were of the right character, Ho could play a key leadership role in Taiwan's future.

But is he? Has he learned from this, or will it simply sour him, instill in him a desire for revenge? I have the power to ruin him right now. Ruin him, or save him. Which will it be?

"Look at me," Chang ordered. Hesitantly, Ho raised his head and met Chang's gaze.

The windows to the soul—and what do I see there? Re-

morse. Sorrow. Deep shame. Yes, he understands. And if he understands, there is hope.

"Wisdom comes from experience," Chang said finally. "My report will contain the recommendation that you be ordered to a shore station in the United States for further liaison duties. Perhaps with their army this time." Chang leaned forward, his voice intense. "Our country's future will depend on knowing and understanding the United States. You have seen yourself how deadly mistakes can be. Some day, I will retire. It would be of some comfort to me if I knew that there were men such as you, men of pride and honor with the willingness to look beyond the surface to find other men of honor in other cultures. Can I count on you? Are you one of those men?"

Ho shook his head. "Not yet, sir. But I will do my best to follow your example."

Chang nodded once. "Then go. Return to the ship, make your apologies and prove that my confidence is not mistaken. I shall be watching, Major. I wish to be proud."

With that, he dismissed the army officer and turned back to the never-ending pile of paperwork on his desk.

The United Nations

Sarah Wexler had never seen the ambassador from China looking quite so—well—what? Embarrassed, perhaps? Chagrined? Or even apologetic? She doubted that anyone who didn't know him as well as she did wouldn't even notice it, but there was definitely an undercurrent beneath the smooth, diplomatic facade he always presented to the world.

He stood in her doorway, motionless, his head inclined slightly. *How long has he been standing there?* Not long, she figured, judging by how Brad, standing directly behind the ambassador, was impatiently shifting his weight.

"Yes?" she said, not really asking a question as much as acknowledging his presence.

T'ing deepened his bow, then said, "May I speak to you privately?"

A request, not an order. That's a good start. Aloud, she said, "Regarding?" She shot a glance at Brad and continued with, "Anything you have to say to me, you can say in front of my staff."

Now that didn't go down well with Brad, did it? I doubt he likes being considered just part of the staff.

"Very well." T'ing's gaze told her he was not pleased. "China is withdrawing her petition requesting sanctions against America." He turned abruptly to leave and bumped into Brad.

"Will there be an apology forthcoming?" Wexler asked, her voice still cold.

"No." He turned back to face her. "You cannot reasonably expect that, can you? Your government will have to be content with what is offered."

That brought her to her feet. "Oh, really? Is that how you see things?"

He gazed at her for a long moment then said quietly, "I would like to speak to you privately. Please."

Please, is it? She nodded. "It's okay, Brad."

Once they were alone, T'ing slipped into the chair in front of her desk and some of the stiffness in his posture slid away. "I have delivered the message from my government. I cannot elaborate on their position, you know. My orders were quite clear. But privately, I wish to assure you that I have been—perhaps not as well advised as I would like." He spread his hands out, palms up. "It is no secret that I have many sources of intelligence. And in this instance, they were sufficiently at odds that I was forced to make a choice. Perhaps I made the wrong one. Had I known the truth of the matter, perhaps things might have gone differently."

So they don't tell you everything either, do they, my friend? She regarded him for a moment, seeing the similarities in how they'd each been forced to operate. "They want all of our skills, don't they? But in the end, we represent our governments, and must advocate their positions. Even when we know better."

His face relaxed. "So you understand, yes?"

"Yes."

T'ing took a deep breath, then let it out slowly. "But we're more than just hired guns, you and I. We do make a difference. For instance, there was some talk of demanding restitution for the attack on our amphibious group. I would like to think that it would have been rejected without my input, but I certainly argued strongly against it."

"Well, then. Where do we stand now?"

"With Japan and Russia arguing over the position of the Kuriles, I suppose. It will come back to this forum eventually, but for now we can safely ignore it."

"For now."

There was a long silence, not an uncompanionable one. Finally, he stood to leave. "Dinner tomorrow?"

She walked him to the door. "Pacini's, eight o'clock."

TWENTY-EIGHT

Advanced Solutions
Washington, D.C.
Monday, September 30
0800 local (GMT −5)

Tombstone fingered the brown official government envelope, knowing what was inside and not wanting to touch it. Somehow, this made his loss seem continually fresh. The monthly arrival of Tomboy's paychecks, because her military pay continued as long as she was listed as missing and not declared killed, was a constant reminder of his loss.

Looks like I'm not the only one who can't believe she's gone. Tombstone stuck the envelope in his top desk drawer, along with the last three he'd received. Someday soon he'd have to decide what to do with them, but ignoring them for now seemed like the most attractive option he had.

"Mister Magruder?" a voice said hesitantly over the speaker on his telephone. "Someone is here to see you."

"Who?" he said, slightly befuddled. No one came to see him here who didn't already have the security codes to all the doors. And if they didn't have the codes, they had no business being here.

"He won't give his name. But he said to tell you it's about going west."

The phrase reverberated in his mind. Go west—the last words his father had etched on the walls of a Vietnamese POW camp. Tombstone shot out of his chair and headed for the front office. His uncle was only slightly behind him.

A small, wiry man was seated in the reception area. He was well-dressed in a dark, pinstriped suit and highly polished shoes. He stood, offered his hand, and said, "Thank you for seeing me."

"I'm not sure we're to that stage yet," Tombstone said. "Want to tell me your name, just for starters?"

The man shook his head. "I could give you a name, but it would mean nothing."

"Then how about telling me what that phrase means to you?" Tombstone shot back, every nerve on edge. He had thought he had finally resolved his father's fate in the cold woods of Ukraine, but to hear those words again . . . was there something he'd missed? Had the grave he'd been assured was his father's been someone else's?

"The more important question is what those words mean to you. I think," and Tombstone now noted a slight foreign accent to the man's voice, "that they will mean hope. Is this room secure?"

Tombstone glanced at his uncle, who shrugged. "The conference room would be better." His uncle led the way past the receptionist and into a utilitarian conference room furnished with a sturdy if decidedly plain table and chairs.

"This is secure enough for anything that concerns those words," Tombstone said when they were inside it and the door shut behind them. "Now start talking."

"A picture is worth a thousand words," the man said. He opened the large brown envelope he was carrying and withdrew a photo. Without words and with a faint expression of pity, he passed it over to Tombstone.

Tombstone drew in a sharp breath. His world reeled

around him, and for a moment he had the crazy idea that
he just might pass out. His uncle moved closer and peered
over his shoulder, then swore quietly.

Tomboy's face, bloody and grim, stared back at them.
The picture captured her from the waist up, and it was
clear from her posture that her hands were tied behind her.
Tombstone saw her iron will etched into every line of her
face, and knew by the hard set of her eyes and the tightness
in her muscles that she was an unwilling participant in this
photo shoot.

A hand intruded into the picture right at about chest
level. It held a newspaper—Tombstone held the photo
closer, and made out the words *NEW YORK TIMES*. The date
was almost too blurred to read.

Almost. A fresh shock reverberated through him, and
his breath froze in his throat.

The man nodded, fresh sorrow in his eyes. "Yes. This
was taken last week."

"Where?" Tombstone gasped, struggling for the words,
not daring to trust the fresh hope blossoming in his chest.
"She's alive!" Joy coursed through him, followed immediately by the deepest anger he'd ever experienced. She
was alive—and she was captive.

"I think we should sit down," the man said gently. "It
is a long story."

GLOSSARY

0–3 LEVEL: The third deck above the main deck. Designations for decks above the main deck (also known as the damage control deck) begin with zero, e.g. 0–3. The zero is pronounced as "oh" in conversation. Decks below the main deck do not have the initial zero, and are numbered down from the main deck, e.g. deck 11 is below deck 3. Deck 0–7 is above deck 0–3.

1MC: The general announcing system on a ship or submarine. Every ship has many different interior communications systems, most of them linking parts of the ship for a specific purpose. Most operate off sound-powered phones. The circuit designators consist of a number followed by two letters that indicate the specific purpose of the circuit. 2AS, for instance, might be an antisubmarine warfare circuit that connects the sonar supervisor, the USW watch officer, and the sailor at the torpedo launcher.

C-2 GREYHOUND: Also known as the COD, Carrier Onboard Delivery. The COD carries cargo and passengers from shore to ship. It is capable of carrier landings. Sometimes assigned directly to the airwing, it also operates in coordination with CVBGs from a shore squadron.

AIR BOSS: A senior commander or captain assigned to the aircraft carrier, in charge of flight operations. The "boss" is assisted by the mini-boss in Pri-Fly, located in the tower onboard the carrier. The air boss is always in the tower during flight operations, overseeing the launch and recovery cycles, declaring a green deck, and monitoring the safe approach of aircraft to the carrier.

AIR WING: Composed of the aircraft squadrons assigned to the battle group. The individual squadron commanding officers report to the airwing commander, who reports to the admiral.

AIRDALE: Slang for an officer or enlisted person in the aviation fields. Includes pilots, NFOs, aviation intelligence officers and maintenance officers and the enlisted technicians who support aviation. The antithesis of an airdale is a "shoe."

AKULA: Late model Russian-built attack nuclear submarine, an SSN. Fast, deadly, and deep diving.

ALR-67: Detects, analyzes, and evaluates electromagnetic signals, emits a warning signal if the parameters are compatible with an immediate threat to the aircraft, e.g. seeker head on an antiair missile. Can also detect an enemy radar in either a search or a targeting mode.

ALTITUDE: Is safety. With enough air space under the wings, a pilot can solve any problem.

AMRAAM: Advanced Medium Range Anti Air Missile.

ANGELS: Thousands of feet over ground. Angels twenty is 20,000 feet. Cherubs indicates hundreds of feet, e.g. cherubs five = five hundred feet.

ASW: Antisubmarine Warfare, recently renamed Undersea Warfare. For some reason.

AVIONICS: Black boxes and systems that comprise an aircraft's combat systems.

AW: Aviation antisubmarine warfare technician, the enlisted specialist flying in an S-3, P-3 or helo USW aircraft. As this book goes to press, there is discussion of renaming the specialty.

AWACS: An aircraft entirely too good for the Air Force, the Advanced Warning Aviation Control System. Long-range command and control and electronic intercept bird with superb capabilities.

AWG-9: Pronounced "awg nine," the primary search and fire control radar on a Tomcat.

BACKSEATER: Also known as the GIB, the guy in back. Nonpilot aviator available in several flavors: BN (bombardier/navigator), RIO (radar intercept operator), and TACO (Tactical Control Officer) among others. Usually wear glasses and are smart.

BEAR: Russian maritime patrol aircraft, the equivalent in rough terms of a US P-3. Variants have primary missions in command and control, submarine hunting, and electronic intercepts. Big, slow, good targets.

BITCH BOX: One interior communications system on a ship. So named because it's normally used to bitch at another watch station.

BLUE ON BLUE: Fratricide. U.S. forces are normally indicated in blue on tactical displays, and this term refers to an attack on a friendly by another friendly.

BLUE WATER NAVY: Outside the unrefueled range of the air wing. When a carrier enters blue water ops, aircraft must get on board, e.g. land, and cannot divert to land if the pilot gets the shakes.

BOOMER: Slang for a ballistic missile submarine.

BOQ: Bachelor Officer Quarters—a Motel Six for single officers or those traveling without family. The Air Force also has VOQ, Visiting Officer Quarters.

BUSTER: As fast as you can, i.e., bust yer ass getting here.

CAG: Carrier Air Group Commander, normally a senior Navy captain aviator. Technically, an obsolete term, since the airwing rather than an air group is now deployed on the carrier. However, everyone thought CAW sounded stupid, so CAG was retained as slang for the Carrier Air Wing Commander.

CAP: Combat Air Patrol, a mission executed by fighters to protect the carrier and battle group from enemy air and missiles.

CARRIER BATTLE GROUP: A combination of ships, airwing and submarine assigned under the command of a one-star admiral.

CARRIER BATTLE GROUP 14: The battle group normally embarked on *Jefferson*.

CBG: *See Carrier Battle Group.*

CDC: Combat Direction Center—modernly, replaced CIC, or Combat Information Center, as the heart of a ship. All sensor information is fed into CDC and the battle is coordinated by a Tactical Action Officer on watch there.

CG: Abbreviation for a cruiser.

CHIEF: The backbone of the Navy. E-7, 8, and 9 enlisted paygrades, known as chief, senior chief, and master chief. The transition from petty officer ranks to the chief's mess is a major event in a sailor's career. Onboard ship, the chiefs have separate eating and berthing facilities. Chiefs wear khakis, as opposed to dungarees for the less senior enlisted ratings.

CHIEF OF STAFF: Not to be confused with a chief, the COS in a battle group staff is normally a senior Navy captain who acts as the admiral's XO and deputy.

CIA: Christians in Action. The civilian agency charged with intelligence operations outside the continental United States.

CIWS: Close-In Weapons System, pronounced "see-whiz." Gatling gun with built-in radar that tracks and fires on inbound missiles. If you have to use it, you're dead.

COD: *See C-2 Greyhound.*

COLLAR COUNT: Traditional method of determining the winner of a disagreement. A survey is taken of the opponents' collar devices. The senior person wins. Always.

COMMODORE: Formerly the junior-most admiral rank, now used to designate a senior Navy captain in charge of a bunch of like units. A destroyer commodore commands several destroyers, a sea control commodore the S-3 squadrons on that coast. In contrast to the CAG, who owns a number of dissimilar units, e.g. a couple of Tomcat squadrons, some Hornets, and some E-2s and helos.

COMPARTMENT: Navy talk for a room on a ship.

CONDITION TWO: One step down from General Quarters, which is Condition One. Condition Five is tied up at the pier in a friendly country.

CRYPTO: Short for some variation of cryptological, the magic set of codes that makes a circuit impossible for anyone else to understand.

CV, CVN: Abbreviation for an aircraft carrier, conventional and nuclear.

CVIC: Carrier Intelligence Center. Located down the passageway (the hall) from the flag spaces.

DATA LINK, THE LINK: The secure circuit that links all units in a battle group or in an area. Targets and contacts are transmitted over the LINK to all ships. The data is processed by the ship designated as Net Control, and common contacts are correlated. The system also transmits data from each ship and aircraft's weapons systems, e.g. a missile firing. All services use the LINK.

DESK JOCKEY: Nonflyer, one who drives a computer instead of an aircraft.

DESRON: Destroyer Commander.

DICASS: An active sonobuoy.

DICK STEPPING: Something to be avoided. While anatomically impossible in today's gender-integrated services, in an amazing display of good sense, it has been decided that women do this as well.

DDG: Guided missile destroyer.

DOPPLER: Acoustic phenomena caused by relative motion between a sound source and a receiver that results in an apparent change in frequency of the sound. The classic example is a train going past and the decrease in pitch of its whistle. When a submarine changes its course or speed in relation to a sonobuoy, the event shows up as a change in the frequency of the sound source.

DOUBLE NUTS: Zero zero on the tail of an aircraft.

E-2 HAWKEYE: Command and control and surveillance aircraft. Turboprop rather than jet, and unarmed. Smaller version of an AWACS, in practical terms, but carrier-based.

ELF: Extremely Low Frequency, a method of communicating with submarines at sea. Signals are transmitted via a miles-long antenna and are the only way of reaching a deep-submerged submarine.

ENVELOPE: What you're supposed to fly inside of if you want to take all the fun out of naval aviation.

EWs: Electronic warfare technicians, the enlisted sailors that man the gear that detects, analyzes, and displays electromagnetic signals. Highly classified stuff.

F/A-18 Hornets: The inadequate, fuel-hungry intended replacement for the aging but still kick-your-ass potent Tomcat. Flown by Marines and Navy.

FAMILYGRAM: Short messages from submarine sailors' families to their deployed sailors. Often the only contact with the outside world that a submarine sailor on deployment has.

FF/FFG: Abbreviation for a fast frigate (no, there aren't slow frigates) and a guided missile fast frigate.

FLAG OFFICER: In the Navy and Coast Guard, an admiral. In the other services, a general.

FLAG PASSAGEWAY: The portion of the aircraft carrier that houses the admiral's staff working spaces. Includes the flag mess and the admiral's cabin. Normally separated from the rest of the ship by heavy plastic curtains, and designated by blue tile on the deck instead of white.

FLIGHT QUARTERS: A condition set onboard a ship preparing to launch or recover aircraft. All unnecessary personnel are required to stay inside the skin of the ship and remain clear of the flight deck area.

FLIGHT SUIT: The highest form of Navy couture. The perfect choice of apparel for any occasion— indeed, the only uniform an aviator ought to be required to own.

FOD: Stands for Foreign Object Damage, but the term is used to indicate any loose gear that could cause damage to an aircraft. During flight operations, aircraft generate a tremendous amount of air flowing across the deck. Loose objects—including people and nuts and bolts—can be sucked into the intake and discharged through the outlet from the jet engine. FOD damages the jet's impellers and doesn't do much for the people sucked in, either. FOD walkdown is conducted at least one a day onboard an aircraft carrier. Everyone not otherwise engaged stands shoulder-to-shoulder on the flight deck and slowly walks from one end of the flight deck to the other, searching for FOD.

FOX: Tactical shorthand for a missile firing. Fox one indicates a heat-seeking missile, Fox two an infrared missile, and Fox three a radar guided missile.

GCI: Ground Control Intercept, a procedure used in the Soviet air forces. Primary control for vectoring the aircraft in on enemy targets and other fighters is vested in a guy on the ground, rather than in the cockpit where it belongs.

GIB: *See backseater.*

GMT: Greenwich Mean Time.

GREEN SHIRTS: *See shirts.*

HANDLER: Officer located on the flight deck level responsible for ensuring that aircraft are correctly positioned, "spotted," on the flight deck. Coordinates the movements of aircraft with yellow gear (small tractors that tow aircraft and other related gear) from maintenance areas to catapults and from the flight deck to the hangar bar via the elevators. Speaks frequently with the Air Boss. *See also bitch box.*

HARMS: Antiradiation missiles that home in on radar sites.

HOMEPLATE: Tactical call sign for the *Jefferson.*

HOT: In reference to a sonobuoy, holding enemy contact.

HUFFER: Yellow gear located on the flight deck that generates compressed air to start jet engines. Most Navy aircraft do not need a huffer to start engines, but it can be used in emergencies or for maintenance.

HUNTER: Call sign for the S-3 squadron embarked on the *Jefferson.*

ICS: Interior Communications System. The private link between a pilot and an RIO, or the telephone system internal to a ship.

INCHOPPED: Navy talk for a ship entering a defined area of water, e.g. inchopped the Med.

IR: Infrared, a method of missile homing.

ISOTHERMAL: A layer of water that has a constant temperature with increasing depth. Located below the thermocline, where increase in depth correlates to decrease in temperature. In the isothermal layer, the primary factor affecting the speed of sound in water is the increase in pressure with depth.

JBD: Jet Blast Deflector. Panels that pop up from the flight deck to block the exhaust emitted by aircraft.

USS *JEFFERSON*: The star nuclear aircraft carrier in the U.S. Navy.

LEADING PETTY OFFICER: The senior petty officer in a workcenter, division, or department, responsible to the leading chief petty officer for the performance of the rest of the group.

LINK: *See data link*

LOFARGRAM: Low Frequency Analyzing and Recording display. Consists of lines arrayed by frequency on the horizontal axis and time on the vertical axis. Displays sound signals in the water in a graphic fashion for analysis by ASW technicians.

LONG GREEN TABLE: A formal inquiry board. It's better to be judged by six than carried by six.

MACHINISTS MATE: Enlisted technician that runs and repairs most engineering equipment onboard a ship. Abbreviated as "MM" e.g. MM1 Sailor is a Petty Officer First Class Machinists Mate.

MDI: Mess Decks Intelligence. The heartbeat of the rumor mill onboard a ship and the definitive source for all information.

MEZ: Missile Engagement Zone. Any hostile contacts that make it into the MEZ are engaged only with missiles. Friendly aircraft must stay clear in order to avoid a blue on blue engagement, i.e. fratricide.

MIG: A production line of aircraft manufactured by Mikoyan in Russia. MiG fighters are owned by many nations around the world.

MURPHY, LAW OF: The factor most often not considered sufficiently in military planning. If something can go wrong, it will. Naval corollary: shit happens.

NATIONAL ASSETS: Surveillance and reconnaissance resources of the most sensitive nature, e.g. satellites.

NATOPS: The bible for operating a particular aircraft. *See envelopes.*

NFO: Naval Flight Officer.

NOBRAINER: Contrary to what copy editors believe, this is one word. Used to signify an evolution or decision that should require absolutely no significant intellectual capabilities beyond that of a paramecium.

NOMEX: Fire-resistant fabric used to make "shirts." *See shirts.*

NSA: National Security Agency. Primarily responsible for evaluating electronic intercepts and sensitive intelligence.

OOD: Officer of the Day, in charge of the safe handling and maneuvering of the ship. Supervises the conning officer and other underway watchstanders. Ashore, the OOD may be responsible for a shore station after normal working hours.

OPERATIONS SPECIALIST: Formerly radar operators, back in the old days. Enlisted technicians who operate combat detection, tracking, and engagement systems, except for sonar. Abbreviated OS.

OTH: Over the horizon, usually used to refer to shooting something you can't see.

P-3'S: Shore-based antisubmarine warfare and surface surveillance long-range aircraft. The closest you can get to being in the Air Force while still being in the Navy.

PHOENIX: Long-range antiair missile carried by U.S. fighters.

PIPELINE: Navy term used to describe a series of training commands, schools, or necessary education for a particular specialty. The fighter pipeline, for example, includes Basic Flight then fighter training at the RAG (Replacement Air Group), a training squadron.

PUNCHING OUT: Ejecting from an aircraft.

PURPLE SHIRTS: *See shirts.*

PXO: Prospective Executive Officer—the officer ordered into a command as the relief for the current XO. In most squadrons, the XO eventually "fleets up" to become the commanding officer of the squadron, an excellent system that maintains continuity within an operational command—and a system the surface Navy does not use.

RACK: A bed. A rack-monster is a sailor who sports pillow burns and spends entirely too much time asleep while his or her shipmates are working.

RED SHIRTS: *See shirts.*

RHIP: Rank Hath Its Privileges. *See collar count.*

RIO: Radar Intercept Officer. *See NFO.*

RTB: Return to base.

S-3: Command and control aircraft sold to the Navy as an antisubmarine aircraft. Good at that, too. Within the last several years, redesignated as "sea control" aircraft, with individual squadrons referred to as torpedo-bombers. Ah, the search for a mission goes on. But still a damned fine aircraft.

SAM: Surface to Air missile, e.g. the standard missile fired by most cruisers. Also indicates a land-based site.

SAR: Sea-Air Rescue.

SCIF: Specially Compartmented Information. Onboard a carrier, used to designated the highly classified compartment immediately next to TFCC.

SEAWOLF: Newest version of Navy fast attack submarine.

SERE: Survival, Evasion, Rescue, Escape; required school in pipeline for aviators.

SHIRTS: Color-coded Nomex pullovers used by flight deck and aviation personnel for rapid identification of a sailor's job. Green: maintenance technicians. Brown: plane captains. White: safety and medical. Red: ordnance. Purple: Fuel. Yellow: flight deck supervisors and handlers.

SHOE: A black shoe, slang for a surface sailor or officer. Modernly, hard to say since the day that brown shoes were authorized for wear by black shoes. No one knows why. Wing envy is the best guess.

SIDEWINDER: Antiair missile carried by U.S. fighters.

SIERRA: A subsurface contact.

SONOBUOYS: Acoustic listening devices dropped in the water by ASW or USW aircraft.

SPARROW: Antiair missile carried by U.S. fighters.

SPETZNAZ: The Russian version of SEALS, although the term encompasses a number of different specialties.

SPOOKS: Slang for intelligence officers and enlisted sailors working in highly classified areas.

SUBLANT: Administrative command of all Atlantic submarine forces. On the West Coast, SUBPAC.

SWEET: When used in reference to a sonobuoy, indicates that the buoy is functioning properly, although not necessarily holding any contacts.

TACCO: Tactical Control Office: the NFO in an S-3.

TACTICAL CIRCUIT: A term used in these books that encompasses a wide range of actual circuits used onboard a carrier. There are a variety of C&R circuits (coordination and reporting) and occasionally for simplicity sake and to avoid classified material, I just use the word "tactical."

TANKED, TANKER: Navy aircraft have the ability to refuel from a tanker, either Air Force or Navy, while airborne. One of the most terrifying routine evolutions a pilot performs.

TFCC: Tactical Flag Command Center. A compartment in flag spaces from which the CVBG admiral controls the battle. Located immediately forward of the carrier's CDC.

TOMBSTONE: Nickname given to Magruder.

TOP GUN: Advanced fighter training command.

UA: Unauthorized Absence, the modern term for AWOL.

UNDERSEA WARFARE COMMANDER: In a CVBG, normally the DESRON embarked on the carrier. Formerly called the ASW commander.

VDL: Video Downlink. Transmission of targeting data from an aircraft to a submarine with OTH capabilities.

VF-95: Fighter squadron assigned to Airwing 14, normally embarked on USS *Jefferson*. The first two letters of a squadron designation reflect the type of aircraft flown. VF = fighters. VFA = Hornets. VS = S-3, etc.

VICTOR: Aging Russian fast-attack submarine, still a potent threat.

VS-29: S-3 squadron assigned to Airwing 14, embarked on USS *Jefferson*.

VX-1: Test pilot squadron that develops envelopes after Pax River evaluates aerodynamic characteristics of new aircraft. *See envelopes.*

WHITE SHIRT: *See shirts.*

WILCO: Short for Will Comply. Used only by the aviator in command of the mission.

WINCHESTER: In aviation, it means out of weapons. A Winchester aircraft must normally RTB.

XO: Executive officer, the second in command.

YELLOW SHIRT: *See shirts.*